FIGHT FOR FREEDOM

THE MERMAID CHRONICLES
BOOK THREE

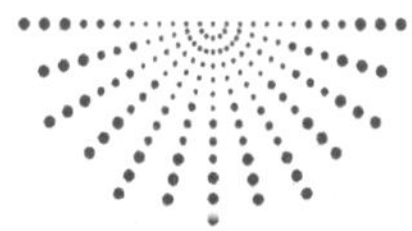

MARISA NOELLE

"A refreshing take on an emerging genre. I found this book so hard to put down. Lots of drama mixed with a dollop of romance and just a touch of the supernatural." – Melissa Welliver, author of *My Love Life and the Apocalypse*

"The premise is laced with conflict, and you'll cheer for Cordelia all the way through as she battle to overcome inherent differences and conflicts." - Author Stuart White, CEO of WriteMentor

"This is a brilliant series! I love it! It's like a mixture of Sirens the TV series and *Aquaman* and a *Romeo & Juliet* forbidden love story." - ARC reader

"Enchanting! Mesmerizing! Captivating! Heart-breaking!" - Book Blogger

"Deliciously romantic!" - Goodreads reader

"This series is so good, it got me out of my slump!" - ARC reader

"My favorite fantasy romance series ever!!!" – Amazon review

"These books are so fast paced and addictive that I usually read them within one or two days—I just can't put them down!" – Amazon review

CONTENT WARNINGS

This book contains themes and references that some readers may find distressing, including, but not limited to: violence, sexual content. death or dying, blood, gore, graphic injuries, mental illness, depression, alcoholism, anxiety, prejudice, swears or curses, murder, war, monsters.

FIGHT FOR FREEDOM PLAYLIST

Mermaid - Train
My Heart With You – The Rescues
Hold On – CaiNo
A Thousand Years- Christina Perri
Fight Song – Rachel Platten
Leave a Light On – Tom Walker
Wellerman – Sea Shanty
Nothing Between Us – Westover
Marry You – Bruno Mars
Love Yourself – Justin Bieber
To Be With You – Mr. Big
50 Ways to Say Goodbye – Train
We Are Never Getting Back Together – Taylor Swift
Wrecking Ball – Miley Cyrus
I'm Not Over You – Scouting For Girls
You're Not Special – McFly
Stay – The Kid Laroi, Justin Bieber
Toxic – BoyWithUke
My Heart Has Teeth – Deadmau5, Skylar Grey
Be Careful - Tommee Profitt, Laney Jones
Vigilante Shit – Taylor Swift

For Petra

RECAP OF BOOK 1 – SECRETS OF THE DEEP

On the approach of Cordelia Blue's eighteenth birthday, she decided it was time to break free from the shadows of her tragic past. The loss of her mother and twin brother in a devastating shark attack had haunted her for five long years, forcing her to abandon her once-promising swimming career. She even shied away from taking a simple bath.

With unwavering support from her best friends, Maya and Trent, Cordelia embarked on a journey to conquer her deepest fears head-on. Little did she know, this leap of faith would reveal a world of enchanting secrets lurking beneath the surface. As she dipped her toes into water for the first time since the attack, Cordelia unearthed her astonishing destiny—she was a mermaid, and her long-lost twin, Dylan, was alive too. Trapped in an aquatic realm, he was unable to shift into human form. Dylan entrusted Cordelia with a mystical pearl, a key to locating the elusive High Council—the sole authority capable of granting mermaids their precious legs once more. However, the mermaids weren't the only ones hunting for this gem. The selachii, shark shapeshifters cursed to the depths, yearned to regain their legs too. And would stop at nothing to find it.

Old flame, Wade Waters, swam back into Cordelia's life. Sparks flew, but lurking in the shadows were Wade's shady cousins, and Cordelia couldn't shake the feeling that he was harboring a deep, dark secret. And keeping her own secret concerning her mermaid lineage under wraps took a toll on their relationship.

When the pearl mysteriously vanished from Cordelia's grasp, she discovered Wade's secret—he was one of the selachii and had betrayed her. Worse yet, Trent, her loyal friend, fell victim to a brutal shark attack and was transformed into one of them.

With trust shattered and alliances uncertain, Cordelia turned to Maya and the ancient tome, *The Mermaid Chronicles*, which held the key to unraveling their intertwined destinies. Maya insisted that merfolk and selachii must unite to reclaim their lost glory. Cordelia delved into the book's secrets, uncovering a forgotten era of harmony between merfolk and selachii on the fabled island of Atlantis.

As Cordelia unmasked Zale, the leader of the selachii, as the thief behind the pearl's theft, she and Wade joined forces to retrieve the precious jewel, but almost cost them Wade's life. When Cordelia and Wade reunited, the pearl's secrets unraveled, whisking them away to another dimension to confront the enigmatic High Council.

The High Council, comprised of representatives from merfolk, selachii, dragon kings, and eelusionists, agreed to grant them legs once more. Yet, it came at a price—Cordelia and Wade were tasked with the monumental quest to unearth their lost homeland, the mythical Atlantis. The epic adventure had only just begun, and the fate of two worlds hung in the balance.

RECAP OF BOOK 2 – QUEST FOR ATLANTIS

When mermaids began mysteriously disappearing, stolen away by humans for display or sinister experiments, the hidden realm of mermaids and selachii was unveiled. Cordelia, Wade, and their friends fought valiantly, rescuing one of their own from a science lab. Yet, the global onslaught continued, casting an ever-growing shadow over their existence.

Their mission was clear: unveil the enigma of the lost island of Atlantis—an aquatic sanctuary where all ocean shifters could find refuge. To unlock its secrets, the team embarked on a quest for the fabled, scattered jewels that held the key to Atlantis' portal. But their journey was fraught with peril.

Beneath the icy depths of Mount Rainier and the treacherous Puget Sound, Cordelia and Wade faced near-death encounters with ice demons. Gal, a formidable dragon king and council member, defied convention to save them. The

Power of the Sea surged through them, healing their wounds and bestowing incredible gifts—a Herculean strength for Wade and the untamed power of fire for Cordelia.

Tensions flared as Wade's ex, Stephanie, intruded on the mission, determined to win him back, fueled by his mother's approval. Cordelia grappled with doubt, their bond tested by misunderstandings and painful infidelities, fracturing their once-unbreakable unity.

Maya's life hung by a thread after a harrowing accident, compelling Dylan to transform her into a mermaid. But the toll of their perilous journey didn't end there—Cordelia's father faced certain death in the unfathomable Mariana Trench, only to be transformed into a selachii through a desperate ritual led by Wade.

Amidst near-tragedies and heartaches, Cordelia and Wade rekindled their love, poised to confront those who sought to tear them apart. Armed with the keys to Atlantis, they crossed dimensions into a magical realm. But a harrowing sight awaited them—an island in ruins, guarded by legions of dragon kings. A savage battle ensued, with Cordelia mastering her fiery abilities to vanquish the malevolent force, at the cost of her dear mentor, Gal.

As the Power of the Sea was plunged into the Fountain of Youth, the island blossomed anew. Amidst the rejuvenation, Cordelia made an astonishing discovery—a long-lost captive, her mother, believed dead for over five years, was alive and well.

In a joyous reunion, Cordelia found her family and a newfound sanctuary where all could walk on land, hidden from prying human eyes. Amidst the serenity, Wade proposed to Cordelia, promising a blissful future, until the pages of *The Mermaid Chronicles* started turning once again.

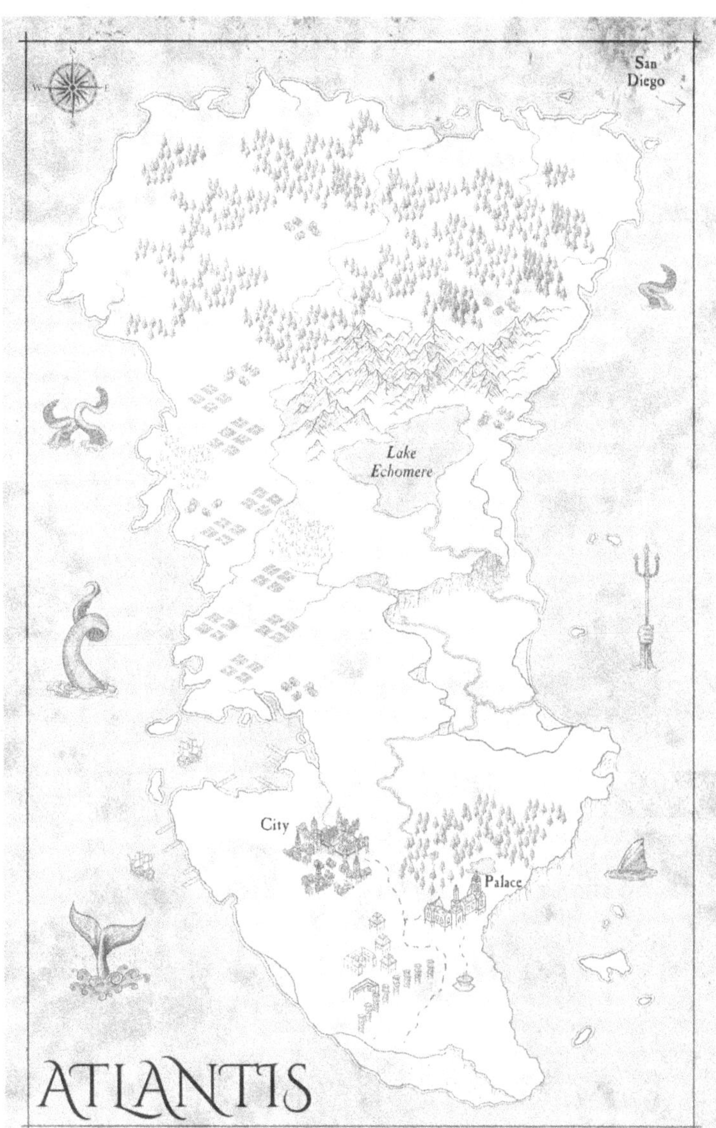

San
Diego
Lake
Echomere
City
Palace
ATLANTIS

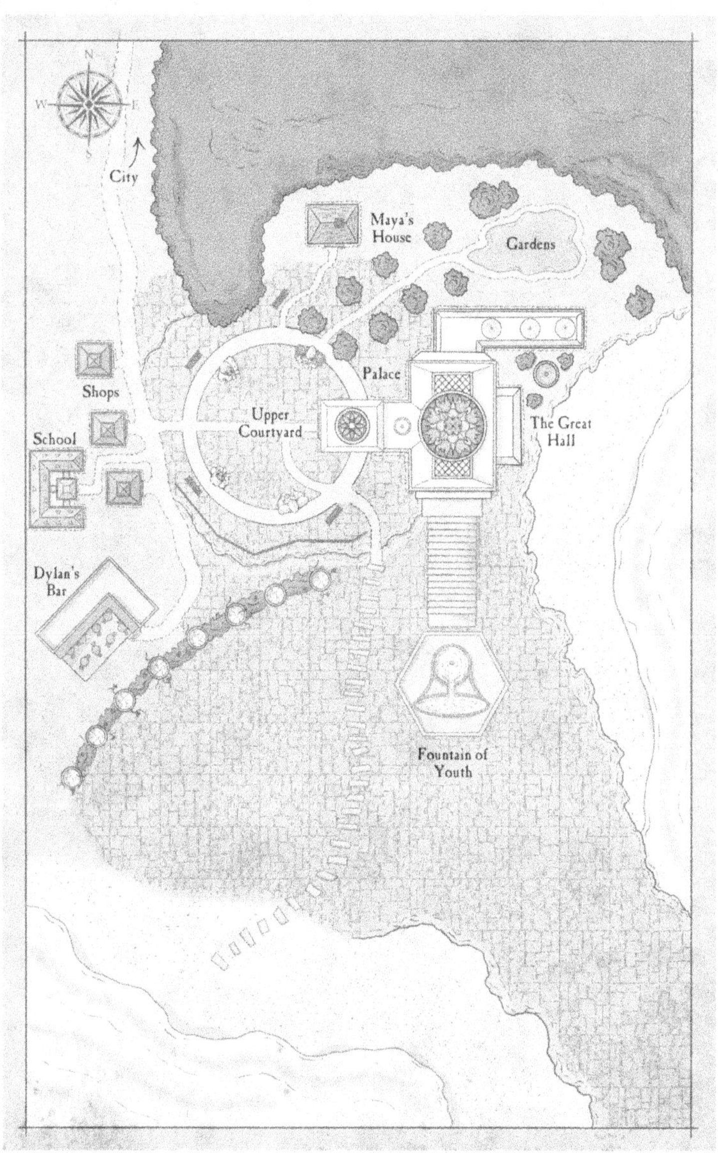

N
W
E
S
City
Maya's House
Gardens
Shops
School
Palace
Upper Courtyard
The Great Hall
Dylan's Bar
Fountain of Youth

"*W*ade Daniel Waters, do you take Cordelia Anne Blue for your lawful wedded wife, to live in the holy estate of matrimony? Will you love, honor, comfort, and cherish her from this day forward, forsaking all others, keeping only unto her for as long as you both shall live?" The minister looked to my almost husband.

"I do," Wade smiled, then added, "always, forever and *united.*"

Standing next to Wade, Trent nudged him in the ribs. "Can we stick to the script?"

"Cordelia Anne Blue, do you take Wade Daniel Waters for your lawful wedded husband, to live in the holy estate of matrimony? Will you love, honor, comfort, and cherish him from this day forward, forsaking all others, keeping only unto him for as long as you both shall live?"

"I do," I replied. "Always, forever and *united.*"

Trent rolled his eyes, and I stifled a giggle. Wade slipped a ring onto my finger, a plain white gold band that sparkled in the sunlight. I slipped the matching one onto his. The minister declared we were now husband and wife. Wade was free to kiss me, as many times as he wanted and for as long as we both desired.

His head dipped, his eyes flashing black. I circled my arms around his neck and forgot about everyone standing on the beach watching us. It was our moment, our first act as husband and wife, king and queen. We would be officially coronated during the wedding breakfast. But I forgot all that as I softened against him. I ignored all the staring eyes, and focused instead on his lips and found myself wishing we could bypass the coming feast and head straight to our new bedroom. But that would have to wait. There were family and well-wishers to greet.

Maya handed me my bouquet, an exquisite arrangement of bird of paradise. Wade walked me back down the aisle, our bare feet sinking into the soft sand, to a thunderous applause and a few loud wolf whistles. Trent was the main culprit. He and Maya stood together at the altar, maid of honor and best man, watching us go.

I lifted my dress as we walked along the cobblestone path. We followed the winding walkway under the aqueduct, vines softening their angular edges and now heavy with plump, ripe grapes, toward the palace steps and the courtyard where the banquet waited for us.

"You're so beautiful. I haven't had a chance to tell you. When you came walking down the aisle, I thought I was dreaming," Wade whispered, his voice thick with emotion. He gently cupped my elbow, guiding me along the flower-strewn path with a tender, protective touch.

I looked up at him, my heart swelling with a rush of indescribable joy. His eyes, glistening with unshed tears, reflected the same overwhelming happiness I felt. The way he gazed at me, as if I were the most precious treasure in the world, made my breath catch in my throat. As we walked together, I marveled at the way the sunlight danced on his features, highlighting the strong lines of his jaw and the softness in his eyes. He looked so handsome, so perfect, that it took my breath away. Every step we took felt like a dream, each moment more magical than the last.

"You too," I managed to reply, my voice trembling with the weight of my emotions. Words seemed so inadequate in that moment, unable to fully capture the depth of my feelings. I was afraid I would cry from sheer happiness, from the magnitude of the whole thing, and from the blissful relief that finally, everything had gone the right way for us.

"We deserve it." Wade read my thoughts. "We've been through so much. It's our time now."

"It is." I clutched his hand as we mounted the marble steps. Halfway up, we turned and waved to our people who were approaching the cobblestone path. "Give me a minute," I said as we arrived in the upper courtyard. "I need to freshen up."

Wade drew me to his side. "Take a few. Now we're married, I won't worry when you're out of my sight."

"Worry?" I questioned.

Wade smiled sheepishly and shoved his hands in his pockets. "Ever since we had that argument on the plane and I realized I loved you more than you loved me, I worried I might lose you."

"Wade..."

"And not necessarily to another guy, but maybe to your family or a career or maybe even to the blue chamber and the High Council or...I don't really know to what. But you've got my ring on your finger now. Two of them. It's the most relaxed I've felt in months." He chuckled. "So take a moment, take a few. We have the rest of our lives to love each other."

I walked back to Wade and gently rested a hand on his cheek, feeling the warmth of his skin beneath my fingers. "Exactly," I said softly, looking into his eyes. "You shouldn't have worried. I was naïve back then, on the plane. It may have only been a year ago, but it's been a long year, and we've been through so much together. I grew up. We both did. We were forced to."

I paused, my heart swelling with the memories of our journey. "I don't regret any of it. It was a stupid argument. If I'd known then that we would be married a year later... But here we are, right where we should be."

I moved closer, feeling the warmth of his body enveloping me, grounding me in the reality of our love. "Don't ever doubt my love for you, Wade. And please, don't hide your worries from me. We're in this together, now and always." My voice trembled slightly as I added, "And for the record, back then, it was me who loved you more."

Wade took my hand from his cheek, his touch gentle and reverent, as if he were holding something infinitely precious. He brushed the ends of my fingers with his lips, sending a shiver of delight through me. "Thank you."

He gestured for me to carry on to the bathroom, but I lingered for a moment, capturing this perfect slice of time.

"Go on," he said. "And hurry back."

Smiling, I disappeared into the bathroom. I stood in front of the mirror and took in my appearance. My ivory dress was a one shoulder affair made from delicate chiffon. A soft trail of chiffon cascaded from one shoulder and puddled on the floor. Attached to the bodice were several white lace butterflies that looked ready to carry me away to a whimsical land. The same butterflies adorned my wild, red hair. I wore Wade's charm bracelet on my wrist, my father's 'C' pendant at my neck, and Trent and Maya's diamond earrings. Presents I'd received for my eighteenth birthday. I looked at the new ring on my finger, nestled close to my engagement ring, a perfect pair. I was now married. To Wade. The enormity of the idea flooded over me, and I had to grip the cold marble sink to steady myself.

Maya found me there. "I thought you might need a few minutes alone."

I splashed water on my face and patted myself dry with a paper towel. "It's all so perfect...too perfect...and I'm afraid."

"You've been through all the bad stuff. We all have." Maya clutched my arm. "This last year on Atlantis has been perfect, and it will continue to be so. Don't start doubting that."

"So you didn't rush back to check *The Mermaid Chronicles* just now?"

Maya blushed. "The pages are changing. They're flapping about all over the place."

A lump of fear formed in my throat. I raised a palm. "No. Not today."

Maya shrugged. "I can't do anything until they stop turning, anyway."

"Well, let's hope it's like last time, after we arrived, a future full of rainbows and unicorns."

"I'm sure." She hugged me. "It's most likely about the future leaders of Atlantis." She looked pointedly at my stomach.

"I am *way* too young to be a mother."

Maya laughed. "There are worse things."

We spent a few more minutes in the bathroom. She touched up my make-up, adding blush to my pale cheeks and a shimmering lipstick to my lips. We faced the mirror again together. Her silk sarong dress of peach-blossom orange complimented my wedding dress perfectly. She had fastened one of the lace butterflies in her blonde hair.

"I love you," I said.

"I love you too," she replied and gave me another quick squeeze. "We should join the banquet. People will start wondering where you are."

I opened the door to the sound of laughter and clinking glasses, animated conversation, and the soft notes of a piano. I followed Maya to the courtyard and prepared myself for the crowd.

A champagne flute was thrust into my hand and Wade appeared at my side, steering me through the crowd with a comforting hand on my elbow. I sipped at the champagne as we made our way through the throng of people, accepting handshakes and kisses on cheeks, congratulations and words of advice. Wade handled them all expertly, never staying too long, but never short enough to appear rude. He refilled my glass when it was necessary, and it wasn't long before we only had our family left to greet.

My parents appeared. My father had tears in his eyes and my mother's spilled freely. She held her arms wide and swept us both up in a hug.

"I'm so happy," she said.

"I am the proudest father on the planet," Dad said, wiping self-consciously under his eye. "This day is so much more than...I don't know what, it's just *more*."

"I know," Wade said. "I feel a little that way myself. I love Cordelia. I always have. I think since I was thirteen. And then we met again, fell in love, and I knew I couldn't be without her. But making it so..." Wade shook his head. "It's a whole other realm of emotion. It's more than I thought I was capable of feeling, more than I thought I deserved."

There was a strange gurgling sound in my throat. My mother choked out another sob.

"I'm going to leave before I don't stop crying," she laughed.

Well-wishers swept by, their effusive affection dazzling and overwhelming. I remained mute. Wade had a way of saying things to me that seemed to stop time. The surrounding crowds blurred into a mirage of whirling colors as I reveled in Wade's words. *He had loved me since he was thirteen.* I could barely breathe. I was afraid the swelling in my heart would pass and I wasn't ready for it to pass.

"I..." I wanted to say something that would mirror his words, that would tell him I felt exactly the same way, more.

"I love you, Cordelia Blue," he said.

I smiled. "You can't call me that anymore. I think you'll find my last name is Waters now."

"You'll always be Cordelia Blue to me."

The sun sparkled over the mountain, beginning its descent, its heat still strong and vibrant. Wade and I leaned against the stone balcony, the coolness refreshing my flushed skin. We stole a brief moment to ourselves, savoring the serenity of the evening. Wade cupped my face in his hands, his touch gentle yet firm, and brought his lips to mine.

The instant our lips met, I felt a jolt of electricity course through me. Though we had kissed countless times before, this kiss was different. It stole my breath, making my heart race as if it had wings.

His lips moved against mine with a fervent passion, each kiss deeper and more consuming than the last. Cocooned in his arms, I had never loved someone more, I had never wanted someone more.

His warmth enveloped me, sending shivers down my spine, heat curling through my stomach, and a deep, desperate ache to settle low between my legs. He nipped at my ear, then traced the length of my jaw with his lips, igniting a trail of fire. When he nestled into the crevice of my neck, I sighed with pure bliss. Every fiber of my being ached for him, and in that moment, I knew our love was a force that would always draw us together, no matter what.

When he pulled away, we were both breathless. He kept his hands on the small of my back and a tingling heat swam up my spine. We stood close, holding hands, whispering to each other, our noses almost touching. I couldn't stand not to be touching him. The feelings that swelled over me were all-consuming, irresistible, addictive...and I wanted more.

With a carnal glint in his eye, Wade skated his hand from my hip, across my stomach, using his thumb to graze the most sensitive part of me. I gasped. He grinned.

"You can't do that to me," I hissed. "We have hours until we can be alone."

He pulled me against his chest, planted his hands on my rear and tightened his embrace so I could feel every inch of his arousal. Dipping his lips to my ear, he said, "I want you as turned on as I am. All. Night. Long."

"You bastard," I laughed, devising a plan to get him away as early as possible.

A bell sounded, signaling it was time for the feast to begin. With a knowing smirk, Wade led me to a pair of ornately carved chairs and pulled one out for me. It was a long, traditional head table. Trent sat to my left, and Maya to Wade's right. Our parents and siblings were further along. Apart from Wade's father. We'd only heard from him twice in the last year.

A band struck up and a buffet was laid for all the inhabitants of the island. Everyone was in attendance.

As my eyes rolled over the feast, a deep sense of loss pulled at my heart. Gal. I missed him terribly. His death had left a thorn in my chest, one I wasn't sure would ever heal.

He had once described a feast like this to me, a royal wedding party with piles of food and plentiful drinks. Closing my eyes against the wave of emotion, I sought his presence. I hoped he was here, somehow, watching over me with a smile on his broad face, proud of how far I'd come.

"It's our turn for food." Wade helped me to my feet and led me to the buffet.

I didn't know where to start. The buffet tables were covered in fine white linen, piled high with glazed food, drink fountains and three-foot vases, each supporting a striking arrangement of bird of paradise that matched my bouquet. A rich green ivy twisted its way down the stem of each vase and spilled over the white tablecloth.

As for the food itself, there were honey-glazed hams adorned with pineapples and sweet cherries, barbequed lambs lathered in a marinade of strawberry jam, beef wellingtons with the puff of the pastry an inch high, chicken kebabs, whole roast guinea fowl. There were piles of mussels, clams, oysters, and shrimp with accompanying Marie Rose, garlic butter, and marinara sauces. The vegetables had been harvested from the palace gardens. There were zucchinis, their meat scooped out and replaced with rice, goat's cheese and roasted peppers, stuffed tomatoes, foot-long ears of corn, a medley of roasted orange vegetables. My mouth watered.

Wade took my plate from my hand and piled it high with food. We laughed when my stomach growled noisily in response.

"Congrats, sis." Dylan stood at my side. He held two glasses of champagne. He knocked one back in an instant. Most of the buttons on his shirt were undone and the shirt itself was creased and stained with the evidence of more than one night of indulgence. "It was a beautiful ceremony." His words slurred and he swayed on his feet.

"Thanks," I replied, grabbing his arm to steady him. "Thanks for organizing all the drinks."

Dylan had taken over the running of the main bar. He spent most of his time there. When he wasn't playing barman and telling stories of his adventures in the water, he was in his apartment above. But never on the balcony. I'd never seen him sitting there. Or in the ocean. Not once. I wondered if he still knew how to swim. Did merfolk tails ever disappear with lack of use?

Wade frowned as Dylan knocked back the second drink. He removed a fraying cigarette from his pocket, lit it, and inhaled deeply. He exhaled the smoke in my face.

"Looks like I'm empty," Dylan said, tapping his glass. "Catch you later." He stumbled away from us.

Something in my chest pinched as I watched him retreat, slapping the backs of some, tripping over the feet of others, but always with the same fake smile plastered to his face. I didn't know how to help him. Every time I tried to raise the subject of his drinking, he shot me down.

"What am I going to do about him?"

Wade rested his head on top of mine. "Dylan is not today's problem."

"But I need to do something..."

"What more can you do?" Wade said. "He needs to learn to stand on his own two feet."

"It's not that easy...especially with everything he's been through."

"I know." Wade kissed me. "But not tonight."

"No, not tonight."

The sun set and the courtyard came alive with laughter and dancing. The dessert course arrived later in the evening. The flowers were removed and a stunning ice sculpture of a mermaid and selachii made an extraordinary center piece. The figures held hands as they swam through an ocean, their tails hovering high above their heads as though they were drifting down the crest of the wave. I ran a finger over the frigid carving, admiring the likeness to Wade and me.

The dessert table held a mountain of sweetness. Cakes, ice creams, a champagne sorbet, a rum flavored frozen yogurt, and a profiterole tower. Syllabubs, mousses, trifles, and puddings. But the best, of course, was the wedding cake. It was a five layered affair, orange bird of paradise sugar flowers decorating its flanks with the real thing adorning the top. Wade and I cut into the cake together and fed each other the first delicious morsels in front of a cheering crowd.

The sun dipped under the horizon and the night sky mantled the distant, snow-capped mountain. The band began a familiar number and Wade took me in his arms and whisked me to the middle of the dance floor. When others floated around us, Wade circled his arms around me and held me tight. Nothing could mar the perfection of this day. Nothing.

Instead of laying my head on Wade's shoulder and soaking up his ocean scent, I scanned the crowd, craning my neck to inspect the more distant groups of people hovering by the buffet tables and refilling glasses by the champagne tower.

"She's not here. I haven't seen her all day," I said.

"That's a good thing, right?" Wade asked.

"I suppose. I didn't know what to expect. I haven't spoken to her once in the last year."

"Me neither. I think she's giving us the space we asked for."

A thread of anxiety weaved through my stomach. The trouble Stephanie had caused was almost a distant memory, but I never expected her to stay quiet for this long.

We danced until the moon was high, until my feet ached, and until the crowds dispersed.

"My feet hurt," I said. "I can't eat anymore, and I can't drink anymore, not if I want to remember today."

"It *is* getting late." A mischievous smile bloomed on Wade's face.

I placed my hand on the small of his back, slipped my fingertips into the top of his trousers. "It is."

Without another word, and without saying goodnight to anyone, Wade led me from the wedding feast. We rushed through the echoing palace hallways, up the marble staircase and into our new suite of rooms. I hadn't yet seen the rooms that had been bestowed on us as the royal couple. I didn't much care to inspect them now. There was only one thing I was interested in. In fact, it had been on my mind for most of the day, ever since I first laid eyes on Wade in his beige chinos and flowing white linen shirt, waiting for me at the altar. The day had been filled with heat, my fingertips often bursting into flames. I ached to be near him, to feel his touch, for him to take me as his wife.

Without another word, Wade circled his fingers around my wrists and pulled me tight against him. He kissed me, his tongue parting my lips, testing, teasing.

"Please...I can't...I need you...now," I begged, tugging at the sleeves of his shirt.

"Patience, Cordelia," he whispered as he kissed me again.

"I've been patient all day."

But he wouldn't be rushed. He unzipped the back of my dress, painstakingly slowly, and after removing the delicate chiffon from my shoulder, let it pool on the floor at our feet. I stood in my underwear, shivering in the moonlight, as he examined me with his eyes. But I wasn't cold for long. He wrapped his powerful arms around me, and my skin flushed with heat.

I pulled his shirt over his head and ran my hands along his defined arms. The Power of the Sea had gifted him extraordinary strength, and it showed in every part of his body. His chest and his back were chiseled to perfection, and I fit perfectly in the fold of his arms.

Wade dropped to his knees, his face level with the very center of me, his warm breath gusting against my swollen bud. I gasped at the riot of sensations swarming over me, my muscles already twitching. He tugged my underwear down and I held onto his shoulders as I stepped out of them, the building damp heat impossible to ignore.

Wade drew my bud into his mouth, pulling it between his teeth, nipping and sucking and tasting. My knees buckled. He held onto my rear, keeping my upright, spreading me wider.

"Wade..." I groaned his name as the pressure built. A heat in my stomach, a coil of tension between my legs. His tongue thrust inside me, finding that other sensitive spot. He nipped and licked and tasted and I could barely stay upright. And then the pressure released and shattered me wide open.

I opened my mouth and let my soft moans fill the room as my body spasmed against his skilled tongue.

Wade stood to face me, kissed me deep and hard, sharing my sweet taste. His hardness pressed into me, the girth and length of it so enticing I could already feel a second orgasm building.

Skating a hand over his length, gliding up and down, Wade released a series of breathy groans. I pushed him onto the bed and swept a leg over him. I hovered over him, his tip at my entrance, circling my hips so slowly that he growled and slammed my hips down, making me take him in one quick motion.

He filled and stretched me, deeper and harder with each of his upward thrusts. His fingers dug into my hips, pulling me down on him each time, the sound of the slap of slick skin surrounding us.

Our rhythm matched, both of us increasing the speed. Both of us exhaling groans and pleas for more. I tipped my head back, drowning in sensation. Ripples of pleasure skated through me. The tension coiling in my lower stomach was intense and biting. It spasmed out to my center. My muscles clenched around him, holding him deep within as shards of pleasure cut through me.

Faster. Harder. Deeper.

Ecstasy burst over me, my voice carrying Wade's name through the echoing halls and out the windows to the party-goers dancing in the courtyard below. But I didn't care, and neither did Wade.

He rolled on top of me and filled me deeper. A third wave of bliss engulfed my body before the second had finished. I clutched his back, pulling him tight against me, spasming against him.

"Cordelia," Wade cried, his entire body jerking, his hands holding me tight. Then he collapsed against me.

We lay in the light of the moon, curled in each other's arms, watching the shadows filter through our arched windows. Wade pulled the duvet over our cooling skin. He entwined his fingers in my hair, teasing the lace butterflies loose, letting them fall to the rug below.

"Are you glad we didn't rush?" Wade asked.

"For now," I replied. "But I'm not done with you yet."

CHAPTER TWO

We sat in the glow of the morning sun, Wade bare-chested and wearing long pajama bottoms, myself in a cotton robe, the tie chord hanging loose and not much caring about it. Wade not much caring about it either. Occasionally he would reach out and rub his thumb over my nipple, arousing me all over again.

Breakfast had been brought to the living area of our suite. We sat on over-stuffed armchairs, sipping steaming coffee, relishing the fix of caffeine that would help us endure the first day of our lives together as a married couple after a sleepless night. *Sleepless in a good way*, I thought smugly.

"Ford wants to talk to us today." Wade sliced into a bear claw doughnut and handed me half.

"Really?" I pulled a face at the mention of the burly security guard's name. He'd sworn to protect us the minute we arrived on Atlantis, wore his promise like a badge of honor, even though Wade and I possessed more power. He'd not once let us down. "Don't we get a honeymoon before we start our reign as king and queen?"

"Yes, but there is one issue we need to address first." Wade flicked a frown at the brightening window and the sounds of the city waking outside. "It's been a year. People want to return to the mainland. Many left family behind."

A tendril of unease slipped into my stomach.

"I can understand it," Wade continued. "We knew we couldn't remain isolated forever."

There was nothing I wanted on the mainland. Everything I wanted, everyone I loved was right here. But others wanted to return, and I worried we would find our world in jeopardy.

"People are growing discontent," Wade addressed my wrinkled face. "They've all been happy about the wedding, helping to prepare, getting caught up in the excitement, but now that it's over, we need to ready ourselves for a battery of requests to return. I guarantee it will start today—"

There was a knock at the door. I raised an eyebrow. "Seems as though it might be starting already."

Wade sighed as Ford swung open one of the tall, wooden doors and stepped inside. He was a giant of a man, with arms and legs as thick as Gal's had been. But he had none of Gal's coloring. Ford was much darker; dark brown skin, dark brown hair, and intelligent eyes that never missed a trick.

"Morning." Ford stood tall and strong, perfect for the role of the head of Royal Security. Atlantis had been peaceful, with little need for a police presence, but it was prudent to build a security team around the rulers of the island.

Although the dragon kings had been defeated, other threats existed. *The Mermaid Chronicles* spoke of many.

There had only been two incidents in the last year that had required Ford's presence. The first when Dylan had become so inebriated after closing his bar one night, that he fell through a stained-glass window. The second when Jordan and Stephanie went missing during one of their wild, adrenaline seeking adventures. They'd been found bruised and injured, but alive.

But if the merfolk and selachii of Atlantis were thinking of returning to the human world, it was prudent to have a protection force in case we were ever discovered. Over the last year, Ford had recruited and trained a formidable army, one I hoped we would never need.

"There's a particularly bouncy young lady here who is desperate to see you. I told her it was your wedding morning, as she well knows—"

Before he could explain further, Maya burst into the room. She plopped onto the couch and pretended not to notice that Wade and I weren't dressed.

"Morning!" she declared brightly as I pulled my dressing gown tighter.

Wade nodded at Ford to allow Maya to stay, so he left, closing the door softly behind him.

"Good night?" she asked, grinning, her blonde curls bouncing. "I didn't see you leave."

"Maya." I glared at my best friend. "What are you doing here?"

The smile slipped from her lips, and it wasn't until that moment I noticed it wasn't a real smile to begin with. She inspected our plateful of food, finally seemed to notice the state of our dress, and had the decency to blush.

"It's this." She pointed to a book in her lap.

How had I not noticed she was clutching *The Mermaid Chronicles*? It barely left her side. She held it tightly, clenching it in white fingers, and said nothing more.

I found myself mesmerized by the glistening blueness of it. Although muted with age and battered by events, there was a faint, blue hue to the cover of the book that glistened when it moved. We still hadn't found an explanation for the symbols beneath the picture of the merfolk on the cover, and Maya was coming to the conclusion it was just for decoration.

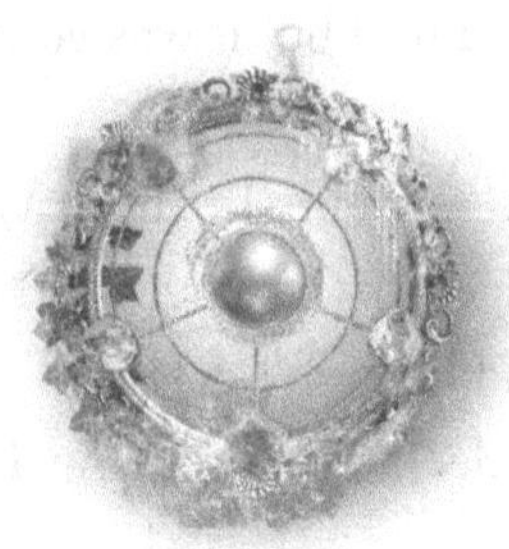

THE THREE OF us stared at the plate of now unwanted food, unwilling to commit thoughts to words. What could be so important the day after our wedding? Nothing good.

I closed my eyes. Wade held my hand. Time ticked silently on.

"What I find interesting about the book," Maya broke the

silence, "is that no matter how many new prophecies or words are written within its pages, the number of blank pages remains the same."

"What are you saying?" Wade asked.

Maya tilted her head. "The book grows. There will always be new prophecies, from now until the end of time."

"But you said there was nothing but happy futures in it." I found my voice. "When we got engaged. You said the pages had stopped changing and that you saw nothing but a bright future for us all on Atlantis."

"I did. But you know as well as I that nothing is set in stone. The book changes. New words replace old."

"So what's changed now?" Wade asked.

A second ominous silence wound between us. A breeze drifted through the windows and irritated the back of my neck.

"We got married," I answered my husband.

I didn't need any confirmation from Maya, her crestfallen face said it all.

"Us getting married was a *good* thing." Wade launched to his feet and jabbed a finger at the ceiling.

"I can't help what appears in the pages," Maya said. "I can only tell you what is says. And now, it seems, there will be another adventure. We must be united once again."

Wade laughed, his shoulders relaxing. "That's easy. We are already united, have been for some time now." He smiled at me and took my hand again.

I rose to stand next to him. "Maybe your book is wrong this time, Maya."

Maya shook her head. She was like a turtle in lockdown mode. "It's never wrong."

"What does it say?" Wade snapped, raking a hand through his hair.

"*To save Atlantis the royal couple must unite with a third, the one who died and lives again.*"

"It *is* because we got married..." I sank back into my chair. Wade rested a hand on my shoulder. "It's never referred to us as the royal couple before."

"Who's the third?" he asked.

"That's all it says," Maya replied. "But I expect it's a human."

CHAPTER THREE

"It's hard to believe we could lose all of this," Wade said.

We stood at one of the arched windows. Maya had left an hour ago, and the only thing we'd been able to do was get dressed and stare at the ocean from our window. My heart was heavy. I struggled to recapture the feelings that had swelled my chest last night, those feelings of hope and happiness and of all being right with the world. They seemed a lifetime ago.

"To save Atlantis—"

"We only just got the island back." I pressed my palms into the coolness of the windowsill, hoping the touch of something solid would reassure me. "It's hard to imagine anything could jeopardize that."

Wade leaned on his hands, chewed on his lip. His eyes flashed black. His selachii eyes always gave his emotions away. "Something will happen when people return to the mainland."

"But we can't stop people returning," I said. "That's not who we are."

"I know."

Standing behind me, Wade slide his arms around my waist, and we stared at our island together. At the courtyard, where we'd celebrated the wedding, lined with marble pillars and plump vines. The cobblestone paths and water channels leading in all directions. The Fountain of Youth that sat in the middle of it, boasting elaborate statues of leaping fish and merfolk. It powered our island. It cured our people. It was a gift from the gods. Then there was my favorite part, the soft white sand and the sparkling blue water.

My gaze snagged on the flat horizon. It used to fill me with possibility. Now it filled me with dread. Anything might appear and break that line of peace.

"Who's the human?" I wondered aloud.

"It could be anyone," Wade replied.

"Is there nothing we can do?"

Wade pressed his chin into my shoulder. "We'll have to wait and hope the person, whoever he or she is, will be revealed to us before too much...heartache and loss are endured."

My heart skipped a beat. Our path to finding Atlantis had caused a wealth of heartache and loss, as predicted by a prophecy in *The Mermaid Chronicles*. Many of my wounds had healed after the battle with the dragon kings, but my scars rested just under the surface. It wouldn't take much to undo me. "There aren't any humans here. It seems we'll have to find the relevant person on the mainland. A place I never thought I would return to."

"But will the act of returning make everything else come to pass?"

"A paradox," I murmured. "Damned if we do and damned if we don't."

"I wish I could enjoy one day with you before we have to deal with this, but I can't have it hovering over us. I need to know what's going on." His arms tightened around me and I wondered if he was offering or seeking comfort. Maybe both.

"I know." I leaned my head back against him and Wade threaded his fingers through my hair, causing heated prickles to break out over my scalp. I wanted to stay here, with my new husband, getting high on his ocean scent, delaying reality for a little longer. Because I knew as soon as I stepped out of the doors of our suite, our long list of responsibilities would begin.

"Ford says there's a line of people waiting to see us, and I can bet you all their questions will be the same; 'when can we return?'"

"What are we going to tell them?"

"We're going to have to come up with something to stop them all rushing into the ocean." He moved his hand from my hair and wrapped his arms around my waist once more.

"I don't know what that could be." I gnawed on a fingernail, hoping for inspiration. "Trent is desperate to go back."

"Trent is a member of the senate," Wade said. "He will understand the importance of prudence."

"We need to gather them."

Wade kissed my neck, my ear, then turned me to face him and kissed my lips. "I'll call for Ford."

There was a knock on the door. Trent and Maya appeared.

"We were just talking about you," Wade said. "Well, *The Mermaid Chronicles*."

Maya flashed him a warning look.

"What's going on with *The Mermaid Chronicles*?" Trent asked, running his hands through his damp curls. He must have recently been in the ocean.

"You haven't told him?" I asked Maya.

Maya grimaced. "Not yet, I was trying to get a better grasp of events before I revealed it more widely."

"But I'm in the senate," Trent said, pointing at himself. "I should know. And more importantly...I'm your boyfriend..."

Maya grabbed his hand. "I know. I wanted to tell you straight away. But some things are bigger than us."

"Shit," Trent muttered. "That doesn't sound good."

Understatement of the fucking year.

"I thought we could plug in first." Maya pointed at the blank TV screen. "Then we might have more information. There is a method to my madness, you know."

"Plug in?" Wade asked. "I thought we were doing that tomorrow?"

"A lot of people want to go back to the mainland," Trent replied.

"I know," Wade said, giving me a look.

"Well, when you start your official duties tomorrow, that's all you're going to hear. I thought if we plugged in now, we could get a jump on what's happening over there," Trent said.

We'd left the network unplugged for the last year. The

Power of the Sea was capable of connecting us to the televisions and news channels and internet of the mainland, but the senate had decided to delay the process. Allowing people to adjust to their new lives on Atlantis without interference from the mainland seemed the best way for people to adapt. Plus, it was glorious to be free of technology. No social media. No phones. No laptops. No Instagram or Tiktok or Snapchat or X...glorious.

"Unless there is a new prophecy you want to talk about first?" Trent asked.

"Later," Maya said, pressing the remote into his hand.

Trent and Maya joined us by the arched window. Trent held the remote to the large monitor fitted in our living suite. Voices below, laughing, floated up to us. Wade leaned out of the window. Stephanie and Jordan, backpacks filled to the brim, made their way down the steps and toward the mountain path. Her hair was longer, reaching almost to her waist, and it swished glamorously against her back as she walked. Dark strands mantled her temples, contrasting against the blonde. Perhaps she was trying something new. The whole effect was quite striking and only emphasized her pale blue eyes.

"They're at it again," Trent remarked.

"What is it this time?" Wade asked.

"They're going to climb the mountain," Trent replied, tossing his curls out of his face. "And I think I heard something about hand-gliding." He leaned out of the window and waved. "I think I'm a little jealous. I could use a thrill-seeking adventure."

Wade, Maya, and I all frowned at the same time. Trent

assessed our serious faces. "You guys are making me nervous. What the hell is going on?"

"Let's just turn on the TV," Wade said. "Then we'll discuss anything else we need to discuss."

The four of us stood in a loose line in front of the screen. Trent swiped a pastry off the plate from the coffee table, the discards of our first breakfast as a married couple. He pointed the remote at the screen, powdered sugar coating his lips, and with a flourish, thumbed the relevant button.

The screen came to life. The channel numbers were big and bold in the top corner, but the rest remained disappointingly blank. Trent pressed a few more buttons. The TV winked off and on again. Still nothing.

"You wired it up, right?" Wade asked.

"Yeah." Trent waved a wrist in his direction. "Took me the best part of a week."

"And you used the Power of the Sea appropriately?" I asked.

He threw me a sarcastic look. "Instructions were simple. It should be working."

He flipped through the channels. The numbers in the corner climbed, but still the screen remained an ominous black.

38...39...40...something...41...

"Wait, go back," Wade said.

Trent returned to channel 40. The screen filled with fire. Licking flames towered high into the sky.

"Forest fire?" Maya suggested.

We stood there mute, knowing in the depths of our bellies

that there was a malevolent quality about the fire. This was no summer blaze.

"Turn it up," Wade said.

Trent thumbed the volume button and a news reporter's voice filled the air. The voice was female and panicked. Her words rambled across the waves to us in a flurry of emotion.

"Look at the date." Maya pointed to the bottom of the screen. "April 7th, that was over three months ago."

The picture changed to show a city. I recognized Washington DC. A skyscraper was centered in the middle of the screen, the sky a smoky gray. Without warning, and with the suddenness of a thunderclap, the building disappeared in a burst of fire and ash. Nothing remained. Moments later a mushroom cloud filled the sky.

Trent flicked the TV off. The four of us stared at the blank screen. My thoughts spun, trying to make sense of what I'd just witnessed.

"What the fuck?" Trent asked. "Did you guys know about this?"

"No," Maya said, her skin turning paler than seafoam. "I had no idea."

Trent's frown deepened, his jaw turned hard. "But you knew something."

A crow landed on the stone sill of the window and cawed at us. Its roving, black eye seemed to size me up. I shivered, despite the heat of the day and the bright sun shining through the windows. Wade collapsed into a chair, his head in his hands.

"The prophecy only came yesterday," I said. "This was three months ago."

"But what does it mean?" Wade asked.

"Is it just DC?" Trent skin matched Maya's sickly pallor.

Maya took the remote from Trent's hand and turned the TV back on.

A terrible story unfolded. The reports were on a loop. The last channel left broadcasting replayed the horrific events to anyone who cared, or was able, to watch. Our world, as we had known it, was no longer.

World War III.

America was a broken land of ash and cloud and radiation poisoning. And it didn't stop there. The Middle East, Europe, Asia...everywhere. Nuclear bombs had been released, and the mainland our people wanted to return to so badly simply no longer existed. A handful of safe havens remained, a few areas of sanctuary outside the bomb blasts where people were gathering. But that was all. Small, desperate communities, disorientated and grief-stricken, clinging to survival.

"Why?" Wade broke our tense silence. "What could have possibly happened to cause a nuclear war?"

That was the million-dollar question.

Maya filled Trent in on the newest prophecy. We sank to the armchairs in the room, mostly silent, but periodically letting out an exclamation of bewilderment.

"Don't tell anyone," I said. "Not yet. We need to understand the situation before everyone finds out."

"Think quick," Trent advised. "Because you'll need a very good reason for denying anyone their opportunity to return to the mainland. To check on their families. Like mine. Who are probably dead."

"I'm sorry, Trent," I said. His parents had suffered loss before, when he'd been turned into a selachii and was unable to leave the ocean. And now Trent had lost them. Heartache and loss were going around in spades.

"Not your fault." He tapped the remote against his palm. "But I'm going to want to find out if they survived. Like...now."

Wade clasped his friend's shoulder. "It's too dangerous. Let's figure out what's going on first, okay?"

White-lipped, Trent nodded.

"We need to inform the rest of the senate," Maya said. "Then perhaps we can think of what comes next."

Wade rubbed at his face. "Assemble them. Bring them here and we'll show them."

Trent and Maya made up half of the senate. My mother and Ford were the other half. Ford was hovering outside the doors of our suite. My mother was found half an hour later in the palace gardens, eyes upward, staring at gathering storm clouds.

"What's the problem?" she asked, taking in my stricken face. She rested her hand on my shoulder, but for once her calm exterior did little to ease the gnawing fear growing in my stomach.

"Not here," I replied, my eyes scanning the clumps of people enjoying the gardens. "Come with me."

The six of us resettled ourselves in the senate's private meeting room. Ford organized fresh pots of coffee and tea. But no one poured.

Maya stood at the window overlooking the courtyard. "Storm's coming."

The clouds turned gray. Dark gray and foreboding, full to bursting with their heavy loads. Was it rain that would fall or something else, something more sinister, something tangible that might signal the arrival of a new enemy? But we didn't need a signal for that. The evidence of the bombs was warning enough. And the prophecy in *The Mermaid Chronicles* was its exclamation point.

"Of course it is," Wade said. "I bet that's written in the book too."

"What's going on?" Mom asked again.

"Show her," I said to Trent.

Trent pointed the remote at the TV hanging on the wall and brought it to life. He found channel forty and we watched again the evidence of the apocalypse. My mother's and Ford's jaws hung open as they digested the grim news. As I watched the horror along with them, I felt I hadn't begun to comprehend the full scale of the disaster or the emotional fallout. What was going on there now?

The six of us watched as city after city was targeted. Manhattan, London, Paris, Los Angeles. Mushroom cloud after mushroom cloud. People fleeing the streets, fiery projectiles of death streaking after them. The horror on their faces, the knowledge of impending death in their eyes. But still they fled until the fire was upon them and they were incinerated in seconds. Those who were lucky enough to survive the initial blasts and managed to find a way to safety were perhaps destined to endure a worse fate. Radiation poisoning.

"Who would do such a thing?" My mother's hands trembled. She reached for her teacup, and it rattled in the saucer as she tried to pour a cup. She gave up and put the cup back on the table.

A great boom clapped over our heads. The first roar of thunder. The rain poured, streaming through the arched windows. Maya ran around the room closing windows. The sky darkened to black and the lightning danced. More thunder, more rain, and more lightning, seeming to signal our own coming apocalypse.

"We don't know," Wade said to my mother. "This broadcast is on a loop, and we don't know the events leading to this war. The internet is down. No one is broadcasting anything on any medium. We just don't know."

Maya chose that moment to reveal the latest prophecy to everyone in the room. *"To save Atlantis the royal couple must unite with a third, the one who died and lives again. Family is important."*

"But it's not Atlantis that lies in ruin, it's the mainland," Ford protested, arms flung wide. "Why does it need saving?"

"It's been over three months since the bombs. We have no idea what the humans are doing now and what that might mean for Atlantis," Maya replied.

"Maya," Mom said. "You are the oracle. You have a special understanding of the prophecies. I know not everything is written in *The Mermaid Chronicles*, and what is written can be rather cryptic, but do you have any insight into what may be coming our way?"

Maya bowed her head. Her blonde hair tumbled around her shoulders, revealing a narrow, delicate neck. She was slim, petite even, but she possessed more inner strength than her body portrayed. What responsibility must lie on those slight shoulders. On all our shoulders.

"I've been thinking of little else since I first saw it written." She raised her head to answer my mother. "But I'm afraid I don't have much to tell you. I don't know what's coming. We need to wait to see what might be revealed, and we need to prepare."

"How do we prepare?" Wade asked, pacing across the stone floor. "If we don't know what's coming?"

Maya splayed her hands. "It will be revealed in time. The third person will be revealed. But it will be almost upon us when it is."

"*What* will?" Wade pivoted sharply, threw his hands in the air, stabbed a finger at Maya. "*What* will be almost upon us?"

"Hey," Trent said, putting a hand on Wade's shoulder. "She said she doesn't know. It's a shock to all of us."

"Fuck." Wade sank into a chair. He threw a decorative cushion on the floor and closed his eyes for a moment. "But what good is *The Mermaid Chronicles* if it can't tell us anything useful?"

"Wade," Mom said. "We're more prepared than we've ever been. We have a haven here on Atlantis. And now an army, thanks to Ford. We're going to be okay."

Wade shook his head, stared at my mother. "No offense, Samantha, but you weren't around for the first two prophecies. You have no idea how bad it got." He looked at me. "We almost lost each other. More than once."

I took Wade's hand.

"We've had such a good year," Wade continued. "I dared

to hope Fate had decided we'd been through enough. I dared to be...at peace."

"We all did," I said.

"How can this be because we got married?" Wade's expression darkened.

"We got married yesterday," I said. "The war happened three months ago. This isn't anything we caused. You can't think like that."

"Listen to your wife," Maya said. "She's smart."

A ghost of a smile flickered on Wade's lips. "I know."

"But why is this happening now?" I asked. Thunder boomed above our heads. Dim light splintered through the windows. Flash puddles and rivers formed on the courtyard below.

"From what I can tell in the pages of *The Mermaid Chronicles*, it's about the anniversary of our time here. An entire year on Atlantis," Maya said. "You remember the big anniversary party Dylan had at his bar? Well, it got people thinking. It gave them pause to question their futures, what they want, and what they've left behind. People want closure."

"I wish everyone could be happy, like us." Wade kissed my hand.

"People have adjusted," Trent said. "For the most part. But happiness is a fleeting emotion and unsustainable in the face of uncertainty. Most people have family on the mainland, like me. I go to bed at night wondering about my parents. At least they knew I was a selachii and hadn't disappeared off the face of the earth, but for everyone else? Their families think they've vanished. And now...with the bombs..."

his voice cracked. Maya wrapped an arm around his shoulders and kissed his cheek. "People need to know."

The earth beneath us shook with each clap of thunder, mirroring my own uncertainty.

Wade glared at the raging storm as if it were to blame. "I reckon, by the time the storm's passed, we'll know what we're facing."

"I wish there was something more we could do." I stood, little flames appearing on my fingertips. "But unfortunately, waiting is all we can do. Maya, I need you to study the book, let us know if anything changes."

"Yes, of course," she replied.

"Ford, I need you near Wade and me. If anything happens...if there is a threat to our land, or us...well...let's look out for each other."

"I won't leave your side," Ford said, eyeing the rain lashing down the windows. He rose and went to stand behind Wade's chair as if he thought the storm carried an imminent threat.

"Trent, if we're able to receive this broadcast, we might also be able to access older internet sites to learn more about the cause of the war and if it has anything to do with what might happen to Atlantis. Can you look into it?" I asked, hoping the task would keep his mind off his parents.

"Yeah, I can do that," he replied, shoving a hand through his thick hair. "Maybe I can find a list of survivors too."

"The rest of us will have to sit it out. We carry on as normal. Wade and I will begin our royal duties..." I fiddled with my engagement ring, prodding the central pearl, thinking things through. "And we wait. We wait for more information."

"You have an appointment this afternoon," Ford said. "A young couple are bringing their baby to you for a blessing."

"I think we can deal with that," Wade said.

Ford frowned. "You should expect to be asked about returning to the mainland at the same time."

We couldn't refuse people their requests to return to the mainland. Neither of us wanted to rule that way, and yet we couldn't tell them the truth. Not yet. Not before we had more information. The last thing I wanted to do was start a panic. But how would we prepare them for what they would find?

I rubbed at a building headache on my temples. "I hate politics."

Wade chuckled. "It's what you signed up for."

"Is it too late to change my mind?"

"You have the senate," my mother said. "It's not solely up to you. We're a team for a reason. Much like the High Council. We're together in this."

"Thanks, Mom," I said.

"We need to allow people to return." Trent clenched a hand, all signs of his usual good humor sadly absent. Unsurprisingly. "We need to tell them what's happened, and we need to let them find the people they left behind. If they still can."

"It's dangerous," Wade said, pacing a line by the windows. "I imagine people are devastated. If merfolk and selachii start popping up again...our people will be captured, or worse."

Maya locked her eyes on me. Dark circles bruised the skin underneath. She cleared her throat.

"What is it?" I asked her.

"I don't know," she replied, fiddling with the hem of her dress. "But I'm scared. I'm scared for our people. I don't want anyone to get caught."

Perhaps she didn't yet know the details of the prophecy, but if she was scared, then we all had reason to be. I trusted her gut, even when I wished she was wrong.

"You have to let them go." Trent's other hand fisted. "I want to go back. And I won't let anyone stop me. I deserve to see my parents. I want to know if they're still alive."

My heart ached for him. "I know, Trent—"

"I'm sensing a 'but.'" His frown deepened. Tears glinted in his eyes. "Ever since we turned on that screen, they are all I've been able to think about. I *am* going to find them."

"I understand." I faced my friend, stared into his honey golden eyes. "But I don't want you caught and shoved in a lab. I don't want you to get radiation poisoning. And I don't want you to find...your parents...not alive."

He stood. "I have to know."

CHAPTER FOUR

The storm descended upon the island with a ferocity unmatched in recent memory. Rain lashed relentlessly against the windows, each drop a bullet of nature's fury, as thunder roared its ominous threats, shaking the foundation of the palace. The wind, a howling beast, circled the structure with malevolent intent, tearing through the once-proud vines that adorned its walls and reducing them to tattered remnants. It whipped the lush vegetation into a chaotic frenzy, sending debris flying through the air like shrapnel. Anyone who dared to venture outside was met with a barrage of nature's wrath, each gust a punishing force that sought to drive them back into the relative safety of the palace. The storm's relentless assault seemed almost sentient, as if it bore a grudge against the island itself.

Wade frowned at the sky. "I hope Jordan and Stephanie are okay."

"They would have returned," I said. We sat next to each other in the great hall, a magnificent room with stone floors and floor-to-ceiling windows that opened onto the courtyard. The room boasted high ceilings and exquisite arches. Two regal chairs and a more comfortable couch were the only items of furniture in the room. "As soon as the rain started. They wouldn't have tried to climb the mountain in this."

I moved to stand in front of a rare fire, warming my frozen toes and wishing for warmer clothes. Atlantis rarely experienced storms. There had only been one other during the last year. When it rained, it was warm and tropical and exhilarating. Running barefoot through the puddles, I felt an incredible sense of freedom, the water splashing up around my legs, soaking me through to the bone. My hair, drenched and heavy, would cling to my back, while my eyelashes, laden with raindrops, made each blink a moment of sparkling clarity. Each drop was a kiss from the sky.

And then, as suddenly as it began, the rain would cease. The world would stand still, wrapped in a serene silence, broken only by the soft patter of the last few drops falling from the leaves. Everything around me glistened with a newfound brilliance, the trees and flowers sparkling like they had been adorned with a thousand tiny jewels. The land, in its glistening nakedness, seemed to pulse with life and beauty.

But there was nothing beautiful about this storm. What little I could see of the ocean had turned a steely gray, and the waves rose and bickered amongst each other, raging in all directions. Thunder clapped above the palace, irregularly, and each time I startled. The rain seemed thicker than liquid. Viscous and solid and full of omens. The lightning came, thankfully without its own sound effects. But the streaking fingers of fire seemed determined to penetrate the palace walls and loose themselves on the hapless victims inside. I shuddered.

"You okay?" Wade rested his hands on my shoulders.

"I think so," I replied.

"It's just a storm."

"Is it?"

Wade turned me around to face him. "They'll be here soon."

"I know."

"Will you be ready?"

"Yes."

"Here." Wade placed my crown atop my head. It was a magnificent combination of white gold, iridescent shells and sparkling gems, each one carefully chosen to capture the essence of the ocean's beauty.

"I really have to wear this?" I asked.

"Our people expect it." He traced a finger along the curve my jaw, then followed it with his lips, his touch leaving warm tingles behind. "And I love you in it."

I laughed and allowed his stirring kisses to drift down my neck and to the hollow of my throat.

"It's all part of the show," Wade said, facing me once more. "If we look the part of the strong, confident royal couple, they'll respect us, and more importantly, they'll listen. And later, I plan to remove your clothes and leave you in nothing but that crown on your head."

I blushed as heat immediately spread to my legs. Despite the number of times we'd made love last night, I was ready for more. I was always ready for more.

"Very well," I replied, settling the crown into a more comfortable position.

As Wade placed his crown on his head, a larger version of the one I wore, there was a knock on the door. Ford pushed open the heavy wooden doors and ushered a young, beaming couple inside. They were fortunate enough to live within the palace walls and not have to venture into the storm. No one should be out in this weather.

"Laura, Brandon, welcome." Wade held his arms wide and plastered a smile on his face.

The couple stepped toward us, beaming smiles turning to frowns as the sound effects from the storm shot through the walls and windows of the room. The flames in the hearth flickered, almost going out, and the lights dotted around the walls dimmed, threating to extinguish.

"Don't worry about the storm," Wade said, squaring his shoulders. "Our land will be beautiful when it is over, and our crops could use a drink."

Frowns turned back to tentative smiles as they stood in front of us.

"This is the baby?" I asked.

A small sleeping bundle was swaddled in white cotton. I spotted the tip of a button nose poking out.

"Yes," Brandon replied.

"It's the fourth baby to arrive here on Atlantis," Wade said. "It's lovely to see children again."

"And we're happy to oblige," Brandon laughed. "It's been a difficult pregnancy. I think Laura is relieved to have her body back to herself."

A pink blush swept over Laura's cheeks. "You'll see one day. It's not so easy."

Warmth rose over my neck and cheeks. "What's her name?"

"Well..." Laura looked at her husband, and with an encouraging nod, she continued. "We hope you don't mind, but considering everything you've done for us, both of you, we wanted to honor you..." Laura placed the sleeping baby in my arms, and I thought how light the bundle was. I stared at her innocent face. She was beautiful. So small and so perfect. One little hand with five tiny fingers stuck out from under the blanket. I placed my finger in her palm and she grabbed on tightly. A lightness flushed through my body, and for a moment, as I took in this small miracle, I was able to forget Atlantis was in danger.

"Cordelia," Brandon finished for his wife. "We have named her Cordelia."

I looked up at the pair, startled such a gift was bestowed on me. I couldn't speak.

"Thank you," Wade said. He came to my side and looked down at the baby with me. "We're extremely touched. But please promise me, if you have a boy next, you won't name it Wade. Not such a great name."

The four of us laughed, and I handed the tiny Cordelia to her father.

"Thank you," I whispered as they walked toward the door.

"Oh, I almost forgot." Brandon turned back.

Wade and I waited. We knew what was coming.

"It's been over a year. Since we've seen our homes. Our

old homes. Now, I'm not so fussed, I was an orphan, but Laura, she has family on the mainland. It's been over a year, and now you two have been married, will we be able to return?"

"No one has prevented you from doing so," Wade replied. He shot me a wary look, and I wondered how he would handle this. "It was dangerous to return before. Nothing has changed. It will still be dangerous to go back now. Before people dive into the water again halfcocked, I would like to organize a scout group to return first. Let this group do the groundwork, understand the situation, and assess if the same dangers remain. If our people can be patient a little longer, I think this will be the safest solution for everyone. After all, it's not only about us returning and risking capture, it's also about keeping Atlantis a secret from the humans."

"That sounds reasonable," Brandon said. "Will you be making an announcement?"

"Yes," I said. "As soon as the storm lets up, we will detail our plan to everyone."

Brandon and Laura left. Ford entered the room in their wake. "I'll start recruiting for that scout group," he said. "That was a good idea."

"It just occurred to me. I'm still reeling from the shock of it all. Bombs. *Nuclear* bombs." Wade shook his head, his mouth pulled into a grim line. "I think a scout group is the right way to go. We need to protect our people. Not only from being captured, but from the pain..."

"We're all reeling," I said, removing the crown from my head. "It's a shock to all of us."

"The team will leave as soon as the storm stops." Staring at the fire, Wade sank into the couch. "We need to see what the humans are up to."

"I'm on it." Ford retreated, closing the doors gently behind him.

Wade dropped his head into his hands. "What are we going to do, Cordelia Blue?"

I sat next to my husband as the storm attacked our palace. "You and me. United. We can do this."

Wade clutched my hand. "I hope so."

Huddled in each other's arms, we listened to the wild storm. Wade stared at the shrinking flames, the fingers of one hand entwined in my curls. We didn't talk, each of us alone with our thoughts. Fear spiraled through me at regular intervals as I tried to picture what we would find on the mainland. A growing anxiety settled into my bones, one I hadn't realized I'd shed over the past year. Before I'd found Atlantis and been reunited with my twin brother and mother, grief had been a constant companion. Anxiety was grief's close friend; a shackle I knew I would be unable to rid myself of for the foreseeable future.

CHAPTER FIVE

$\mathcal{E}$ ight volunteers joined the scout group. Four selachii and four merfolk, and seven of them were already members of the Royal Guard. There was one who was not, but insisted on being part of it. Trent. He was determined to find his parents.

"Are you sure?" Wade asked him.

"I will fulfill my duties as part of the scout group." Trent stood with his hands on his hips. "But I need to know whether this ball of hope in my chest is justified or if I should give up...hope...I can't stand the uncertainty. I have to know."

"Okay," Wade agreed. "I don't doubt your loyalty, Trent. I hope you find what you're looking for."

"Thanks, buddy."

They left immediately, even though the storm was still waging war with our island. They would dive deep into the ocean where the depth would protect them and hope that when they emerged on the mainland, it had passed. Although, as it had been observed by Wade's father when out on his fishing boat, the mainland experienced different weather patterns to Atlantis.

The eight of them ran to the beach, and by the time they dove into the water, they were already soaked. Maya joined Ford, Wade, and me at one of the tall windows and watched as their tails emerged and disappeared beneath the squabbling waves.

"I can't stand this," Maya said, fidgeting with a delicate chain hanging around her neck. Trent had given it to her for their first anniversary. "The not knowing."

I held her hand. "Over the last year, I've learned to trust your instincts when it comes to *The Mermaid Chronicles*. If you're not feeling anything, if you can't see anything, then we must wait until things are clearer. That's all we can do."

"Maybe we could wait somewhere else." Even though Wade's voice was low, it echoed off the stone and marble in the palace. "Dylan's bar? You could have that chat with him, Cordelia. And I'd like to show my face to our people. Show them I'm unafraid."

"How are we going to get there?" Maya pointed at the aggressive weather.

"I'll take you through the tunnels," Ford said.

Joined by my mother and father and armed with a flashlight each, Ford led us down a winding stone staircase to the cellar beneath the palace. We walked past aisles of red wine laid flat for storage and fought off thick cobwebs that wound around my wrists and ankles, attempting to cover me in a belated, macabre wedding veil. More stairs led to a gently sloping tunnel which ended in a black abyss.

"Are you sure about this?" I asked Ford as I peered into

the darkness. I covered my nose and mouth as dust and mildew filled my nose. A heavy coolness hung in the air, thick with the unseen. "This is creepy."

"The tunnels go under the entire city," Ford said, his booming voice bouncing off the narrow walls, causing a few cascades of loose dirt to trickle to the floor. "They were used as escape routes for the palace in times of war. Wade has got me charting the entire area."

"What for?" Dad asked.

Ford hesitated. Wade didn't volunteer an explanation. A silence as thick as the cobwebs hung between us.

"Wade?" Dad asked.

"In case we need them," Wade replied eventually.

"You anticipated the prophecy." Maya turned her flashlight on him. "You expected something like this to happen. You've been preparing."

"Expected? No, not expected." Wade sighed and brushed dirt and cobwebs from his shoulders. "I hoped we would always have peace here, but I felt it prudent to be prepared."

He hadn't even told me. It had been his and Ford's little secret. I'd been so happy to have my family back, preparing for my wedding, reveling in the blissful status of our relationship, that I hadn't thought to examine what Wade's royal duties entailed. Not the specifics.

Wade had kept it from me. The thought sat uneasily under my skin. Although his secret mission only showed how much he loved me and that he wanted to spare me from pessimistic thoughts, I was uncomfortable with the idea of him shouldering the responsibility alone. We were married.

A royal couple. I ought to be involved in every decision. It was my job to support him in all matters, as he supported me. Maybe if he'd confided in me, the shock of our new situation wouldn't have buried so deep.

"Please don't keep things from me again," I said, keeping my voice light in front of the others.

Wade's eyebrows gathered as he took my hand and passed his thumb over the pearl in my engagement ring. "I'm sorry. I didn't want to worry you. You've been through so much."

"As have you," I said. "We're in this together, remember? United?"

Wade dipped his head. "You're right. I'm sorry."

I stopped walking. "Is there anything else I should know?"

"Of course not," he said, cupping my elbow and gesturing for me to keep walking.

"Good."

It was time to grow up.

Before I'd found Atlantis, I'd felt older than my years, learning to live with overwhelming grief. The last year had been full of so much brightness that I'd allowed myself to feel free again.

I had thought finding Atlantis was the answer to all our prayers, that we would live out our lives in a blissful bubble of romantic idealism. I'd assumed the battle with the dragon kings had been my quest, my one and only epic battle, and that I had been rewarded with a life of peace and love. How foolish.

Wade was right. We had been through so much. I was a

queen. I was the fire mermaid. Ordeals would continue to come my way. It was time to lift my head out of the sand and face my turbulent future. But Wade would always be with me. And that was enough to ease my fears.

I walked through the tunnel next to Wade, allowing my remaining naivety and innocence to leach away. It was time to face the future.

"The route to the bar was one of the first I charted," Ford chuckled, unperturbed by the grim undercurrents of our conversation. "Figured your brother might need a helping hand every once in a while."

I sighed. It was only a week ago that Ford had had to deal with Dylan. When my brother had appeared in the middle of the courtyard after closing his bar last week, drunk and disorderly, Ford had hefted him over his shoulder and carried him away. Dylan had passed out before he'd walked the short distance to his room. And two nights later, he'd stumbled his way into Tammy's bedroom. That was the fourth time in two weeks, and she wasn't the only one.

"Whoever thought it was a good idea for him to run the bar?" I shook my head.

"He's trying to find his place here," my mother said. "He grew up in the ocean, without his family. It's hard on him."

"I know."

"I blame myself," Mom said. Regret lined her face, sorrow flashed in her mermaid eyes.

Dad took her hand. "It's not your fault."

"It really isn't," I agreed.

Silence fell like snowflakes, cocooning us in our own thoughts as we trudged along the tunnel.

"Please tell me we're getting close to the end of this infernal tunnel," Maya said after she jumped at another shadow and sneezed five more times.

"Not far now," Ford said.

Five minutes later, the slope ascended, and we found ourselves in front of an arched wooden door. The door led to the alley that flanked the bar. We dashed through the rain, slipping on the flooded cobbles, and tumbled through the back door.

"Welcome," Dylan said from behind the bar, his hand wrapped around a glass. He wore a black shirt, only half buttoned, and a beige pair of shorts. His feet were bare, how most of us preferred it on the island.

Candlelight filled the room. Every table boasted an elaborate candelabra and sconces hung on the walls. Dylan claimed the dim lighting created a better atmosphere for his patrons. They drank more. And he drank with them.

A roaring fire crackled in the hearth at the far side of the room, and a large seawolf skin was centered between two large cozy couches. Leather chairs and stools were positioned to create small, intimate areas, while high-backed booths lined one side of the room. Dylan stood behind a long wooden bar. Wine and champagne glasses hung from racks above his head. On the shelf behind him were the spirits, reflected in a mirrored backdrop along with delicate candlelight.

Customers filled the seats and stood in clumps in the aisles, obviously caught by the storm. The spot in front of the fire was free, and so after ordering drinks and baskets of French fries, my friends and family made their way to the vacant area. After a meaningful look from Wade, I slid onto a stool at the bar opposite my twin brother.

"What are you drinking, sis?" Dylan asked, a cigarette dangling from his lips.

"Water."

He gave me a look. "That's not an option."

I stared right back at him. But I didn't want our conversation to start with an argument. "Cider."

Dylan pulled the pump and filled a pint glass. He slid it along the bar and watched as I took my first sip. "It's good."

"From our own orchards. We had a good harvest this year," he said, wiping non-existent drops on the counter. "Have you come to ride out the storm? Thought you would have been comfortable enough in the palace."

"We needed a distraction." The words were out before I had a chance to take them back.

His hazel eyes didn't miss a trick. "From what?" He might be drunk half the time, but he was still intelligent. And he knew how to read me.

"Forget it. I shouldn't have said anything." He would find out about the prophecy eventually, and the state of the mainland, but now wasn't the time. I refused to push him over the edge of the precipice he was so precariously balanced on. "It's nothing important."

He laughed. "Cordelia, I'm not stupid. What's going on?"

"How much have you had to drink?"

He frowned. "Don't you start with that. Mom and Dad are bad enough."

I put my glass down. "I care about you."

"I know," he said. "Care enough to know I'm okay. I'm an adult. I can look after myself."

"Can you?"

"You're trying to piss me off," he snapped, then glugged the rest of his drink. Defiance rolled off him. "And it's working. But I know you're hiding something. What is it?"

"Chill."

"I'll find out, eventually."

"I'm sure you will. But tonight's not the night."

"I'm not going to fall apart at the slightest whiff of trouble." He poured another drink for himself. "I can handle it."

I arched an eyebrow at him and sipped my drink to avoid his scrutinizing stare.

"Really," he insisted.

"It was only last week you had your stomach pumped, Dylan." I slammed the pint glass back on the counter, spilling half of it over the wooden bar top.

"Sipping from the fountain because I drank a little too much is not the same thing as having my stomach pumped."

"If we didn't have the fountain, that's what you would have needed."

"Relax, Cordy. No harm done." He made a cross over his chest.

I threw my hands at him. "Your behavior isn't normal."

"What's normal, anyway?" He had the gall to grin at me.

"You know what I mean."

"Do I?"

I will not lose my shit.

"For fuck's sake, Dylan. Pull yourself together."

"You sound more like Mom than Mom does."

I glared at him. "You bring out the best in me."

"I aim to please."

I jabbed at the counter with a finger, a flame coming to life.

"Don't burn my bar! Jeez."

"You're not taking this seriously. You were drunk at my wedding last night. *Really* drunk. I thought you could have held it together for one night. For me."

"That's not fair."

"Isn't it?" I gritted my teeth to prevent the prickle of tears. "I'm surprised you were able to open the bar today."

"I have a high tolerance."

"You were a mess."

He leaned over the counter. One lone fleck of emerald green glinted at me meaningfully, a hint of something from a time before. "You're not my mom, Cordelia. I don't need a lecture from you. I don't need one from her either. I lived without parents for five years. I do not need any more interventions. I can take care of myself."

"Can you?" I asked, meeting his steely gaze. We had been born minutes apart, but I felt like the protective older sister. Especially considering I had been lucky enough to have one parent while he'd had none. "When's the last time you slept in your own bed? When's the last night you didn't have a drink?"

"It's none of your business." He turned his back and unloaded glasses from a dishwasher. From the dangling cigarette, a trail of smoke wound its way into Dylan's right eye. He killed the cigarette in an ashtray and swiped at his watering eye. Then he coughed into his elbow, a hacking, gurgling smoker's cough.

"When did you start smoking? Of all the asininely stupid things..."

Dylan arched a derisive eyebrow. "It's not like I can get lung cancer. The Fountain of Youth is just over there." He pointed in its general direction.

"Still...that's like jumping off a cliff into the fountain as some sort of sadistic pain experiment, just because you can."

"Maybe I should try it," he said and turned his back on me again. "Maybe then I'd feel something other than this dead sense of nothingness."

"Dylan...*Dylan*..." How was I supposed to respond to that?

"No, Cordelia. I don't want to talk about it." He remained with his back to me, his shoulders high. He hummed quietly under his breath, blocking me out.

I'd gone too far. I always did. Every time I tried to speak to him, I promised myself I would go easy, but frustration always won, and I ended up nagging him like a sea witch. I didn't know how to make him stop. I didn't know how to talk to him. I didn't know how to make him happy. I didn't know him anymore.

Reaching for my drink, I took a long sip.

"I'm sorry," I sighed. I picked up a handful of peanuts from the bowl on the bar. Instead of eating them, I let them fall back into the bowl, one by one. Then I swirled a finger through the bowl, making a figure of eight until Dylan rested his hand on mine. I jolted at the surprising touch.

"People have to eat those, Cordy," he said, his voice

portraying his exhaustion. He put the bowl of nuts on a shelf out of my reach.

"I want you to be happy," I said, tracing the rim of my glass with a finger.

"That's all anyone wants."

He was lost, and I didn't know how to find him. His once bright eyes were dim with despondency. Until he started drinking. Then they'd sparkle with mischief and the pretense of happiness. He'd act like the life of the party, everyone's best friend, always ready with a joke or a shoulder to lean on, all the while ignoring his own festering problems.

Dylan looked at the bar top. He polished the wood with such force that I was sure he would leave an indentation.

"What is it you want, Dylan?" I asked.

He raised his gaze, but he didn't look at me. I followed his eyes across the room, toward the fire, where they came to rest on Maya. Her blonde hair turned golden in the firelight, and her face was eager and animated as she listened to a story my mother was recounting.

"Maya? Are you still in love with Maya?"

He shook his head and turned his attention to his rag and polishing the bar top into oblivion. He cleared his throat, and his eyes glistened.

"No," he said softly. "She and Trent are meant to be. That much is obvious."

"But that doesn't mean you can turn your feelings off."

"It's okay, really. I don't feel that way about her anymore. I mean, I love Maya, I always will, but I'm not *in love* with her. I wish..." he stared at the fire where our family and friends were gathered. "I wish..."

"What?"

"I wish I knew," he said, his gaze far away. "I wish I knew."

That I had someone too.

I heard his thoughts, our telepathy powers emitting powerful signals despite not being in the water. Perhaps it was a twin thing.

It broke my heart. I had Wade. Maya had Trent. My parents had been reunited. Even Jordan and Stephanie were a couple of sorts. So many of us were paired off. But Dylan? He was alone, seeking comfort in warm beds and naked skin, and when that didn't work, the bottom of a bottle.

CHAPTER SIX

The storm continued to battle outside, relentless gusts hammering against the windows, our faces illuminated by the sporadic flashes of lightning that pierced the heavy clouds. The wind howled like a banshee, its eerie wails mingling with the insistent pounding of rain against the roof. Dad's eyes flickered nervously towards the rattling windows. Each clap of thunder reverberated through the floorboards, causing us to flinch and grip our drinks tighter, as though the alcohol could somehow shield us from the encroaching doom. The next howl of wind sent the candles flickering into nonexistence. Dylan relit them with a pack of matches and settled next to Maya on the seawolf skin rug.

The front door burst open. Jordan, Wade's cousin, stumbled over the entrance, bringing gallons of frigid rainwater with him. It streamed over the front step and puddled on the floor below. Backlit by streaks of violent lightning, his dark figure brought an ominous air into the previously cozy bar.

He staggered down the steps, shaking water out of his hair, his drenched backpack hanging from his shoulders.

Wade was on his feet immediately. "What's the matter?"

"Stephanie. Is she here?" Jordan's wild eyes roamed the gathered patrons. The bar was full, but Stephanie wasn't present.

"I thought she was with you?" Wade pulled his cousin out of the storm and allowed the wind to slam the door shut.

Jordan shook his head. "We got separated on the mountain path. There was a flash flood. A massive one."

Wade paled. "I thought you would have turned back when the rain started."

"Should have," Jordan said, inspecting his ripped clothing. "But you know what we're like. It made the adventure more exciting. I didn't think it would be a problem. We're selachii. We can't drown." He bit down on his lower lip. "I'm a fucking idiot."

"Everyone can drown," Wade said. "Even us."

Stephanie had almost drowned once before when we were attacked by a ball of electric eels. In her panic, she'd transitioned to her human form and passed out under the water. Wade had saved her life. If she was caught unawares this time, she might not think to produce her tail.

"I've looked everywhere," Jordan said, dropping his drenched backpack on the ground. He raked a hand through his dripping hair and pressed his face close to the window. "I can't find her."

"She'll be fine," I said. "She's a tough girl. She's most likely holed up somewhere waiting it out. You'll see. When the storm's over tomorrow, she'll come bounding down the mountain path with a big smile on her face and a bigger story to tell." I felt the falseness of my words even as I spoke them. Atlantis had never witnessed such a storm. Whatever force was ravaging our island was more than mere nature.

"I can't leave her out there. It's so cold." Shivering, Jordan stared at the door as if he hoped she would come waltzing through it. "The rain feels like acid, the wind is cracked up on speed. I can't leave her out there."

"No one should be out there." Ford raised a hand to block Jordan's path to the door. "We can't send people looking for her now, it's too dangerous. Cordelia's right. She's a smart girl, she'll have found shelter somewhere. God knows you two have discovered every nook and cranny on this island."

Bonded by their mutual need to find and conquer any adrenaline-fueled task, Jordan and Stephanie had become close. Neither of them would declare themselves a couple, but more often than not, they could be found in each other's bedrooms. But there was an obstacle which prevented their relationship becoming any deeper than day hikes around the island, coast-steering from cliff heads, and the occasional shared body heat at night. That obstacle was Stephanie's previous feelings for my husband. Jordan had confided to Dylan one night that he didn't trust she was over Wade.

"There's nothing we can do tonight," Wade said, a strong arm around his cousin's shoulders. "Come and warm yourself by the fire."

Jordan allowed himself to be led to the couch. He shrugged out of his wet T-shirt and Dylan placed a beer in his hand. He nodded his thanks.

With his back to me, I examined the changes in his

Medusa tattoo. The previous wriggling snake hair and wide, baleful eyes now depicted a group of swimming merfolk, their tails undulating when he moved. Although I'd forgiven him long ago for his part in the battle for the pearl, transforming the tattoo into merfolk was a nice touch, and tipped a metaphorical hat toward our united species.

"We'll send a search party at first light," Wade said. "We'll find her."

Conversation stalled as we sat by the fire, each of us nursing drinks and muttering the occasional exclamation at the fierceness of the weather. No one mentioned Stephanie's name again, but concern pooled in all our tense gazes when we happened to catch the eye of another.

No one slept. No one spoke. The air was thick with tension, and every breath felt like an effort. Outside, the wind howled like a tormented spirit, tearing at the trees and lashing the island with unrestrained ferocity. The rain fell in torrents, a ceaseless deluge that turned the ground to mud and threatened to flood the bar. Each lightning strike illuminated the landscape in stark, blinding flashes, revealing the tempest's unbridled power and the ominous clouds swirling above, thick and black as ink. Wade held my hand. I could feel the heat of my fire power simmering just beneath my skin, flames dancing on my fingertips, mirroring the turmoil within me.

When dawn arrived, Dylan organized food for everyone who'd taken shelter in the bar during the night. Before we could eat, Jordan shot out the door and headed for the mountain pass. We hurried after him, the storm vanquished, but the ground slick under our feet. He ran, calling Stephanie's name, banging on doorways, waking anyone who had fallen asleep.

"Get the army," Wade said to Ford. "We need to go after him. Quickly."

Ford turned and ran without another word, calling for his soldiers to be ready in five.

It didn't take long for the people of Atlantis to organize themselves into groups and spill off in different directions. Wade, Ford, Maya, and I formed our own group. We spoke only to offer suggestions of a direction, then headed toward the mountain where Stephanie was last seen. I told myself not to worry, that she knew all the caves and shelters the mountain had to offer, but I couldn't deny the fear in my quickening pulse.

Atlantis was a new land after the storm. But it wasn't welcoming or beautiful. It had become a foreign island. The stench of damp smoke and something more dreadful hovered in the air. Deformed glass sculptures dotted the beach where lightning had struck. Bushes and trees smoldered. More than a few houses smoked from their roofs. Rain clung to grass, making it slick and precarious. The cobblestone pathways lay in ruin, only useful for breaking an ankle, and a few of the ancient fountains had crumbled into marble messes.

Enormous holes of nothingness pocketed our island. New murky rivers flowed through the streets, flooding through doorways and into homes. Trees and branches caused more than one obstacle and impeded our progress.

"It's almost as bad as when the dragon kings were here," Ford mumbled.

"It makes me remember Gal." I stood on a broken column, eyeing the horizon, thinking of my dear dead friend.

Thankfully, the destruction didn't last. The power of the Fountain of Youth repaired Atlantis as we walked, deleting the destruction from our land and our hearts.

We searched for Stephanie until dusk hovered on the horizon. Jordon continued to shout for her, his voice wretched and gravelly.

"Take a break," Ford said to him when we found him pulling at rocks covering a cave entrance.

"She might be in here, running out of air," Jordan said.

Wade used his enhanced strength to shift the rocks, but Stephanie was not inside.

When darkness made it too dangerous to continue the search, we retreated to Dylan's bar. Jordan remained on the mountain, no longer yelling because he'd lost his voice. We sat by the fire in silence, waiting for news. Hope dwindled. I didn't know how to feel. Stephanie had made my life hell for so long, and then oddly kept her distance for just as long. Was it wrong to want her out of my life? A certain relief came with that. But I never wished her dead.

Dead.

The truth of it sank into me.

Jordan trudged through the door at midnight. Defeat rolled off him. He looked at us but didn't see us.

"Where is she?" he asked. "Where could she be?"

"Maybe she's in the water," I lied.

"Maybe she went back to the mainland," Wade said.

Jordan shook his head. "She didn't want to go back to the mainland."

Ford stood. "We've searched every inch of this island."

"And yet she's still missing," Jordan growled. "So you can't have done a very good job."

"Jordan." Wade approached his cousin. "There's only one reason I can think of to explain why we haven't found Stephanie."

"She's dead," Jordan said, hanging his head. "She's been taken by the storm."

CHAPTER SEVEN

Twelve hours later, Stephanie was still missing.

During our hours of searching, when the whispered theories as to the cause of her disappearance had died down, there was only one other topic of conversation that spread through the crowd; when we would return to the mainland. Some thought finding a lack of Stephanie's body was evidence she had left us, that she had decided to leave Atlantis behind and return on her own.

"Do you think she might have gone?" I asked Wade as we stood in the palace's foyer. "I didn't think there was anything left for her on the mainland."

"I don't think there's anything here for her either," Wade said.

"Jordan," I said, knowing in my heart her feelings didn't run deep enough to make her stay.

Wade frowned. "She wouldn't stay for him, not if there was something better on offer."

"But there's nothing on the mainland," I said. "*You're* not on the mainland. You're here."

"We're over all that."

"Are we?"

"Have you and Stephanie been arguing—"

"No, I've barely spoken to her. But I'm not going to pretend to know what she's thinking."

People swarmed around us, leaving the palace to assemble in the courtyard where Wade had called a meeting. It was time to address their concerns.

Wade lowered his voice and leaned close to my ear. "Perhaps we will find a body eventually."

"She may have been swept out into the ocean," I said. "We may never know."

"We'll talk more about this later." Wade took my hand and led me outside. "Right now, we need to deal with our people."

We stood on the top of the marble steps and waited for conversation to subside. People gathered on the steps, filled the courtyard and paths beyond. It seemed the entire population of Atlantis was here.

A trickle of nerves raced down my spine. How would we tell them about nuclear war? That the families they'd left behind were most likely dead?

"Many of you want to return to the mainland," Wade said. "It has never been my intention to deny you that wish."

A resounding cheer rippled through the crowd. I couldn't bring myself to smile. I'd never questioned the responsibility of being queen. It was a blessing I accepted as part of being with Wade. But now ominous prophecies shadowed our happiness once again, and I wondered whether I was up to the task.

"But before you decide to go, please heed these words." Wade raised a palm to quiet the crowd. "The mainland is not what you remember. Much has changed. I have sent a scout group to assess the situation and bring us news of the world and what our return might mean. I strongly advise you wait until the scout group is back before returning. Let's hear what they have discovered and form an intelligent, well-advised plan for your return."

Murmurs swept through the crowd. A sea of alarmed faces stared back at us. People shouted questions.

"What about you? Will you be returning?" A voice yelled from the gathering.

"I have no desire to return," Wade said. "My job is here, my people, my wife, my life, my heart, my soul."

There was a swell of noise as people offered us favorable gestures. A few clapped and whistled. Wade gave me a hopeful smile.

"What's wrong with the mainland?"

"Is there something you're not telling us?"

"Is the politics as bad here as it was there?"

I gritted my teeth harder with each damning question.

"What do you mean, it's *not as we remembered?*"

Wade pinched the skin at his throat, an angry red mark appearing. "Shit," he muttered, only loud enough for me to hear. I took his hand and gave it an encouraging squeeze. We would never lie to our people, but the truth was...ugly.

He pressed his lips into a grim line and let his gaze roam the faces of the attentive crowd. "That's not something I can answer, not until the scout group returns."

"What does *that* mean?"

"It means I don't have all the facts and I can't possibly give you a knowledgeable answer without them."

"What kind of answer is that?"

"Bullshit," someone shouted.

"Cordy..." Wade whispered.

"Something happened," a measured voice rose above the growing speculations. "Something big."

Panic surged through the crowd. Stephanie's disappearance had put people on edge, and now Wade's evasive words fanned confusion. Heated whispers flew through the courtyard. People hurled assumptions and accusations.

Wade cut me a nervous glance, then raised both palms. "Please don't panic. The scout group will return soon, then we'll know."

"Know *what*, exactly?"

A roar of conversation muted Wade's words. The fire of speculation spread quicker than my flames. There was nothing we could do to stop it. People gathered in small groups, voices worried and raised. Not once did I hear anything close to the truth, nothing half as devastating.

"What are we doing to do, Cordy?" Wade asked.

"There's nothing else we *can* do," I replied. The prophecies Maya had quoted tumbled through my head. It seemed we were now on a pre-destined path of no return. "What will be, will be."

"We've lost them," Wade sighed.

"We'll get them back."

"It's too late," Wade said. "It's only a matter of time until they discover the truth."

"I hope no one attempts to return tonight."

"God help us if they do."

The crowd surged up the steps, deep concern alight on their faces, questions hurled at us like torpedoes.

Ford blocked their path with an arm and pointed us up the stairs. "Let's get you two inside."

"They wouldn't hurt us," I said.

"They're confused. Scared," Wade said. "People do all sorts of things when they're scared."

He swept his arm around me and escorted me up the palace steps, through the marble halls, and into our chambers. We spent the evening standing at one of the arched windows, watching the dark ocean for anyone brave enough to dare the return.

"We should get some sleep," Wade said, his touch light on my skin.

"I can't," I replied. "I'm waiting for the scout group."

"It could be days." He kissed my shoulder and circled his arms around my waist.

"We don't have that long."

"I know."

His hand trailed a delicate line across the small of my back, circling lower, pulling me against him.

"I'm not sure I'm in the mood."

"You can't stand here all night."

I turned to face him. He pinned my lips with a hungry kiss and held me tight against him. Aroused, I wrapped my arms around his neck and dug my fingers into his hair.

"Shall we go inside?" he asked.

"No," I whispered. "I like being out here."

I encircled my legs around his waist, and he lifted me onto the stone balcony. My thin dress was no barrier to the coldness of the balustrade, but it did nothing to diminish my desire. Locking his eyes on mine, Wade lifted the hem of my dress, pushing it over my knees, over my thighs, until it came to rest across my hips. He tugged off my panties with one quick yank, staring at me the entire time. I blushed. The intense desire in his eyes always made me shy.

"I love you, Cordelia Blue," he said, burying his face in my hair. The cool night air swept against my exposed skin, making me shiver and sending a pulse of expectation low in my stomach. Wade's fingers crept along my thigh, drifting higher, until finally they pushed into my warmth. I muffled a groan against his neck.

"People might hear you," he laughed.

"Let them." Our balcony overlooked the courtyard. Anyone could see us.

His thumb circled my sensitive bud, causing a pleasurable shudder to whip through me and I bucked against him, digging my fingers into the meat of his powerful bicep. His fingers moved slowly, in and out, taking his time as the damp heat built. My bud pulsed with need as he continued to circle his thumb over it. And then he kissed me again, his tongue parting my lips, his mouth devouring me from the inside, sending a new wave of heat to barrel through my body.

Wade removed his fingers, undid his shorts, and released the aching length of him. The sight of him sent a delicious shudder through my center. With a long, drawn-out sigh, he pushed himself into me, filling me deeply as I shifted my hips to meet him.

We settled into a position, me sitting on the balcony, my legs hooked around his waist, my hips tilted toward him, and him standing there, facing the courtyard, twitching inside me with delicious cruelty. He gripped my rear and thrust into me, making me shout his name. I clung to his shoulders, lifting myself to meet every one of his powerful strokes, determined to take him deeper with each one.

Moonlight pooled around us and the scent of honeysuckle growing in the courtyard filled the air. A crescendo of bliss built within me as he moved, spreading heat and desire through my limbs, into my veins, into every cell of my body. Heavy lidded, my eyes drooped as a surge of sensation pulsed through me.

"Harder," I murmured. I needed him to take away my distracted thoughts. I wanted to consume myself with only him.

With each thrust he brought me closer to the brink. He held me against him as I arched over the balcony. He kissed my breasts, tangled his hands in my hair, and moved my hips in a mutual rhythm. My mind blanked out as a rush of sensation spiraled into my core and flashed through my entire body. My heart raced as my pleasure peaked and my body trembled uncontrollably as a shattering release consumed me and I fell over the edge.

To keep myself from crying out, I bit into his neck, and he

cradled my head against him. His climax occurred simultaneously. He shuddered against me and called my name.

"I think the entire island heard that."

"Let them," Wade said. "Let them see they too can be happy."

CHAPTER EIGHT

Days passed, and there was no sign of Stephanie or the scout group.

I hoped she had merely used the cover of the storm to flee. But the sinking feeling in the pit of my stomach told me we hadn't seen the last of Stephanie Bowers. In what form, I didn't know. But I hoped she was alive.

Wade and I spent an afternoon in the great hall with Maya and Ford. The Power of the Sea rested on a pillar, the swirling blue orb casting a peaceful glow into the room, bringing with it the salty scent of the ocean. It powered our island, lending its magic to the Fountain of Youth, and giving Wade and I our extraordinary powers when we'd both been mortally wounded during a battle with ice demons.

"When do you expect them to return?" Maya asked, pacing a circle around the dark blue orb. "People are getting restless. Including me."

"Tomorrow." Ford leaned against a marble pillar. "I told

them to spend no longer than a week. With a day's travel each way, they should be back tomorrow."

"Then we'll know how bad it is," Wade said, sinking into a chair.

Without warning, a blue light flashed into the room. I glanced at the Power of the Sea to see if it was responsible, but found the three members of the High Council had appeared instead. Esmerelda, Shane, and Edward gathered in front of the cold fireplace and cast their eyes over the assembled group, until they fixed on Maya.

"What is it?" Maya asked. "What's wrong?"

Esmerelda fiddled with the mermaid brooch at her throat and dispensed with any form of pleasantry. "You're concerned."

"Of course," Maya replied. "I'm worried about Trent's safety."

Esmerelda's expression softened. "Trent will be fine." She glanced at the other two High Council members, who gave her brief nods of encouragement. Esmerelda tugged her velvet jacket tight. "You haven't looked at *The Mermaid Chronicles* lately, have you?"

Maya's fists opened and closed. "Yes, of course. There's a new prophecy about being united with a third."

"More recently than that," Esmerelda said.

"Well...no." Maya frowned. "We've been busy with Stephanie disappearing and our people wanting to return..."

The expressions on all three members of the High Council caused anxiety to bloom in my stomach and flames to flicker on my fingers. "What's going on?"

"I'll get the book." Maya ran to the doors, her blonde curls streaming behind her.

"Not now, Maya," Esmerelda called. "The book can wait. In the meantime, we have something we'd like to share with you."

Maya retraced her steps to the middle of the room. Wade stood with hands on hips. Ford's expression was nothing more than a frown. I shook the flames from my fingers and attempted to remain calm. A state of mind I was becoming increasingly bad at.

"We need to share with you an emotional past event," Esmerelda said, fiddling with her brooch once more. "I don't quite know how to say this..."

I had never seen Esmerelda lost for words. The idea of it made my stomach churn.

Shane, the selachii representative, permanently dressed in a tuxedo, stepped forward. "We need to show you the instance of your parents' demise."

"My parents...*what?*" Maya gaped at them. "I already know how they died. Samantha told me."

"Samantha wasn't there," Edward said, the sinuous nature of his stature revealing his eel heritage. "She doesn't have all the facts."

"Why now?" I asked. "It's been so long."

"Events are changing," Shane said.

Wade and I shared a glance. The mainland was a nuclear wasteland. Stephanie was missing. Our people were restless and untrusting. How much worse could it get?

"We wouldn't normally show you something so...awful," Esmerelda found her voice. "But I feel it is necessary. For the particular events surrounding their...deaths...I think you need the knowledge."

Shane walked to the pillar supporting the Power of the Sea and poked the nebulous material with a finger. The orb cleared, forming an image for us all to see, much like the strange screens which had appeared in the High Council's chambers when Wade and I had first contacted them. Screens that revealed every moment of our lives, proving the High Council had always been watching.

Within the orb, a scene played out. A smiling couple with a baby held close. Wade and I had already seen our pasts. Now it was Maya's turn.

The couple sat in a rowboat in the middle of the ocean, the baby settled between them. Merfolk surrounded them in the choppy waters. But not just merfolk. A sea witch was present. A figure ten times more terrifying than Aquaria. Her sister.

Maya's hands flew to her mouth as she watched. I stood next to her and held her hand. "It's going to be okay, remember they're at peace now."

"Is this really necessary?" Ford asked, striding in front of the swirling image, his broad shoulders blocking most of it.

Esmerelda silenced him with a hand. Ford bristled. He'd had little to do with the High Council during the year we'd lived on Atlantis and was yet to learn how particular they could be.

Maya gripped my arm as the scene continued. The sea witch rose from the water and hung above the choppy surface, eyes turned to the swirling heavens, invoking a spell of evilness. The rowboat teetered and baby Maya cried.

Maya's mother held her close to her chest and protected her against the swelling waves and driving rain. Her father stood in the boat, his widening eyes glued to the horizon.

I glanced at the three High Council members, a reprimand on my lips, but their gazes were fixed on the orb.

"You don't need to watch this," I said to Maya.

"I think I do," she whispered. "If I'm to prevent the same fate for us all."

A heavy weight landed on my chest and a sour taste prickled the back of my throat. Sea witches were mostly immortal. Aquaria lived in a whirlpool prison. But what if she broke free?

Within the orb, the scene revealed a developing vortex, churning the waves to angry heights. Screams filled the air as merfolk were sucked into the spinning whirlpool, disappearing into its tumultuous depths.

"Oh, God," Maya murmured, her grip turning icy on my arm.

The sky turned bullet-gray and shot icy needles of rain upon the steel blue ocean. The waves rose, rocking the boat, lapping over the sides. Maya's family capsized. Struggling for breath, Maya's mother held her above the bickering waves. The surrounding merfolk helped them find air. But the whirlpool gained in size and velocity.

A deafening scream reigned over the ocean, a scream that stole courage and spurred even the fiercest fighters into panic. The sea witch hovered above the ocean, the merfolk, and Maya's family, chanting her strange incantation, her arms raised to the sky. A wild madness glowed in her unforgiving eyes, while her snake hair struggled against her scalp in anticipation of a macabre feast. From the depths of the whirlwind, a new terror emerged.

"What *is* that?" Wade asked, drawing closer to the orb.

The High Council members remained silent.

"Nothing good." I swallowed the anxiety crawling up my throat and blinked to prevent flames escaping. My flames had always mimicked my emotions, and during the last few days my eyes had sparked, and steam had poured from my nostrils, and I had to keep shaking the fire from my fingertips before I hurt someone. Did my power sense it was needed?

An enormous snout appeared in the middle of the whirlpool. Its terrifying teeth ripped through the waves searching for a victim.

Ford passed a hand over his face as he gaped at the devastating scene. "I've never seen anything like it."

A scaled monster emerged, a creature of darkness. Toxic fumes of gas spewed from its nostrils as it swam toward the cornered merfolk. The gas cloud billowed over the waves, eliciting screams from every merfolk it touched, burning their skin from their bodies.

My eyes watered as I watched the carnage. "That's...horrible."

Beside me, Maya whimpered.

The sea witch smiled triumphantly, but her arrogance didn't last. Maya's father thrust a pointed blade through her heart, the only area of weakness a sea witch possessed. She died instantly. But it was too late to stop her evilness. The monster continued its rampage, decimating the merfolk.

"It's too much," Wade said, casting a sharp glance at the

High Council. "You could have told us. You didn't need to subject Maya to this."

No one replied.

"I demand an answer." Wade's voice rose.

Esmerelda swiveled a raised eyebrow in his direction. "You will get one." She pointed at the scene within the orb.

Beside me, silent tears streamed down Maya's face as we witnessed a terrible battle. The merfolk launched their spears at the gargantuan beast. It possessed legs and clawed paws, but could swim well in the ocean. It had no fire, but the noxious gas flaring from its mouth and nostrils was equally devastating. The humped body ended with a long, clubbed tail reminding me of beasts from another time. But this one was far worse. And a thousand times worse than a murderous dragon king.

The spears found purchase within the beast's body. Blood poured from its wounds. But the merfolk were injured, their ranks devastated. In the middle of the chaos, Maya's parents battled to keep her above the water. The beast loomed over Maya's mother.

"You don't need to see this," I said to Maya.

She gritted her teeth. "I have to."

As the creature opened its nightmarish mouth, Maya's mother plunged her under the water. The toxic gas plumed out of the creature's snout and caught Maya's parents in a cloud of agony. They screamed as the skin dripped from their faces, stripping them to the bone within seconds. They screamed long past the time when I thought they should have been dead. I didn't know anyone could survive with half a face and no eyes. At the edge of the picture, a mermaid swam away with a tiny bundle. Maya.

"Jesus fucking Christ," Wade hissed, glaring at the three High Council members. "Was that really necessary?"

Esmerelda touched the orb and the picture paused, clouded over and then dissolved until the pulsing blue returned. "I'm sorry you had to see that, but yes, it was necessary."

"What happened next?" Ford asked. "The battle was far from over. Did the merfolk defeat the...what *was* that?"

"The Hound of the Ocean," Esmerelda replied. "And to answer your question, sort of. They banished it back to the depths, but it lives still, ready to be called forth by any who know how and care to command it."

"We didn't show it to you just so you could see the fate of your parents," Shane said, pulling at his bowtie as if he'd suddenly realized he was inappropriately dressed.

"No, I thought not." Maya wiped her tears with the backs of her hands.

Fear was a powerful emotion. Just enough and it could make you brave, allow you to face an ordeal. Too much, and it would break you, move you to destruction. I thought I'd reached my limits before, but the Hound of the Ocean was an unimaginable horror. Something even my fire power would struggle to contend with.

I looked at Esmerelda. "It's coming back, isn't it?"

"Yes," she said. "I'm afraid it is."

Maya blew out her cheeks. "That's the new prophecy you were alluding to?"

"Yes," Esmerelda replied. "It came to us last night. If you study the book, I think you'll find it there."

"Why?" Wade asked. "I thought only a sea witch could summon the Hound of the Ocean. During that battle, the sea witch was killed. And since then, Aquaria has been vanquished. There are no more sea witches."

Esmerelda frowned. "I can't tell you anything more." She looked at me meaningfully. "Cordelia, it's one of those situations..."

"...if you tell me too much or intervene, you can alter our fate," I finished for her.

"The fate of all of you," she whispered, fiddling with her brooch. "All I can say is its weakness is its throat. And now I have told you what we can. The rest is up to you. I'm sorry. And good luck."

The three High Council members departed as suddenly as they had arrived. It was a quiet departure, but I flinched as though a door had been slammed.

"But the sea witches are gone," Wade said again. "They're *gone*."

"Unless, of course, one of them is not," I said.

CHAPTER NINE

The sudden departure of the High Council left me feeling stranded and uncertain. I stared at the Power of the Sea, wondering what other secrets it could impart, what other ordeals we might have to face. But it only had the power to reveal the past.

"Gal killed Aquaria," Maya said. "He did."

"No," I said. "He couldn't bring himself to kill her, I'm not sure why, so he vanquished her to an eternal whirlpool. Like Zale and Caol. He said, if I remember correctly; 'that whirlpool is a fate *worse* than death.'"

"I thought there was no escape from those whirlpools," Wade said. "That has always been my understanding."

"No one has escaped so far," Ford said. "But that doesn't mean it can't happen."

"Aquaria may have returned," Maya said.

"Why couldn't he have killed her?" Wade wrung his hands.

"He couldn't," Ford said. "He loved her."

I gaped at him. "Say *what?*"

"You didn't know?" Ford asked.

"Know *what?*" I asked.

"He loved her," Ford replied. "They were together once. He could never have killed her."

I looked at Wade. "How did we not know?"

"He never spoke of his personal life," Wade replied. "He was always so focused on helping us not screw up."

"Which we were all doing spectacularly well," Maya said, a gentle smile on her lips.

I dipped my chin, thinking of my old friend and mentor. "Despite all his muscle and strength, Gal had a gentle heart."

"So," Ford said. "We now have a missing inhabitant, the aftermath of a nuclear war on the mainland—which suddenly all our people are desperate to return to—and subsequent battle with whatever humans are left, an escaped, evil sea witch, and a murderous sea monster to deal with. Does that about sum it up?"

No one replied. His words hit home like the force of a hammerhead shark. Although the Power of the Sea continued to swirl and sparkle with its mysterious magical powers, it no longer appeared benign. Tragedy threatened our future. My chest tightened and my throat closed.

"I'm not sure if I'm ready for this," I said, as the anxiety trickled through me, making my hands shake and my flames reappear. I looked at my hands. They contained such power, but would it be enough? Could I protect all those I loved?

"None of us are." A muscle ticked in Wade's jaw.

"We need to prepare. Study the book. Learn as much as

we can about Aquaria and the Hound of the Ocean," Maya said.

The door swung open. Sunlight streamed into the room, highlighting a familiar figure. Trent.

"We're back." He wore only a pair of shorts, and dripped salt water over the marble floor.

"Trent!" Maya ran to him and threw her arms around him. She kissed his cheek. Trent automatically circled his arms around her, but his face held no pleasure.

"What's wrong?" I asked.

Trent kissed Maya's cheeks, then buried his face in her hair.

Ford, Wade, and I gathered around the couple.

"Trent?" I said softly. "What's happened?"

He pulled away from Maya. "The mainland is...everything is gone..." his voice caught. "It's as we feared. Worse."

The ounce of hope I'd been carrying and protecting deep inside slipped away. There was no avoiding the coming devastation. It was tempting to remain on Atlantis in its protected dimension, to live in its magical realm and never return to the mainland. But our people needed closure. Wade and I would never deny them that. But if they discovered the truth, they would return from the devastating events of the mainland in despair, making us vulnerable to Aquaria and the Hound of the Ocean. I could see it all so clearly.

Although I was afraid, my determination to protect our island grew. We'd only just recovered it after hundreds of years of searching. Battling the dragon kings had left deep scars, and damned if I was going to let anything destroy what we had only recently built.

I was Cordelia Blue. Waters. I was the fire mermaid. Atlantis and the people in it were my destiny, and they deserved whatever protection I could offer.

Wade's expression turned grim. "Worse?"

Maya led Trent to a winged armchair. He eased himself down and leaned his head back against the soft fabric. "My parents..." his face crumpled, and he covered his eyes with a hand. Maya sat on the arm of the chair and cradled him.

Trent's parents were kind and loving people, always supporting him at his surfing competitions with wide banners dripping with fresh paint.

"I'm sorry," Wade said, touching his shoulder.

Trent swallowed, wiped the tears from his cheeks and faced us. "They died in the initial blast. They were vacationing in New York. It was one of the first."

"It would have been quick," Maya said.

"I know," Trent replied, staring at the Power of the Sea. "I never considered when I came here that I wouldn't see them again."

"None of us could have predicted this war," Ford said.

Trent gripped the armrests. "But it was all our fault."

Confusion spun in my head. "*Our* fault?"

"How do you figure that?" Wade asked.

"You all need to sit," Trent said. "And get Dylan in here with a cart of drinks. Something strong."

Maya left briefly to retrieve dry clothes for Trent. Dylan arrived with a drinks trolley from his bar, a few bottles of hard liquor, and glasses. Trent and I reached for the bottle of tequila at the same time. Our fingers brushed over the neck, sparking a memory. He poured a shot for all of us.

"What's going on?" Dylan asked, sitting and dangling a leg over the side of a chair.

"You're not a member of the senate." Ford frowned at him.

I waved a hand at Ford. "It's okay. Dylan won't say anything."

Ford pressed forward. "If we go against protocol now—"

"Ford, please," I said. "It's not important right now."

Dylan downed a shot and turned the glass around in his hand. "I repeat, what's going on?"

"The mainland is a wasteland," Trent said once we all had a drink in hand and were adequately seated. "The nuclear war was total and quick. It only lasted twenty-four hours. It started with the baron in Europe."

"The one who turned his wife into a mermaid?" I asked, thinking of the time when the truth about merfolk and selachii exploded into the world. Everyone wanted their own mermaid, or to become one. The rich baron in Europe had turned his wife into a mermaid and kept her on display at their estate. She was on Atlantis now, relieved the carnival show was over, safe from persecution.

"The very same," Trent replied.

"But why?" Dylan asked, refilling his glass.

"He wanted his wife back," Trent replied. "He searched the world high and low for her. Not only for her, but all the merfolk. He couldn't figure out where we'd gone, so thought a threat would make things more transparent. Then people began drowning in the ocean. Kids venturing out too far, teenagers on a drunken night out, boating accidents...and the merfolk and selachii weren't there to save them. So he turned it into a crusade. Blamed us all for the increase in water deaths. Said we should have stayed to protect those in the water. Threatened war if we didn't reveal ourselves."

"They didn't know about Atlantis." Wade passed a hand over his brow. "We were here. Unable to protect anyone."

"We couldn't know what was going on," Maya said. "This is not our fault."

"Isn't it?" Dylan asked.

"No," I said. "We can't be held responsible for the war crimes of an insane person."

"But it's always been our job to protect people," Dylan said as he refilled his glass.

"And where was their protection of us when they stuck us in labs?" I snapped. "No, they don't deserve our protection."

"Cordy..." Wade pressed me with a look.

"I'm sorry," I said. "I didn't mean that. Of course those vulnerable deserve our help, but those who stuck us in labs, this baron...they deserve nothing." The flames on my fingers flared, separated from my hands, and raced around the room, looking for a target. I stared at the empty hearth and directed them there before they could hurt someone.

"Jesus, Cordy, get a hold," Dylan said.

I glared at him. "Excuse me for being emotional, for expressing my feelings, for letting people know how I feel."

"Whatever," Dylan said, swigging another shot.

"Both of you, calm down," Wade said. "This is bigger than both of you."

"I'm sorry." I stood and marched to the Power of the Sea, stared at the swirling blue, demanding it give me answers.

But of course, it didn't respond. "What are we supposed to do?"

"It's not our fault," Maya said. "It's the baron's."

"Assigning blame will do nothing at this late date," Trent said. "The baron pinned us as the scapegoats, and that's how the world sees it. What's left of it, anyway."

"Fuck the world. I never liked it anyway," Dylan said.

Ford rolled his eyes. "And you wonder why you're not on the senate."

"Never asked for it," Dylan replied. "Thankless job."

A sour taste flooded my mouth which I struggled to swallow. My gills spluttered into existence despite the lack of surrounding water. I couldn't seem to get a breath past my throat.

"You okay, Cordy?" Wade asked.

"Not even a little bit," I replied.

"Watch you don't burn us all with that fire power," Dylan said.

I quashed the urge to scream at my brother and instead heeded his warning. I laced my hands behind my back.

"The baron had ten nukes," Trent said. "He targeted DC, New York, Los Angeles, London, Istanbul, Sydney, Singapore, Beijing, and Tokyo. They were his first targets. Of course, all those cities defended themselves. Those who possessed nukes launched a counterattack. God may have made the world in seven days, if you believe that, but man destroyed it in twenty-four hours. Fuck me."

"Is there anything left?" I asked.

"There might be a tribal village in South America still intact somewhere, or maybe one of the Pacific islands." Trent stared at his drink, unable to meet anyone's eyes. "The radiation fallout is the only silver lining."

"How so?" Wade asked. "I thought nuclear bombs caused cancer for years..."

Trent shook his head. "Not anymore. Most of the radiation disappeared within a couple of days of the original blasts. Don't get me wrong, there will be a shit load of people with cancer and extra limbs and stuff, but there will be survivors."

I returned to the table for my glass, swallowed a double shot, but it did little to comfort me other than produce a warmth in my stomach and stop my hands from shaking. "This can't be happening."

"Somehow, it just doesn't feel real," Wade said, his hand a reassuring pressure on my hip.

"Oh, believe me," Trent said. "It's real."

I stared at my friend. No matter how tough things had gotten in the past, he was always ready with a joke, always ready to lighten the mood. Not anymore. Instead, he wore a haunted look in his eyes. The weeklong trip to the mainland had aged him, given him knowledge he couldn't unknow.

"I'm so sorry, Trent," I said. "For your parents."

"Thank you."

"Me too," Dylan said. "I'm sorry too. I always liked your parents."

"Thanks, buddy," Trent said. "They were good people."

"My foster family?" Maya asked, her eyes bright with pain.

Trent shook his head. "I'm sorry."

Maya stood and walked to a window, stared at the ocean.

"I don't know what to say." Wade marched an irregular pace around the chairs. "I really don't know what to say."

My mother entered the room. She joined us quickly. "I heard the news from one of the other members of the scout group." She looked at Trent. "It's true?"

"It's true," Trent replied.

My mother had been missing from my life for almost six years. I couldn't count the times I'd prayed I could ask her a question. About life, growing up, boys, the future, becoming an adult. And now I had her by my side, we had spent many evenings together talking and getting to know each other again. She had become more friend than parent. How I wished she could make this all go away. But no one in this room, or on the island, had that kind of power.

"What can we possibly do?" Mom asked.

"Nothing," Ford replied. "There's nothing *to* do."

I wrapped my arms around my waist. "But all those people..."

"A lot of them need help," Trent said. "There are masses sick with radiation poisoning. Most of those who are well are struggling for survival."

"There are survival camps?" Mom asked.

"Two we know of," Trent replied. "One of them is inland from San Diego, in the desert. Seems relatively benign. The army and navy make up a large percentage of their numbers, must have been stationed at Miramar or nearby. But they're inactive. The camp is mostly a makeshift hospital."

"And the second group?" I asked.

"Hmm. Headed up by a guy called Sean Wilson, an ex-mercenary," Trent said.

"Holy shit," Dylan muttered. "What's he up to?"

"He has a lot of special forces in his camp," Trent said. "They're looking for revenge."

"Us," Wade whispered.

"Ding, you receive the main prize of ten thousand dollars," Trent said. "Will you keep it or gamble it for more?"

"But there's nothing we can do," I protested to the air.

"Have you spoken to him?" Wade asked.

"We've observed," Trent said. "There's no reasoning with him. Although most of his group want revenge, there are others who seek Atlantis as a refuge. They've already started their searches. Their intel is scarily accurate."

"But they won't be able to find us." Maya said. "You have to be a merfolk or selachii to step foot on Atlantis."

"It won't stop them trying," Trent said, slapping the table in front of him, causing the drinks to jump and spill. "Especially as not all members of the scout group made it back."

The silence that descended on us was coiled tighter than a spring.

"Maybe you should have led with that," Ford said.

Dylan smirked. "I say nuclear war has the bigger headline."

"Sean Wilson has taken a selachii prisoner," Trent said. "None of us were trained in torture evasion...who would have thought we needed that? So now Sean knows where to look. We'll see their boats before long."

We rose as one and approached the windows, looking for a hint of foreign sails.

"The veil will stop them entering," Mom said.

"What if they find a way through?" I asked.

Dylan pointed. "There. Do you see it?"

A boat hovered on the horizon. A scientific research vessel like my father used to use. Far from shipping lanes, I'd never seen a boat on the water which didn't belong to Atlantis. We were surrounded by shallow water and jagged rocks. No one had ventured here before. But now they knew where to look.

"How does the veil work, exactly?" I asked.

"It's the magic of the Power of the Sea," Maya said.

"Yeah, and how does *that* work?" Dylan piped up.

"No one knows," Mom replied.

"They could find something out there to break it," Wade said. "Like we found the keys to Atlantis buried around the mainland."

"We can handle this," Ford said, both hands clenched around the hilts of the two swords he always wore. There were no guns on Atlantis. "The Royal Guard have drilled for invasions."

"For invasions by desperate people with nothing to lose?" Trent asked. "With guns."

"But where do Aquaria and the Hound of the Ocean fit into all of this?" I asked.

CHAPTER TEN

"*To save Atlantis, the royal couple must unite with a third, the one who died and lives again. Family is important,*" I said, quoting the newest prophecy for the millionth time as I paced the length of the windows in my chambers. "What the hell does it mean?"

"That is oddly specific, and yet I have no idea," Wade said.

"Tell me about it."

"Maya can't shed any more light on it?" Wade sat on our bed, his hands folded in his lap, his shoulders hunched.

"She's with the book now. Looking up the Hound of the Ocean too." I stopped pacing to stare out the window. I counted over fifty boats. "They keep coming."

"Remember, the veil is protecting us. They may know our location, but they'll never be able to set foot on the island."

"Yeah, and I thought Dylan was dead, and my mom, and dragon kings were the thing of nightmares and Atlantis was lost forever...but none of that turned out to be true."

"But those are good things."

"Bad things can happen too."

"We need to stay positive."

"Do we?" Dread coated my throat, making my voice harsh and scratchy. "I think we need to be realistic. Prepare for the worst. We have no guns on Atlantis. A human army would annihilate us in a matter of hours."

"It won't come to that."

I turned to face my husband. The only man I'd ever loved. Concern shadowed his handsome face and his eyes flashed black, an emotional selachii reaction. "I love you, but it's time to get our heads out of the sand."

Wade frowned. "When did you become so cynical?"

"Life experience," I muttered.

"Has it been that bad?"

I approached him and laced my arms around his neck. "Not with you. Never with you...apart from when you cheated with Stephanie."

Pain glimmered in his eyes. "I'll never forgive myself for that."

I waved a hand at him, kissed his lips. "I didn't mean to bring it up. I'm sorry. It's forgotten, truly. And I wasn't exactly girlfriend of the year either. It's behind us."

Wade stood and circled his arms around my waist. "I'm scared if I don't stay positive then I'll...I don't know..."

"Sink into a pit of despair?"

"Something like that," he said. "We've been through so much heartache and loss. And now we have multiple enemies to face. What if we don't make it?"

A reflexive whimper escaped my throat. "I don't think I like it when you're realistic. Go back to being positive."

He rested his forehead against mine. "I can't lose you, Cordy."

"And I can't promise you we'll both survive."

His arms tightened around me. He held me fiercely against his body. His breath came in shaking gasps at my ear. "I can't lose you. I *need* you. I can't...I just *can't*."

I clung to him, his words piercing my heart. It brought back the memories of when I thought Wade had been killed. An experience I never wanted to live through again. I wasn't strong enough. This time, we would face things together. We wouldn't separate, we wouldn't leave each other to deal. Together. United. Always.

I cleared my throat, swallowing the emotion. "It's not just up to us. We have Maya and Trent and Ford and my mother and the Royal Guard...it's not just up to us."

"Do you think our people will vote to get rid of us if we fail?" Wade asked. "Lock us in a tower? Go back to old-fashioned beheading?"

"I hope you're joking."

"I am." Wade released me and slumped back onto the bed. "I've always known I came from selachii royalty, and that if we ever found Atlantis, it would be mine to rule. I pictured...I pictured...peace. Not this."

I took his hand. "The responsibility is not yours alone."

He rested his head against my stomach. "Thank God for you, Cordelia Blue."

Maya burst into the room. "*The united three must battle ancient enemies in the face of great betrayal.*"

I pivoted to face her. "A new prophecy?"

"Yes," she said, *The Mermaid Chronicles* in her arms. She laid it on the bed and pointed to the words.

"I can't read that," I reminded her.

"It's part of the original prophecy, like an extension."

"Christ, now we get amendments to prophecies?" Wade asked.

"Just this one," Maya said. "It's set in the page now, no more changing. Whatever events have led to this moment, well, it's done, and we can no longer change what's coming."

"*To save Atlantis, the royal couple must unite with a third, the one who died and lives again. Family is important,*" I said. "*The united three will need to battle ancient enemies in the face of great betrayal.* I don't think it even makes sense in English. Are you sure you've got the translation right?"

Maya scowled at me, pointing at the glowing page. "I'm sure."

There it was written within the pages of the heavy tome in black and white, in a forgotten ancient language. Not being able to read it myself didn't make the message any less potent.

"We need to tell our people," Wade said, storming toward the doors. "We cannot deny them the truth any longer. Anyone can see the fleet in the ocean." He yanked the door open. "Ford? It's time."

Maya and I hurried after him.

"Wait," I called. "What are you going to say?"

Wade stopped in the middle of the hall. "I'll figure it out. Just be by my side, Cordelia Blue."

"Always," I replied.

Only a few minutes later, the entire Atlantean population gathered in the courtyard. Perhaps they had been waiting for an announcement.

Wade addressed the crowd. "There's no easy way to tell you this, so I'm not going to form a long, drawn-out speech about the merits of Atlantis or how lucky we are to be here. We all know we are. Especially as it has been confirmed that while we've been here, there has been a nuclear war on the mainland. Pretty much every city has been destroyed. The families you left behind are likely dead. If that isn't tragedy enough, the humans now know of our hidden land. Some of them seek sanctuary, but others want revenge."

The news was received in silence. Not a single whisper among the gathering. Not a single breath of air in the packed courtyard.

"We are a kind race of people, and I would love to offer sanctuary to those humans who seek it and mean us no harm. Even if I knew how to drop the veil that separates us from the human world, it is impossible to allow some and not all. And so, I urge you to remain here on Atlantis where we are safe. The humans cannot reach us here. They've already captured one member of the scout group. I know many of you will feel the need to return and see the aftermath for yourselves, to search for family members who may have survived, but I urge you to wait a little longer. Let these humans who have sailed to our doorstep become bored and give up on their quest. Then it may be safe to return."

Our people remained stoic. I was proud of them. They vowed to protect our land, to unite behind us, which they had done so many times before. Wade called the Royal Guard to ready themselves. Our civilian inhabitants went to bed with pickaxes and baseball bats. Fire flickered intermittently on my fingertips.

Wade and I slept fitfully. Occasionally, one of us would rise to peer out the window and check on the status of the enemy fleet. The moon highlighted their white hulls. But they remained stationary for the time being, anchored in the sea, a growing wall of impending war. Weren't they sick of war?

In the middle of the night, when neither of us could sleep and words seemed either insufficient or too ominous, we made love, urgently and fiercely, perhaps sensing our time together was not eternal. There was nothing in *The Mermaid Chronicles* that spoke of our personal fate.

The morning sun broke over a new day, but I'd learned long ago that bad things still happened when the sun was shining.

Wade and I walked the paths around the island, reassuring our people. But many wouldn't meet our eyes. Several groups huddled in whispered conversations, locking us out of their thoughts. With the presence of numerous human boats anchored off our shores, tension became a physical thing, clenching around the heart of each inhabitant.

"Wade, look." I spotted a small group of selachii slip into the water.

"They're probably going to the mainland to see for themselves," Wade said. "I knew this would happen."

Slow movement on the horizon caught my attention. A massive vessel approached the island, its horn blasting the smaller boats out of the way.

Wade stood. "It's my father."

"At least we know he's safe."

"He would have been on the water when the bombs hit. But why he didn't come back to warn us..." Wade's expression darkened.

The Albacore, a boat I'd once had the displeasure of being a passenger on, tunneled toward the port, propelling the smaller human boats out of its path.

"Something's wrong," I said.

A handful of smaller boats gave chase. The Albacore slowed at the last moment, slipping through the veil to the marina. The trailing human vessels farther out to sea turned in circles.

"It disappeared before their eyes," I said.

"At least we know the veil is working." Wade gripped my hand. "But look."

A small, determined sailboat followed the path of *The Albacore*, hurtling toward the veil. Without warning, it vanished.

"Where did it go?" I asked.

Wade scanned the horizon. "There."

The missing vessel appeared on the other side of the island by the craggy rock face where Stephanie had disappeared.

"Are you sure it's the same one?" I asked, shielding my eyes from the sun.

"Same idiotic Jolly Roger flag."

My shoulders dropped a couple of inches. I didn't pretend to know how the Power of the Sea worked, but at least I could trust in its magical powers to keep us safe.

Daniel Waters disembarked from *The Albacore*, following the cobblestone path leading to the palace. We waited for him in the courtyard, under the shade of the circle of columns supporting aromatic honeysuckle and hanging grapes. The fragrant scents turned my stomach.

"Wade. Cordelia." He shook hands with his son and pecked a kiss on my cheek.

"We're glad to have you back safely," I said.

"It was touch and go for a while," he replied.

"There are new prophecies," Wade said to his father. "There's a war coming."

"Let me know what you need me to do." Daniel laid a hand on his son's shoulder.

Wade's eyes narrowed. "A warning would have been nice."

"I came as soon as I could," Daniel said. "We've been in hiding."

"I'm sorry to hear that," I said, attempting to lessen the tension between father and son.

Daniel gave me a curt nod, then turned to Wade. "I'm going to find your mother and sister."

Feeling utterly helpless, Wade and I continued to walk the island paths, reassuring anyone we could. I was disappointed to see other groups approach the water. A few sought our permission to return, so we kept a list of names.

When we reached the lower mountain trails, I glanced at the snow-capped beauty. Not being a fan of the cold, the mountain was one of the few areas I hadn't explored.

"Where the hell did she go?" I glared at the rocks.

"Who?" Wade asked.

"Stephanie."

"I don't know. But I think she's alive. I think I'd feel it if she was dead."

I raised an eyebrow at him. "Losing your virginity to someone doesn't make you eternally connected."

Wade chuckled.

"I'm serious."

"I know you are." Wade pecked my cheek. "You're never going to get over her, are you?"

A flush spread over my face. "I think I've done rather well over the last year."

"Cordelia Blue, if there's one thing I know about you, you do like to hold a grudge."

I scowled at him. "I think you'll find that's Stephanie's key personality trait, not mine."

"You two are more alike than you realize," Wade muttered.

"What was that?"

"Nothing."

"Uh-huh."

"Are you not relieved by her absence?"

I considered. A life without Stephanie would be much smoother. But she'd already caused her damage, and nothing could take that away, so what did it matter now whether she lived on Atlantis or the mainland? "I hope she's okay."

"And that's another reason I love you," Wade said as he cupped my rear. "Your giant heart."

We found our way to the beach as the sun kissed the horizon, turning our sky into a brilliant pastel rainbow. Human scientists dove into the water armed with an array of tools to measure whatever it was they thought they could measure.

"Good luck to them." Wade kissed the back of my hand.

In the fading light, we stumbled onto a mermaid stretched out on the sand. Beached, her yellow tail glistened with salt and sand, and her gills spluttered irregularly.

"Quick, Wade, go to the fountain."

Wade dashed away, and I kneeled by the mermaid.

"Where have you been?"

The mermaid panted, her ribs heaving, her skin encrusted with salt, body battered by relentless waves. Her chest rose and fell with labored breaths, each gasp a struggle. Her once luminous skin was now encrusted with a layer of salt. Her eyes, swollen and nearly sealed shut from the saltwater, fluttered weakly as she tried to focus on her surroundings. Tangled in her hair, which was matted with seaweed and debris from the ocean's depths, were remnants of her underwater journey.

"Rest, don't talk," I said, stroking her hair and brushing the sand from her face.

Wade returned with a cup of water from the Fountain of Youth, as well as my mother and Dylan. He held the cup to the mermaid's dry lips. The healing liquid bubbled down her throat until she coughed and swallowed.

The transformation was instantaneous. Her skin radiated color, her eyes cleared of their milky cloud, her tail glistened with new strength. Her hair lengthened and surrounded her waist in long waves of tumbling strawberry blonde. The tail was the same color as her hair, an unusual occurrence considering merfolk only possessed tails of blue or green or purple.

Except for me. Mine was fiery red and the only one of its kind. Finally, with the completion of the cure, her tail gave way to her legs.

"Radiation poisoning," Dylan said.

"From the nukes? She was there?" Wade asked.

"Obviously," Mom said, taking a step back. She looked over her shoulder, then out at the water, then finally her gaze settled on the recovering mermaid. Her hands trembled.

"She's going to be okay, Mom," I said, taking her shaking hand.

Mom nodded, then wiped away a stray tear.

"I thought everyone was here," I said. "I didn't think anyone had left."

"They hadn't," Mom replied. "Not then."

"Then how did she get radiation poisoning?" I asked.

"Because she didn't know she was a mermaid until now," Mom replied. "She never knew. She grew up in the middle of the country and never had the opportunity to access her birthright."

Dylan stared at our mother. "Huh?"

"What are you talking about?" Wade asked. "How do you know anything about her? None of us have seen her before." He was still cradling the woman's head. She was coming to, trying to sit up.

"I've seen her before," Mom murmured. "A long time ago. Years. But I'd recognize her anywhere." She crouched in front of the woman. "Because she's my daughter."

CHAPTER ELEVEN

I kneeled in the sand as a myriad of thoughts cluttered my head. The sound of the waves faded to the background as I stared at my mother. She had another daughter?

Dylan's expression mirrored my incredulity. And Wade looked equally nonplussed.

The woman sat up, sipping from the cup containing the Fountain of Youth, which my mother held for her while she whispered reassuring sentiments.

I stared at the stranger, taking her in all over again. Her tumbling blonde hair with a hint of auburn, her pale skin, the freckles scattered across her nose. Her eyes so bright and blue it was like looking in a mirror.

My mother's revelation hung in the air. I couldn't find an appropriate way to respond. Dylan stared at the sand, refusing to look at my mother, his mouth a twisted line.

The woman glanced at my mother. "What did you say about daughters?"

Mom's hands worried at her waist, her movements as rapid as a hummingbird's wings. "You're my daughter."

Even though Dylan and my mother were more alike in looks with their dark hair and hazel eyes, the family resemblance was striking. Something about the shape of her chin, the slant of her nose, the curl in her hair. If I was honest, she looked more like me than anyone else.

My mother swiped at tears sliding down her cheeks.

"I..." My throat gurgled and words refused to flow.

Wade shoved his hands in his pockets. "Maybe I should leave you all alone."

"This is as much to do with you as it is me," I said, finding my voice.

"Explain, please," Dylan demanded.

"Let's get her inside. Some dry clothes," Mom said. "Then I'll explain."

We got to our feet and picked a path through the cooling sand.

"Does Dad know?" I asked as we climbed the palace steps.

My parents had met in college. They were young and I'd assumed they'd been each other's first serious relationships. It never occurred to me that my mother might have a past. A past that came with an infant.

I cut another surreptitious glance at my sister. She was older than me. Not an affair. My mother must have been a teenager.

"Yes," Mom replied, without offering further explanation. "Raina? Are you still called Raina?"

"Yes," she replied.

My mother smiled, held her hand, and led her up the palace steps. The rest of us trailed behind, lost in a dense fog of bafflement.

"The sapphire keyring," I said.

"Yes," Mom replied.

Sometime ago, when I'd decided to face my fear of water and braved taking a bath for the first time in five years, I'd rummaged through the kitchen drawers looking for a box of matches to light the candles in the bathroom. Dad and I had found Mom's old keyrings that she'd used for her car. Three jewels dangled from the spiral fasteners. Two opals and a sapphire. It was obvious the opals represented Dylan and me because it was the birthstone for October, the month we were born. But the third sapphire jewel had presented a mystery. These were the jewels that had started our quest for Atlantis. Keys my mother protected in case the rubies were taken from her. Now it all made sense.

"Is your birthday in September?" I asked Raina.

"Yes," she replied.

"What are you talking about?" Dylan asked.

"Mom's keyring."

"Oh."

Conversation dwindled. The important things were too big to say.

Inside the palace, Raina was given a sarong dress of salmon pink and slippers for her unprotected feet. Most Atlanteans chose to walk barefoot to ease the transition between water and land, but Raina's feet had yet to harden.

We gathered in the courtyard around a table. Dylan brought a carafe of wine. Someone fetched my father. He arrived, looked Raina up and down, smiled at my mother, and folded them both into a bear hug. I reminded myself he had known.

"Out with it," Dylan said.

I swatted my brother's hand. "Less tone, more tact."

Someone brought a basket of bread and fresh cheese, which Raina dove into ravenously. "It's been so long since I've eaten. I don't know how long I swam for..."

None of us said a word, we just stared at her.

"Where am I?" Raina asked, toying with a damp curl.

"Atlantis," Wade replied.

"It's real..." Raina leaned back in her chair. "I wasn't sure the stories were true. I thought it was a provincial tabloid trying to sensationalize everything." She smiled at me secretly. A special kind of smile reserved for a younger sister. It was kind and thoughtful and wonderful and made me bristle with the pride of existence.

"It's true," I said to my sister.

Sister. *Sister.* I had a sister. An older sister. I felt a sudden pang of regret, a yearning for lost time.

"Mom?" Dylan looked at our mother. "Why didn't I know I had an older sister?"

Mom took a sip of wine. "I had Raina when I was sixteen."

Dad held her hand. "It's okay."

Mom frowned, dipped her chin, stared at her lap as if gathering her thoughts. There was a shadow over her life. A shadow I'd never been aware of. Something worse than Zale and Caol.

"I went to the movies with a friend one night." She

looked at me, then Dylan, then Raina. "And I walked home alone in the dark."

"Jesus," Wade muttered. "I'm so sorry."

"You were attacked?" Dylan asked.

"I was." Mom patted at the wetness on her cheeks. "I didn't tell anyone about it. I was ashamed."

"Oh, Mom," I cried.

Raina, her face paler than bleached coral, drained her glass. "I never knew."

"I never wanted you to," Mom said. "But I'm tired of secrets. Everyone deserves to know their truth."

"Did you tell your parents?" I asked.

"Eventually. When it became obvious I was pregnant," Mom said. "They were supportive, they would have helped me care for you, Raina...but it was impossible."

"Why?" Wade asked.

"*The Mermaid Chronicles*," Mom replied.

I closed my eyes. That book brought nothing but angst.

"I knew one of my children was destined to find Atlantis, that they would endure a lifetime of heartache and loss. And I refused. I thought I could simply send her away and none of it would come to pass. How foolish I was."

My mother reached for her wineglass, and seeing it was empty, placed it gently back on the table. Moonlight danced in the courtyard, brushed the surface of the Fountain of Youth, and rested on my mother's face.

"I gave you up for adoption on the condition that whoever took you home would continue to call you Raina. I wanted you to have a little piece of me with you, always, even if was only your name. The second condition was that you had to live in Kansas, or a similar land-locked state."

"So she would never discover her tail," I guessed.

"Yes," Mom replied.

"You can't keep a mermaid from water." My gaze drifted to the dark ocean, to the white crests highlighted by the lights of a hundred circling boats.

Mom ran her hand over the surface of the iron table. "I was sixteen. Terribly naïve. I made a lot of mistakes."

Dylan plucked at the honeysuckle snaking behind his shoulder, shredding its leaves, destroying its blossoms. "But there are lakes, streams..."

"But nowhere to go, and with none of the threats the ocean poses," Mom replied.

"It obviously worked, because Raina has only recently discovered she is a mermaid," I said.

"Twenty-nine years of life and then out pops a tail." Raina raised her eyebrows. "Gave me a hell of a scare."

"I bet it did," I said. "How did it happen?"

"I grew up in Wichita, Kansas." Raina tucked her hair behind her ears, giving us all a quick glance. "I didn't see the ocean until recently."

"Why not?" Dylan asked.

"Never went near it," she said. "We went on camping vacations in vast woodlands. Never near a body of water. My mother almost drowned when she was little. She was terrified of water. Although she insisted I learn to swim in a pool, she'd never let me approach a stream or a lake. So I never knew."

"You found out when the bombs dropped," I said.

"I suspected something before that," Raina said. "Once I graduated from college and got a job as a reporter, I became curious about my past. I did some digging. The more I dug, the more obscure things got. My curiosity was piqued. When I went on assignment to San Diego, I was drawn to the ocean. I'd never been near it. And then the bombs."

"Were you in San Diego when it happened?" Wade asked.

"No, I was back home," Raina replied. "None of the bombs landed nearby, but I didn't escape the radiation clouds. I knew I needed to get to water. Maybe it was a dying wish. And so I walked, and hitchhiked, and sometimes crawled, vomiting on the sides of roads when the sickness overcame me, until I reached the ocean. I was so sick by the time I got there, I could barely roll down the sand."

"Christ," I muttered.

"The waves tugged me into the current," Raina said. "I thought I would die, and I remember thinking it wouldn't be so bad, that there are worse ways to go. But I didn't die."

"You discovered your tail," I said.

"Yes," Raina said. "And it felt glorious. I loved the water and I wanted to swim. I'd heard rumors about merfolk and shark people...incredible. I still can't believe I am one."

I thought of Gal. I often felt his presence as a guiding force, a comforting essence that sometimes followed me through the palace and filled my heart in such a way that I knew guardian angels existed.

"I'm so sorry," Mom said to her. "I was only trying to protect you. But it seems I've caused you more pain."

"I don't blame you," Raina said. "I've had a good life. Finding all of you now makes it better."

"Your parents?" Wade asked.

Raina shook her head. "They didn't make it."

"I'm sorry," Wade said.

My mother looked over her eldest child, following the length of her wild hair to her waist, not quite able to meet her eyes. "You have a life with us here now. If you want it."

"Thank you." Raina bowed her head. "I'd like nothing more than to get to know all of you, my family, my birth family."

A natural silence descended over us as we shared looks and held hands, filled glasses and whispered emotional sentiments.

"I can't believe I have a sister," I said. Raina smiled and squeezed my hand.

"Twin brother wasn't good enough for you?" Dylan winked. But I could no longer tell when he was joking.

I threw a napkin at him, which he caught and balled into his pocket.

Raina looked at me. "By the way, what is a fire mermaid?"

"*The* fire mermaid," Dylan said. "There's only one."

"Cordelia is," Wade said, draping an arm across the back of my chair. "Show her." His eyes flashed black, then twinkled with delight. A demonstration might provide a brief reprieve from the prophecies that bound our futures.

"It *is* getting dark," I laughed. "None of the lanterns have been lit. It would be a shame to waste these beautiful candles."

I shot ten flames from my fingertips to light the candles

of the courtyard. They formed center pieces on every table and hung from the columns lining the pathways. After one candelabra came flickering to life, the flames streaked through the courtyard to find others waiting for illumination. The courtyard was aglow with soft lighting in a matter of seconds.

"Wow," Raina said. "When you said fire mermaid, you actually meant *fire*."

"It was the Power of the Sea," Wade said. "Cordelia and I ran into...problems on our quest to find the island."

"We almost died," I added.

"The Power of the Sea saved us," Wade said. "It's an ancient power created at the beginning of time to stand dominion over the ocean. It granted us abilities. Fire for Cordelia. Strength for me."

"Hercules," Raina marveled.

Wade blushed. "Nothing like that."

I nudged him with an elbow. "It's exactly like that."

"Well, I'm sure as hell glad I wasn't injured and granted sobriety," Dylan chuckled, downing his drink.

Mom leaned closer to him. "Dylan—"

He raised a palm. "Kidding."

Raina skimmed over the forming tension. "But mermaids and fire? That's...strange, isn't it?" She smiled, a charming smile which put me immediately at ease.

"Don't forget dragon kings can breathe fire too," Wade said. "And they're a water species."

"They're gone now," I said, tempted to make the sign of the cross, even though I'd never been religious.

"Does it work in water?" Raina asked.

"It does," I replied. "It can burn through anything. In fact, I think it works best in water."

"What else can you do?" she asked.

I lowered my head as I cast my mind back to the terrible battle with the dragon kings. Although I had felt my power building, I hadn't known it was capable of such destruction. The complete and utter decimation of an entire race. An outcome which sat uncomfortably on my shoulders. But I'd had no choice. War was war. And it seemed we were about to face another.

"The power is deadly," I said, unwilling to reveal more.

Dylan put his glass on the table. "It is much more powerful than the magical lighting of a few candles."

"And you're married, I see," Raina said to me, inspecting the two rings on my finger.

"Yes," I replied, raising my hand. "Recently."

"I wish I could have been there."

"Me too." I smiled at my sister.

We sat in the courtyard until dawn appeared on the horizon, catching Raina up on all she had missed, attempting to make up for a million lost moments.

"These prophecies," Raina said. "They always come true?"

"So far," I replied.

She toyed with the melting wax from the elaborate candle arrangement. "So who on this island would betray you?"

I'd thought of little else since Maya had informed us of the addition to the prophecy. I didn't think there was an Atlantean capable of it.

"I have no idea," I said, staring at my sister, wondering for the first time if she was who she claimed to be.

CHAPTER TWELVE

"Jordan's gone!"

I sat bolt upright in my bed and looked for the source of the intrusive bellowing, unsure whether the fearful yells were originating from a yawping monster in the depths of my dream or if Dylan was really standing there at the foot of my bed shaking my foot and shouting. Wade sat up next to me, rubbing his eyes. It was still dark. We'd only been asleep a couple of hours.

"Jordan's gone," Dylan said more quietly, but no less urgently.

I blinked a few times, trying to adjust to the darkness. I lit a candle with a fingertip.

"You mean he's no longer passed out on that awful seawolf rug in your bar?" Wade said. "That's a *good* thing, isn't it?"

"No. I mean yes. No! He's *gone* gone," Dylan replied.

"Where?" I asked.

"To the mainland."

Wade and I leaped out of bed, dressing quickly.

"Why?" I asked.

"He's upset about Steph," Dylan said. "He's angry. He wants to take his grief out on someone, and who better than the humans who are trying to invade us?"

"Oh, no," Wade said.

"We have to stop him," Dylan said.

"We do." Wade pulled off his clothes, preparing himself for the water. "We can't let him go off halfcocked. He's in a delicate state. He can't be the one to cast the first stone."

"Bombs have dropped," Dylan snapped. "I think we're a little past stone throwing."

"You know what I mean," Wade said.

"When did he leave?" I asked.

"About half an hour ago," Dylan replied.

"We might be able to cut him off. If we move now." Wade marched to the door.

Dylan and I followed him to the water's edge to find Trent and Maya waiting for us.

After a brief strategy session on the beach that consisted of no more than; dive, swim, follow, catch, and retrieve, Maya ran back to the palace to inform Ford and my parents of our plans and the four of us dove into the ocean.

There was a moment, when my skin met water and my tail transitioned, that I felt perfectly happy. It happened every time I submerged myself in the ocean, and I had denied myself the primal need for over a week. The longer the denial, the more agonizing the anticipation, and the more blissful the release when I finally allowed my need to consume me. But now was not the time to revel in the glory of my tail. I shook off the feeling and followed the three men. Diving deep, we swam under the reaches of the nets and scientific instruments of the human fleet. With powerful strokes, we flicked our tails hard and fast, but there was no sign of Jordan.

We swam for the rest of the night and most of the day, and when we reached Ocean Beach, we stumbled up the shore and lay under the pier to catch our breath.

"I can't believe we didn't catch up with him," Trent said, casting furtive glances up and down the deserted coastline.

"Maybe he didn't come this way," I said, shaking water and sand out of my hair.

"He might have had a bigger head start than I thought," Dylan said.

Voices above my head drew my attention. An altercation on the pier. Jordan's voice.

I gave Wade a questioning look, but he only splayed his hands in return. Dylan laid a finger across his lips and indicated we should listen.

Goosebumps swarmed over my skin as I stood under the pier in the dying day, feeling guilty for eavesdropping.

"How could you?" Jordan screamed as the wind gathered.

"It wasn't hard," a familiar voice shot back, but it was altered, veined with a caustic edge that during all her past misdeeds, I'd never detected before.

"I've been searching for you everywhere. Everyone has, the whole island."

"I didn't ask you to." She was calm, eerily calm considering she usually wore her emotions on her sleeve. But things had changed during the last year, things I hadn't noticed, or had perhaps ignored. That much was evident.

"No, because we all thought you were dead. People tried to tell me you might have returned. I didn't believe them. I told them you would never leave me. I told them we were kindred spirits. I told them I loved you and you loved me. I know you've never told me that last part." Jordan sniffed loudly. "But it was implied...wasn't it?"

I imagined the two of them on the pier, facing each other, staring each other down. Jordan's face full of anguish. Stephanie's full of...I had no idea what. I stepped out of the shadows, but Wade grabbed my arm and tugged me back under.

"Wait," he whispered. "We'll learn a whole more like this than if we confront them."

"It doesn't feel right," I said.

Dylan raised an eyebrow. "We're long past things feeling right."

"I'm not sure anything does anymore." Wade's eyes flashed black.

"I didn't think you would leave me," Jordan said, the last uttered so softly it barely reached me over the sound of my shallow breathing.

"Leaving you was the easy part," Stephanie replied.

"Bitch," Trent muttered.

I couldn't disagree.

"Poor Jordan," Wade murmured.

"I love you," Jordan said.

"But I never loved you."

Silence fell, the only sound the irregular gusts of wind. Sand stung my legs and salt tightened my skin.

"You're a bitch," Jordan snarled. "A hateful witch."

Stephanie laughed. "You don't know the half of it."

"Maybe we should go up there," Trent mumbled.

"I wish you were dead," Jordan said, his voice so twisted with pain it was barely recognizable. "You betrayed me. You are the worst kind of traitor. I can't believe you led the humans to Atlantis. Just you wait until..."

I blanched. Wade stumbled backward in the sand. Trent shot me an incredulous look before his expression hardened. I missed his easy laughter, his spontaneous jokes, but life had changed for everyone.

"Come now, Jordan, the sergeant's waiting," Stephanie said.

I dared an upward glance at the pier and caught sight of their silhouettes. Jordan, bare-chested and wearing only cropped jeans, stood with his shoulders squared and his chin raised. His tattoo jerked with angry defiance as he moved. I startled when I noted the presence of an entire troop of soldiers, and almost dove back into the shadowy belly of the pier. But I had to know what the hell was going on.

Jordan's wrists were handcuffed behind his back, and he was guarded by a couple of high-ranking soldiers in combat uniforms. There were dozens more footmen holding a tight perimeter around the arguing couple. One soldier pushed Jordan to the mouth of the pier, and then into a waiting armored car. The car drove away. The rest of the soldiers climbed into jeeps and followed behind.

"What the actual...?" Trent stared at the now empty road.

"I have no idea," I said.

"She's been up to something," Wade said. "Scheming something while we were playing happy families on Atlantis. I should have known. Dammit."

"No one could have known," Dylan said. "Not even Jordan had a clue."

I watched the trail of cars disappear over the hilltop. It was then I took in the war's destruction. The houses of Ocean Beach were nothing but broken windows and looted goods. Doors hung from hinges, the brown grass of front lawns struggled for life, fire hydrants spewed their loads onto the roads. Parked cars showed missing hubcaps and wheels, smashed windows, dents and holes in roofs. Trash skipped along the streets, skittering with jagged bursts of wind, producing an eerie sound like a march of murderous beetles.

Broken buckets and spades were scattered along the empty beach. Perhaps decades from now, centuries even, archaeologists would unearth the colorful plastic toys and wonder who they belonged to and what they were for. But they would know from the telltale signs of the surrounding earth that there had been a nuclear war and that the owners of these toys had most likely perished.

"Do we go after him?" I asked, raising my voice now the four of us were alone.

Dylan mimed zipping his lips shut. "Stephanie is still here."

I glanced at the pier but couldn't spot her. She had to be there somewhere. She hadn't left with the soldiers.

"I need to talk to her." Wade climbed from the shadows of the pier.

"Wait." I grabbed his arm. "Didn't you hear them? She's behind it all. *Stephanie* is behind it all. She is our great betrayer. The one in the prophecy."

"So we deal with her now, and maybe things don't get too bad," Trent said, jerking his head at the pier.

I blocked his path. "Or any one of us could be captured too."

Wade clenched his hands into fists. "She wouldn't do that to me."

"We don't know what she's capable of anymore," I said. "If she still has affection for you...or not."

"I need to try. I can't just let her walk away." Wade kicked at the sand. "I need to try and make her see."

"Okay," I said. "But be careful."

Dylan, Trent, and I followed Wade from the shadows. We climbed the steps of the pier and mounted the concrete pathway. Stephanie stood in the middle of the tarmac, her face lifted to the dipping sun, her eyes on the horizon.

She pivoted to face us. "I knew you were here." Her eyes locked on Wade. "I could feel you." She smiled. But it wasn't the arrogant smile of superiority I had become familiar with. This smile contained touches of evil. Were we too late?

"Stephanie," Wade said, a reproach in his voice. "What have you been up to?"

"Many, many things."

"What? Why?" Wade asked, taking small steps toward her.

"You should know by now that I don't take rejection well."

"It wasn't personal," Wade said.

"Of course it was personal!" she snarled, jabbing a finger in the air. "You love Cordelia. Irrevocably. Eternally. It's written in the damn book!" She narrowed her eyes at me. "You love Cordelia, not me. You told me enough times. It doesn't get more personal than that."

"Would you rather I be in a loveless relationship with you?" Wade asked. "Because, Stephanie, I think you'd hate that even more. I know I would. And Jordan—"

"It doesn't matter anymore," she said. "It's too late."

"So what's your plan?" Wade inched closer. "You plan to bring down Atlantis and everyone on it just because I didn't return your feelings? To lead our people into the waiting jaws of vengeful humans? We've been on such a journey together, our quest for Atlantis, and now you want to destroy it all?"

Stephanie's black selachii eyes blazed.

"All our memories..." Wade looked at his feet, then raised his eyes again. "I may not want to be with you now, but I still treasure the memories. You've just stomped all over them."

"We all make choices, Wade-y," Stephanie said. "And choices have consequences."

"Yes, they do," Wade said. "Mine. Yours. Everyone's."

Stephanie crossed her arms over her chest and narrowed her unforgiving eyes.

"So what now?" Wade asked, splaying his hands. "What have you done, and what happens next?"

"For starters, the humans have given me immunity," Stephanie replied. Never had she looked so arrogant, so haughty, so superior. God help us if Wade had stayed with her. She'd be Queen of Atlantis and drive it to ruin. She was no better than the dragon kings. "In exchange for scientific subjects, they have allowed me freedom on the mainland."

"Scientific subjects?" Wade gaped at her. "Do you not remember when merfolk and selachii were put in tanks across the world? Their freedom stolen? Did that mean nothing to you?"

"Do not scold me, Wade Waters."

"The humans aren't looking for scientific subjects. Don't you see? There's no reason to study us when their world is a wasteland. No. Now they want revenge. Now they want to imprison and torture and inflict pain upon us in their deluded vindication of fairness. It's an eye for an eye. More than that."

Stephanie tossed her hair over her shoulder, her high eyebrows revealing her disdain. "I don't care."

My anger blazed. I bit my lip to prevent my flames from appearing on my fingers, or the fireballs streaking from my eyes. That had happened only once before, during the battle with the dragon kings. But I could feel the heat building behind my eyes.

"And then what?" Wade asked.

Stephanie smiled. "And then Aquaria."

I was sick of that smug little smile of hers. She'd pointed it in my direction countless times before. My flames sparked into existence.

"No, Cordelia." Wade shook his head at me. Did he think she could be saved? Did he not see her for the evil person she'd become?

I ignored Wade's plea and pointed my hands at

Stephanie. As I was summoning the courage to release my flames, they winked away.

"You can't even control your own stupid power," Stephanie laughed. "You'll never stop me."

Gritting my teeth, I strained to bring my flames back, but my will would not be obeyed. I shook my fingers, blew on them, pinched their tips...and nothing. A wave of nausea consumed me, and my knees buckled. My power was tied to my emotions, and the one person I could guarantee would inflame my rage was Stephanie. But I couldn't explain the absence of my fire. Stephanie should be consumed by a fire-ball right now. Not that I was trying to kill her, but I wanted to inflict pain. Enough pain that she would stand down and put right her wrongs.

"Are you okay?" Dylan asked, as Wade and Stephanie continued to argue.

I went down on my knees, vomited on the concrete ground.

"Just about." I wiped my mouth with the back of my hand. "Something weird is going on. My fire power isn't working..."

A startling presence interrupted my thoughts. Aquaria appeared. She stood next to Stephanie. She had swapped her purple tail for legs, but the snakes in her hair remained, exactly as we had seen them before, black and evil and wriggling with murderous intent.

"I thought you were in prison?" Trent asked.

Aquaria's snakes hissed. "The only sure way to keep someone down is death."

"I'll remember that when I kill you," I snarled, eliciting a manic peel of laughter from her.

"Now?" she asked Stephanie.

"Yes, Aquaria, now please," Stephanie replied.

Aquaria closed her eyes. An incantation twitched on her whispering lips. "It's done."

"What's done?" Wade asked.

Stephanie smiled.

"*What's* done?" Wade demanded, charging at her, ready to catch her wrist in his hand.

Stephanie's long hair turned dark and whipped around her face, her black selachii eyes glinted with malevolent desire. "The veil has been dropped. Atlantis will now belong to the humans. You are a king of nothing now."

CHAPTER THIRTEEN

The wind picked up, growing proportionally stronger with the widening of Stephanie's smile.

"No," I whispered. I shook my hands again, desperate to evoke my devastating power. But the flames eluded me.

Wade said nothing. He let his hand drop to his side. Hope dwindled in his eyes, and his shoulders sagged. The humans would be all over Atlantis by the time we swam back. We were right where Stephanie wanted us, and there was nothing we could do.

"Stephanie," Wade choked out her name. "*Please.*"

"You had your chance," she said.

Without another word, Stephanie and Aquaria jumped over the side of the pier and disappeared into the ocean below.

"No!" Wade ran to the metal balustrade and peered over the edge. "No!"

As a tense silence descended on us, the nausea slipped

out of my stomach and the flames reappeared on my fingers. "Typical," I muttered.

Wade turned and faced us. "We need to go back. We need to save our people."

"How?" Dylan asked. "The humans will have swarmed the island before we get there."

"Maya is there," Trent said, looking at the horizon. "I can't leave her there."

"We need to do something," I said. "We can't stand around here. Even if we are late, we still need to go back. I have my flames, and Wade has his strength. We need to try."

The four of us stood at the pier's railing. A cloud shadowed the drooping sun and the ocean turned a bleak steel-gray. Before we jumped, I glanced over my shoulder. A procession of army jeeps approached the beach. Fear licked the back of my spine. We were wedged between a rock and a hard place, and I couldn't tell if the humans surrounding Atlantis, or these soldiers were the worse obstacle.

We held hands and jumped into the water. As we fell, I spotted a young woman climb out of a jeep and shield her eyes to watch us. There was something familiar about her, something about the shape of her chin and the way she wore a ponytail high on her head. As the water engulfed me and my tail appeared, realization struck. The woman was Babette, my high school nemesis, who I'd had to fight for Wade's arm. Were all the females in Wade's past making an appearance in this latest battle? What was Babette doing here? Did she know what I'd become? Did she also want to make me pay?

My thoughts spun the entire swim back to Atlantis. We emerged on the cliff face to find smoke hanging in the air.

The report of gunfire sounded from all pockets of the island. I didn't know whether to cry or scream.

Most of the human fleet was docked at the harbor, and the sound of marching feet filled the island. Humans charged up the cobblestone pathways, wielding shotguns and automatic weapons.

"These are Sean Wilson's people," Trent said, his eyes narrowed. "They're here for revenge."

We concealed ourselves against the rocks. The humans dashed by with twisted mouths and hate in their eyes. They were here for one reason only. To decimate our island.

"Most of them are in civilian clothing," Wade said, turning in a slow circle. "Where's the rest of his army?"

I scanned the immediate area, searching for a second wave of attack, but all I saw was the melee of human civilians and Atlanteans in a terror-filled exchange. Gray clouds filled the sky, the sun but a hopeful wish hidden deep.

"I don't know," Trent replied. "But he's calculating and cold. I'm sure he's got a plan."

I looked at my brother, into eyes sunken with exhaustion and stress. I couldn't lose him again.

"What do we do?" I asked, as a group of Atlanteans ran by, horror in their eyes and only blunt weapons in their hands. "How do we help them?" Fire leaped from roof to roof as my people attempted to extinguish the blaze amongst searing bullets and flying punches.

"The palace." Wade urged us forward, into the dense fray of slaughter and beyond.

The four of us ran, weaving our way through the humans, covering our ears as explosions punctuated the air. We ran past the Fountain of Youth, now a brown and putrid mess, as if disgusted by the inhumanity of the humans. We ran up the marble steps and when we reached the top, Esmerelda was waiting. She clutched at her skirts, her eyes wide and her body visibly trembling.

I followed her eyeline. Blood lined the pathways, churned in the water channels, covered masses of darting people. Screams and smoke and panic filled the air, filled me with dread, filled the island with terror.

"What are you doing here?" I asked Esmerelda.

"You were away," she replied, a hand trembling against her lips. "You were away, and I saw what was going to happen." She looked at me. "I fear I revealed too much."

"Is it too late?" Wade asked.

"I don't know," Esmerelda replied.

"Shane? Edward?" I asked.

"They're here somewhere," she replied.

Esmerelda held a small portion of The Power of the Sea in her hand. She ran down the steps and thrust it toward the nearest firing humans. They died immediately, the blue orb shooting deadly projectiles of agonizing heat and venom, killing them instantly.

"I don't want them to die," I said. "Can't we talk to them?"

"I think it's too late," Wade said, ducking at the sound of nearby gunfire.

Esmerelda whirled around to face us, a triumphant smile on her face. How long would she stay to help us? How long until she aged too quickly, and died?

While she stared at us, a human teen launched himself at

her with a knife, stabbing the mermaid High Council representative in the neck.

"Noooooo!" I yelled, my flames bursting into existence.

Wade charged down the steps, grabbed the human teen by the neck, and threw him into the air. The teen somersaulted over our heads, over the moldering fountain, and landed on the rocks, shattering his skull.

Esmerelda's knees buckled. Her hands grasped the arterial spurt at her neck. She tried to smile, but only a gurgle left her lips.

The small portion of the Power of the Sea recollected itself into a spherical shape and buzzed away to rejoin its mother orb.

I kneeled by Esmerelda, held her in my arms as her eyes dimmed. She died quickly. Her body dried and shriveled, releasing itself from centuries of life within the eternal chamber of the High Council. Her skin cracked and broke apart. Her bones shattered and turned to dust. In seconds, there was nothing left of her apart from the mermaid brooch she wore at her neck.

"Inside." Wade pulled me away from Esmerelda's remains and led us toward the palace entrance. As soon as the four of us tumbled through the doors, he locked them with the deadbolts. Locks that hadn't been used the entire time we'd lived on the island.

The noises of the battle diminished, but I couldn't deny the way each scream pierced a new stab of guilt into my heart. The nausea accosted me again. I stumbled and leaned against Wade for support. I heaved up bile and water all over the marble floor.

"Cordy?" Dylan rushed to my side. "Are you okay?"

"Too much smoke. I sucked in a lungful," I replied, using his arm to get to my feet. "More than a lungful."

A loud and piercing scream peeled through the palace. Raina came running around the corner, her hands covered in blood.

"Cordelia, thank God, please help!" She led me through the hallways, deep into the palace, where we found our mother lying crumpled in a heap, blood pouring from a shoulder wound.

"She needs medical attention," Raina said, squatting by her side, pressing a blood-soaked towel against my mother's shoulder. "I removed the blade, but...she's not in good shape."

"The Fountain of Youth," I replied, turning, intending to retrace my steps to the palace door and down the marble staircase.

"It won't work," Mom said weakly. "It's tainted. As soon as the veil dropped, it turned brown."

"Stephanie," I snarled. "She doesn't want us to survive."

"Our island is being destroyed." Mom's face was white and clammy.

"She needs help." Raina flicked her hand, wiping the blood on her dress. "I don't know what to do."

"Where's Dad?" I asked.

"I don't know," Mom replied. "I lost him outside."

My heart surged into my throat. *Help Mom, or...look for Dad.*

"The wound isn't so bad." Mom sat on the floor, sagged against the wall, her arm resting across her lap, the other supporting it. Her face was devoid of color and sweat beaded on her forehead and her upper lip. She was lying.

"Her breathing isn't good." Raina stroked my mother's back. "The blade was tipped with something...poison...I don't know. It's in her bloodstream." Raina held a towel to the wound and periodically peeled it back to inspect its severity. Each time she grimaced and hastily replaced the towel, attempting to hide the grisly evidence of my mother's indeterminate future. But her face said it all. "I saw stuff when I was a journalist...but this is...this is...we need to do something."

"We need to get you to the mainland," Dylan said. "You need a doctor. An anecdote. Something."

"Isn't there a doctor here?" Raina asked.

Dylan shook his head. "We've always had the Fountain of Youth. We've never needed anything else."

"Our fight is here," Wade replied, his shoulders stiff. "We can't leave our people. Stephanie and Aquaria...I'm sorry, Cordelia."

"Stephanie is alive?" Mom panted a few breaths, then asked, "Aquaria is alive?"

"Aquaria escaped. Or Stephanie released her. It doesn't matter how," I replied. "Stephanie's been on the mainland organizing the human invasion. She summoned Aquaria to help."

"It's all my fault," Wade whispered.

I reached for my husband's hand. "It's not your fault."

He stared at the floor. "I never thought she was capable of such merciless, narcissistic destruction."

"It's not your fault, son." Christina Waters, Wade's mother, rounded the corner with Maya. Maya dashed into

Trent's arms. "It's entirely hers. You can't blame yourself for other people's reactions or subsequent choices. It's a question of free will. Stephanie has made her decisions, however unwisely, and now she will have to see them through. As will we."

Wade nodded at his mother's words. "How do we defeat Aquaria?"

"Through the heart," Maya said.

"But you must avoid those venomous snakes," Christina added. "They are deadly."

Wade frowned. "I thought they'd be here. Haven't you seen them?"

"No," Mom murmured.

Raina checked the wound again and this time her face didn't contort into a picture of dismay. "The bleeding is slowing."

"If Aquaria is alive, then she can summon the Hound of the Ocean," Mom said, attempting to sit straighter. "I bet they never left the mainland. Easier to perform the spell over there, not here in the middle of a war."

"We need to go back to the mainland," Dylan said.

"Agreed," Wade said. "We need to find Stephanie and Aquaria before they call on the Hound of the Ocean."

Raina looked at me. "We need to help Mom."

"I know," I replied. Tension invaded my limbs, clenched my heart. I barely had the courage to look at my mother. She'd only been back in my life for one year. I couldn't lose her again. Or Dylan. Or my father. Or Wade...the list went on. It was likely we wouldn't all make it out of this war alive.

Dylan looked out one of the tall windows. "Maybe we

should stay there this time. Away from this infernal island. What's it brought us after all? We lost people to find it. We're losing people trying to keep it. What's the fucking point?"

I whirled on him. "Dylan!"

"What?" He swiveled toward me. "I'm just voicing what everyone is thinking. Atlantis is no longer our sanctuary. We might have better chances back on the mainland. It's much bigger, with plenty of places to hole up and hide from the humans. Or we could always blend in and pretend we've never heard of merfolk and selachii. Look." He pointed out the window.

The rest of us gathered around him. Merfolk and selachii gave up on dousing the fires and fled to the beach, to the water and the safety only it could offer. Humans fired on them as they ran, cutting them down on the pathways, causing new pools of red to bloom in the water channels.

"Let's go," Wade said. "Now."

"We can't abandon them," Maya said.

"We can't do anything for them," Trent said.

Christina gestured to me. "Unless you use your fire power."

I glanced at my hands. "I can't kill all the humans. I can't...I *was* a human...they're not like the dragon kings. I can't..."

"Don't you see what they're doing to our people?" Christina asked, an air of disproval in her tone.

I hung my head. I still lived with the guilt of killing the dragon kings, of the destruction my flames could cause. I didn't want to be forced to use that kind of power. I refused to fight like that. It was the same as dropping a nuclear bomb.

Not every human here deserved to die. I had to give the good ones a chance.

And even if I wanted to use the power, it hadn't been reliable during the last twenty-four hours. I could end up getting us all killed instead.

"Leave her alone," Wade snapped. "I agree with Cordelia. I'm not so into the idea of *genocide*. Plus, the latest prophecy says we must be united with a human. One of *them*." Wade pointed outside.

Christina threw her hands in the air. "Have it your way."

"So we go back," Trent said.

Raina helped my mother to her feet.

Wade raised an eyebrow at his mother. "You're coming?"

"Yes." She marched toward the locked doors. "If we can find Stephanie, I think I might be able to reason with her."

"I've already tried," Wade said, lifting my mother into his strong arms.

"Don't hold your breath," Trent added.

Ford appeared as we turned to the doors. "Not that way. They're on the steps now."

He led us deeper into the palace, down several flights of stairs, into the cellar where the secret tunnels began.

CHAPTER FOURTEEN

Ford led a fast pace through the winding underground tunnels. "Keep up."

Rough slabs of stone paved the floor, which spread up the walls until waist high. The arched ceiling consisted of densely packed earth, spilling claw-like roots of long dead trees. With only one flashlight in our possession, we tripped and stumbled and knocked into each other. Wade carried my mother, cradling her listless body close to his chest, and protected her head from falling debris.

As we ran, earth crumbled above our heads, trailed down the walls in tiny avalanches, bringing a skittering of insects. An ancient smell filled the damp air, soaking my lungs. A decaying mustiness that evoked images of long-dead kings and queens who may have used these tunnels to run for their lives. Much like we were doing now.

"Cordelia!" Raina shouted my name.

I turned to see Wade on his knees, holding my mother.

Raina crouched next to them. My mother's eyes were closed, her chest pulsed with shallow breaths.

"There's nothing we can do for her here," I said. "We have to keep going."

Come on, Mom.

Before we started off again, I caught sight of something encrusted within one of the walls. It was a symbol, one I recognized. Five orbs circling a larger sphere in the center. It was carved into one of the stone walls. But I didn't have time to inspect it now.

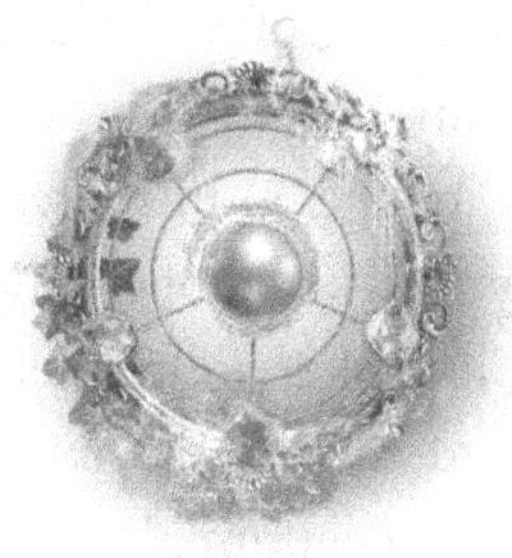

We hurried through the pitch-black tunnels. After half an hour of stale air and winding pathways, we emerged at the bank of an underground lake. Elaborate stalactites stretched from the ceiling, attempting to unite with their counterparts on the ground. Cool air whispered over my cheek.

"I found this the other day," Ford said, shining his light over the lake. "If we dive deep, there's a tunnel, a river that leads to the ocean. There's a drop. A hundred-foot waterfall, but it comes out on the other side of the island. We'll be able to swim to the mainland from there."

I looked at my mother, now unconscious in Wade's arms. Would she be able to transition?

Wade nudged my shoulder. "We don't have a choice."

"We can't leave her here," Raina added, inspecting my mother's wounds.

Chewing my lip, I nodded, my fear poisoning what hope I had left.

"Keep her safe," I said to Wade.

"I'll do my best," he replied.

"Let's get on with it," Dylan said, disappearing into the water.

We followed him. All of us. Maya, Trent, Christina, Ford, Wade, Raina, my mother, and me. When we hit the water, despite my mother's unconscious state, her tail emerged, and her eyes flickered open briefly. I heaved a sigh of relief before my gills took over my breathing.

We followed Ford toward the middle of the lake, his flashlight incapable of penetrating more than three feet into the inky water. I kicked with my tail fin, arrowing my body deeper into the darkness, sticking close to Ford's waning light.

We found the tunnel, and one by one, we swam through the opening. A turbulent darkness descended as a current pushed us through the rocky passageway. I scraped my back along the roof, drawing a ribbon of blood. The telepathic thoughts of my friends came in chaotic bursts. Ford, ahead, signaled we were almost there.

Light burst over me. I had a split second to savor the sun

before I fell through the foamy water. I windmilled my arms, instinctively looking for a handhold, but the relentless flow of water carried me down. My tail changed to feet, back to tail, back to feet. A cycle I couldn't keep track of. I gulped water, the icy terror freezing in my lungs.

My friends screamed their panic. My mother's weak thoughts drifted in the background. The rocks below loomed toward me. I threw my hands in front of my face, but I landed in water.

As I spluttered for oxygen, I spotted a smudge of the mainland in the distance. I swam to my mother and Wade. Her eyes were open, and she offered me a weak smile.

"That was some ride," Trent said. "Almost as good as a board. Might have to give that another go when we get back."

Maya nudged him. "On your own."

It was good to see a smile on his face, even if it was brief.

As the descending sun reddened the sky to the same color as the battle on our land, we pointed ourselves in the direction of the mainland and swam. I kept an eye open for Stephanie. Another for Aquaria. And my entire body tingled in anticipation of meeting the Hound of the Ocean.

I glanced over my shoulder once before we left Atlantis. Our people, those who were not being sprayed with bullets or slashed with knives, ran toward the beach and leaped from the clifftops in their desperate bid to reach the ocean. They would take their chances on the mainland and leave our island in the hands of the humans.

We swam as a pack, my mother in the middle for her protection. Ford led our closely knit group, setting a swift pace. Fear knotted my throat as I swam, ballooning with each mile we sped. We no longer had a home. We no longer had a safe place. And we had a multitude of enemies to face.

When we emerged on Ocean Beach, we scrambled out of the water under the protection of the pier. The moon carved a slice out of the black sky. Many Atlanteans huddled on the beach, but their relieved conversations were short-lived as the army made its presence known. A line of armored jeeps on the coastal road. Countless soldiers swarmed over the low beach wall, aiming their weapons.

"Hide," Wade said, circling his arm around me and dragging me deeper into the shadows.

We huddled beneath the pier, ready to take to the water if we were spotted.

Warnings shots slammed into the night, but thankfully took no mortal targets. It didn't take much for the defenseless Atlanteans to concede. They'd jumped from one hell to another. The soldiers of Sean Wilson's rebel army gathered them up as easily as a child's net catching minnows, and threw them into the armored vehicles, their screams muted with each slamming door. Had this been their plan all along?

Dylan narrowed his eyes at the line of army personnel. "They're going to pay."

"Mom first," I said as I glanced at her laying in the sand. "Then the rest."

He removed a cigarette from a plastic baggie and lit up.

I knocked it to the ground, jerking a thumb at the army. "Not the time."

A bulky man stood on the beach wall, arms crossed, eyes scanning the dark horizon. I assumed it was Sean himself. The air of arrogance and authority surrounding him left little doubt. Atlantis now belonged to him. A radioactive-free island of beauty and peace. But they had ruined the Fountain of Youth, which didn't work on humans anyway. His initiative was entirely pointless. Unless he had other plans to make us pay.

"Oh, no," Wade whispered under his breath.

Shouts and cries peppered the air as more Atlanteans were taken. We clumped together under the flimsy protection of the pier, hoping to remain unnoticed until we could pick a safe path past the army.

Wade marched to the edge of the shadows. "I can't let this happen. I can't let my people get hurt."

"Wait!" I called after him, grabbing his wrist, be he was too strong and easily shrugged me off. "Wade!"

Dylan grabbed me and dragged me back, put a hand over my mouth to muffle my shouts as I struggled against him. When I noticed Wade was already halfway up the beach, I sagged in defeat. The cone of an enemy flashlight picked him out.

"I'll get him, Cordy," Ford said as he dashed into the open after Wade and was quickly followed by Trent.

"Stop!" I half shouted. But they too quickly disappeared among the soldiers.

Maya sat next to Raina in the sand near my mother. "And so it begins."

I swiveled toward her. "What does that mean?"

She watched Trent's broad shoulders disappear into the night, but did not attempt to go after him. "The book said he would be captured if he gave himself up."

"He's hardly giving himself up," Dylan said. "He might

not have Wade's strength, but he's been pressing in the gym every day."

I whirled on my brother. "They have guns."

"No one fucks with an angry Trent and gets away with it," Dylan said, a ghost of a smile on his lips.

"Can we please do something about Mom?" Raina said. "She's burning up."

I looked at my mother draped across the sand, her breathing weak, her face pale, her eyes closed. My fingers heated in their tightly clenched fists. But my fire would only give me away.

"We shouldn't have let them go," I said, watching the broad square of Wade's back.

"Not letting them go would have brought worse fates," Maya said. "*The Mermaid Chronicles* has begun showing the pathways of the most likely choices."

"The possibilities must be endless," Christina said, helping Raina to tend to my mother. Someone had thought to bring a dry bandage and she wound it around my mother's arm.

"They are," Maya said. "It's a lot to keep in my head."

Dylan toyed with his lighter. "What happens next?" he asked Maya.

Maya clutched her arms to her chest. "I'd rather not."

"That's my husband who just walked away with Trent," I said. "I think I deserve to know."

"Nothing is set in stone," Maya said. "We should concentrate on getting help for your mother."

"We can't go anywhere without getting caught." I thrust a

hand toward the knots of soldiers dominating the beach. "They're going to find us any minute."

I couldn't deny my mother needed urgent help. She sat propped against Christina, which almost evoked a bitter laugh from my throat. I'd never seen the two of them together before. And yet, here we were, Atlanteans helping each other, as had been our norm during the last year.

"What do we do about them?" My heart raced as I watched Wade, and then kicked painfully against my ribs.

"There's nothing we can do for them," Maya replied. "We must find the united third."

I watched the brave trio approach the army standing on the beach wall. A soldier pointed Wade toward a car. He refused. The soldier thrust his rifle into Wade's chest. Wade swatted it away as if it were no more than a stinging weever fish. He was rewarded with a backhand to the chin and two more rifles thrust into his chest. He wrenched them both from the soldier's grips and sent both startled men flying with one powerful fist.

Yes. Maybe it wouldn't be as bad as Maya thought.

"We need to go," Raina said, dusting sand off my mother's face.

"There is nowhere to go," I replied, my heart sinking. "We have to wait until they're gone."

The fight turned ugly. With Wade's enhanced strength, and Ford and Trent's burly physiques, they held their own against an army of fifty for a full ten minutes. Fists were thrown and men doubled over as they were punched in the gut, winded, and taken out of the immediate fight. Several were knocked out with well-placed right hooks. One unlucky contender had his knee broken by Ford's swift karate chop. But more swarmed the beach, hesitant to use the deadly force of their weapons, until Sean Wilson raised a pistol and leveled it at Wade's chest.

"Enough," Sean said, his voice reaching me.

Wade raised his hands. Ford and Trent, with matching cuts and bruises, followed suit.

Maya stood next to me, holding my hand, a look that passed for courage on her face. Fear nipped at my lungs. "Are they going to be okay?"

"I don't know," Maya replied.

Sean held the gun only a foot from Wade's heart, both of them panting. My heart ached in my chest as Sean's finger twitched alarmingly on the trigger. The endless ways this could play out flooded my mind with terrible images.

Wade stood with his hands held either side of his head, his breath pluming thready wisps. Without a word, Sean Wilson removed his finger from the trigger and I let out a sigh of relief. My knees buckled. Sean gestured to an armored car with the barrel of his gun. The three of them disappeared inside. My husband. Gone.

I clutched my stomach as a wave of nausea consumed me. Fear streaked through my veins. Images of what could be... no...I shook my head to dispel my morbid thoughts.

As the car sped away, I dropped to my haunches and buried my face in my hands.

"How are we ever going to be united with a third if Wade is stuck in a prison cell somewhere?"

Or worse. But I couldn't voice my inner fear aloud. I

couldn't bear to see the same thought mirrored back to me in the eyes of my friends.

Christina laid a hand on my shoulder but said nothing. Her gaze lingered on the distant car carrying her son away.

"That's enough for tonight," Sean Wilson called.

The remaining soldiers climbed into the line of jeeps and Sean led them in a quiet procession through the streets of Ocean Beach.

"We need to go. Now," Raina said, trying to lift my mother into her arms.

"Cordelia?" Maya whispered, gesturing toward the other side of the pier where the shadows were hungriest.

I looked at my friend and followed her gaze to a looming shape.

"What is that?" Maya asked, her voice strained.

Flames flickered on my fingers, which I hid behind my back. I needed to pass as human. The looming shadow enlarged, snuck around the side of the pier, and hesitantly entered our conspicuous hiding place. Everyone gathered in a tight circle behind me, Dylan and Raina supporting our barely conscious mother. A clock ticked loud seconds in my head. How long could we wait to get my mother help before it was too late?

The shape emerged into a female figure. A young woman with a tangled mess of blonde hair and dressed in army fatigues. I was two seconds away from attacking her with my power.

Recognition dawned. Of all the people to survive a nuclear holocaust, I would never have bet on Babette.

CHAPTER FIFTEEN

*B*abette and I stared at each other, silently daring the other to speak first. My flames remained on my fingers behind my back.

Babette cut a quick assessing glance over our small group, her eyes brightening when they fell on Dylan. Interesting. She refocused on me, her eyes narrowing once more. What was she doing here and what the hell did she want?

"Babette..." I inched toward her, shielding the others.

"Cordelia," she replied neutrally.

We continued to stare at each other. The sound of her breaths and my pounding heart formed an irregular rhythm. We'd always been out of synch, destined to never understand each other.

Determined to reset the rules of our relationship, I waited her out. Seconds jerked by.

"You're a mermaid." It wasn't an accusation. More a statement of fact.

I tensed for more. For a judgement or a sentence that

indicated dark dungeons and bowls of gruel. She had to be part of Sean Wilson's army. What else would she be doing here?

Her face broke into a wide smile, and I heaved a confused sigh of relief. "And Wade's one of those shark people…"

"Selachii," Christina said, stepping forward. "We're called selachii."

"Noted," Babette replied, taking in Christina's presence. "You look like him."

"He's my son," Christina replied. "And who are you?"

Babette's smile faltered. "An old friend."

I almost laughed.

"You don't have to hide from me," Babette said, her eyes raking over our small, huddled group. "Jared? Is that you?"

"Bette?" Dylan handed our mother to Raina and stood to greet 'Bette.' He wrapped her in a tight hug, the two of them squeezing and rejoicing until I couldn't stand it anymore. She offered him a cigarette, which he lit immediately.

"Thanks, Bette," Dylan said. "Needed that after such along swim. My sister trashed the one I had."

"What the hell is going on?" I asked, ignoring his barb.

Neither of them answered. They only had eyes for each other.

"I'm so glad you're okay," Dylan said, his hand resting on her waist. He was touching Babette. Bette. Or whatever she liked to be called now.

"You too." She kissed his cheek. "How are you caught up in this?"

"Cordy's my sister," he replied, releasing her.

"*What?*" Babette gaped at me. "Cordelia doesn't have a

brother anymore...his name was Dylan, and he died a long time ago."

I was surprised she knew anything about me. During her vitriolic outpourings at high school, I assumed my presence didn't give her more than a passing thought. Or if it did, only in reference as to how to get me out of Wade's life so she could have him to herself. But it seemed she had acquired at least one pertinent fact about my past.

"Dylan is my real name. When I died, I became a merman and I couldn't leave the ocean, not for five years. Not until Cordy braved the water and broke an ancient curse. But I couldn't return as Dylan, I had to invent a new identity for myself," Dylan said. "That's when I met you."

I'd almost forgotten about Dylan's secret identity. Jared Stoltz. With an ID that gave him access to an unending supply of beer. Not much had changed.

"Dylan," I said, "Babette and I didn't exactly..." How could I put this delicately?

"See eye to eye," she finished for me.

He turned to look at me. "It's okay. I trust Bette."

"Well, I don't," I said.

Conversation stalled as a thread of tension licked through the group.

"I'm sorry you feel that way," Babette said. "I don't harbor any negative feelings."

I raised an eyebrow. With only one sentence, she'd reduced me to a warring teen. I allowed my evaluating gaze to size her up. She was still blonde, still beautiful, still confident. At least that's the face she presented to the outside world. I had no idea who she really was. Not then, and not now.

"Trust is earned," I said.

"I'm in agreement with you there," Babette replied.

Raina tugged on my hand. "We need to help Mom."

"Raina's right," I said. "This can wait. We need to get Mom help."

"What's wrong with her?" Babette asked.

"She was attacked," I said. "On Atlantis. By humans. *Your* kind. She was stabbed with a poisoned knife."

"We have medicine at our camp," Babette said, ignoring my jibe. "I can take you there."

I chewed on my lip. It could be a trap. It most likely was. I looked at Maya, but she only offered me a helpless look. "She could be our third," she mouthed.

Fuck, no.

"I want to help," Babette said, splaying a hand. "Really."

"We don't have another option," Raina said.

I glanced at the deserted streets, the now empty beach, then back at Babette. "How are you involved? Aren't you with Sean Wilson?"

Her jaw clenched and anger flittered through her eyes. "No. Fucking. Way."

"I told you we could trust her," Dylan said, exhaling a smoke ring toward the sky.

"So?" I pressed.

"Let's just say I'm with the good guys." Babette's voice was as flat as steel. "I'm different to how I used to be in high school. A lot has changed. The war..." She looked along the coastline, her eyes misty. "Well, the war happened, and it changed everything and everyone. I grew up, Cordelia."

"You're not the only one to face trials," I said. My flames winked out, perhaps sensing they weren't needed.

"I know."

"Do you know where they've gone? The *bad* guys?" I asked.

"They have a base over the hills somewhere." Babette waved her hand inland. "I assume you'll be wanting to find Wade and Trent and that other muscleman friend of yours."

"You got that right," I said.

She squared her shoulders, but it didn't make her any taller than her five foot two inches. "I can help you with that too."

"How?" I asked.

Raina stood. "As much as I love a reunion, we seriously need to get Mom help."

"Your mother, Cordelia?" Babette asked. "Your mother is alive too?"

"It's a long story," I replied, realizing there was a second pertinent fact about my life that Babette had knowledge of. "For another time."

"More curse breaking and ancient mystical lands?"

"Something like that," I said. "Now she needs medical attention."

"I'll take you to my father," Babette said, turning her attention to Dylan and letting her eyes roam unabashedly over his sinewy form as he kneeled at our mother's side. "He'll have everything you need."

"Who's your father?" Dylan asked. "Didn't you tell me he was the head of FEMA, or something?"

"That's right," Babette replied. "Now he's the head of the army. The good one."

"Let's get her up," I said to Dylan.

"I've got a jeep on the road, can you get her there?" Babette asked.

"Yes," I said. Raina and I helped Dylan carry my mother across the sand and into Babette's open topped jeep. It reminded me a little of my red Jeep Wrangler and I felt a pang of loss.

We positioned my mother in the back seat and let her head slump against the headrest. She was unconscious again but breathing regularly. The rest of us piled in and kept our heads low as Babette drove into the night.

"She's the one." Maya turned from the front seat and whispered to me as we drove through the empty streets.

I balked at the suggestion, but kept my cool.

"How do you and Dylan know each other, anyway?" I asked, ignoring Maya's excited gestures. No way was I going to let Babette, of high school bully status, be my united third. No way. Maybe I hadn't grown as much as I thought. Wade was right about me holding grudges.

"Senior year," Babette replied.

"Dylan didn't finish high school," I said, satisfied I'd already caught her in a lie.

Babette glanced at me in the rearview.

Dylan frowned at me. "We were both working at the garden center."

"Oh, right. Yeah."

"We used to talk," Dylan said, eliciting a smile from Babette.

"We potted plants together and talked," Babette said.

"Sounds so boring now," Dylan laughed.

Babette winked. "Never. I quite enjoyed it."

"Me too," Dylan said.

"Keep your eyes on the road," I said to Babette when she'd glanced at Dylan in the rearview one too many times. Her eyes caught mine, then slipped away.

As Raina tried to get Mom to drink small sips of water from a flask Babette had given us, I fixed my eyes on the window, wanting to be anywhere but here. The thoughts cycling in my mind were too scary to indulge. My mother in danger. Wade captured...I couldn't go through this again. So I stared out the window, examining my old home, yearning for the days when life was less complicated.

Mountainous piles of trash littered the sidewalks, scattering in the onshore winds, filling front yards with shrines to the apocalypse. Toilet paper hung from the palm trees, presenting the illusion of arms and legs spreading wide to capture innocent souls. Cars lay rusting in their drives. The carcasses of numerous animals peppered the roads. The night sky was a hazy blackness, forbidding the stars to shine.

"What happened here?" Dylan asked after a long silence. "We know there was a nuclear war because of us, but why are there now two different armies?"

"Those who want revenge and those who only want to rebuild their lives," Babette answered.

"And you're one of those who wants to rebuild their lives?" Christina asked.

Babette nodded. "But we're being increasingly drawn into this battle between the other army and the Atlanteans."

"How so?" Maya asked.

"For starters, they keep capturing our people and trying to turn them, like they're vampires or something," Babette sighed. "Let me start at the beginning. When the war happened the president was killed, along with the vice president, secretary of state, secretary of defense, surgeon general, chief of staff, press officer…let's just say so many government officials were killed, it was unclear who was in charge. It didn't take long for the Americans to realize this and a second, civil war broke out between those who wanted to rebuild their lives and those who wanted to rampage the country; stealing, looting, raping and murdering their way to hell, or glory, depending on your perspective."

"Jesus," Dylan muttered.

"Makes being Zale's prisoner in the water seem like a vacation," Christina said.

Babette paused in her story to ease onto the deserted freeway entrance. She stopped on the slip road, scanning the distance. Cars lined the road, some burned out, a few looted, others overturned. Suitcases and clothing were caught on the central reservation, and huge potholes threatened to puncture the toughest of tires.

"What are you looking for?" I asked.

"Signs of an ambush," she replied.

"Which are?" Maya asked.

Babette cocked a shoulder. "Hard to say. Wandering kids, no birds, too quiet, stuff like that."

I scanned the road but couldn't spot anything that looked out of the ordinary, if an apocalyptic landscape was ordinary.

Dylan touched Babette's shoulder. "What happened next?"

"It was only a matter of a few weeks when the reason for the nuclear war became apparent—"

"It was *not* our fault," I said.

"Laying blame is moot, pointless, and totally unhelpful," Babette said, edging onto the road. "But people did. Those who had been stealing and murdering turned vengeful. They now had an object for their anger, and they were determined to make the merfolk and shark people pay."

"Selachii," Christina corrected.

"Selachii," Babette repeated. "Anyway, no one knew where any of them, you, had gone. You simply disappeared, so how could you be found? But that didn't stop Sean Wilson looking or building an army for the day the Atlanteans were located."

"Today," I murmured.

"Our people are exhausted," Babette said. "As if dealing with the aftermath of a nuclear war wasn't enough. Everyone fears being kidnapped by Sean Wilson's group and turned. And if you don't turn...well, let's just say no one has come back to tell us what happens."

"I don't know how you live like that," Dylan said, drawing a mushroom cloud on the inside of the window.

Babette swung the wheel to avoid a capsized truck. "My life has become learning to shoot a gun to defend our camp and nursing the sick until they die." She spoke softly, wearily, but the impact of her words hit like bullets. "As for me, I want to be with my father and not get killed. I want a little piece of the world where I can dream again and not worry about survival."

"That's all any of us want," I said.

"But first Sean Wilson needs to pay," Babette's voice hardened.

"Kumbaya to that," Dylan said.

"How is the rest of your family?" I asked.

"Dad is alive," Babette said. "As I mentioned, he was the head of FEMA. He also has a military background. People looked to him when the radiation sickness set in. As he was here in San Diego, tons of people traveled this way. Now he's the leader of the army. The good one."

"And how did Sean Wilson get here?" Raina asked.

"He heard rumors that Atlantis existed somewhere off the coast of San Diego and made his way across the country to the coast, collecting survivors like charms as he went. They're the ones with the blame problem. They're the ones who want to make you guys pay. And rumor has it, he has an informer."

I looked at my merfolk and selachii friends and family. Who the hell would betray us? Who would give up our sanctuary? Stephanie, that's who.

"He's turned his attention away from us for now, and onto you," Babette said. "Which gives my father and I the opportunity to free the merfolk and selachii he's captured so far."

"Why?" I asked. "Why would you care what happens to us?"

"How can I not?" Babette shot back, swerving into the middle of the road. "Remember a little thing called the

Second World War? Exterminating a race of people isn't something I'm on board with. Although I suppose, strictly speaking, you guys are a different species."

Dylan barked out a laugh.

"I can't stand by and watch the human race make the same mistakes all over again," Babette said. "We can't let history repeat itself. We have to do better."

"We do," I agreed. "That's what we were trying to do on Atlantis."

"There's not much of this world left." Babette's eyes met mine in the rearview. "But I'm damn well going to fight for it. I like to think I'm a decent human being and that our world and our people are still capable of goodness, if we have the courage to fight for it."

Maya shot me a look over the seat. "She's the third."

"Third what?" Babette asked.

"Babette, have you ever died before?" I asked.

She frowned. "Why?"

"Nothing for you to worry about right now," Maya replied with a smile.

"But why hasn't the army tried to invade Atlantis before now?" Christina asked. "We've been on the island for over a year and never seen a human boat until a few days ago."

"Stephanie," I answered. "Wade and I got married and Stephanie got angry."

"You got married?" Babette asked, looking over her shoulder, her eyes going to my rings. "Congratulations."

"Thanks," I replied. *I think.*

"The world needs all the love it can get," Babette said.

She said all the right things, but I was struggling to let my guard down.

Christina's lips set into a thin line. "Stephanie has always been a handful."

I was tempted to remind her of when she wanted Stephanie as a daughter-in-law instead of me, but kept my thoughts locked inside. We'd put all that behind us and there was no point dredging it up now. When, if, our current predicaments were resolved, I'd have to spend time working on my grudges.

"Stephanie approached my father with the location of Atlantis first," Babette said. "But he wasn't interested. So she took her vengeful ideas away and found Sean. She promised him paradise. Clean air, bountiful food, pure water, and so much more...the Fountain of Youth."

"The Fountain of Youth doesn't work on humans," I said.

"That's a shame." Babette's eyes dimmed. "Sean doesn't know that. His people won't be healed."

"It's been poisoned anyway," Dylan said. "Which is why my mother needs help here on the mainland."

"Can we go any quicker?" Raina asked, her eyes on the darkness outside.

"It's not far now," Babette said as she exited the freeway and navigated a series of dusty roads. The narrow trails led inland, into the desert. The tires kicked up dust, clogging my throat and irritating my eyes.

"What are Stephanie's plans?" I wondered aloud.

"I don't know," Babette replied. "She walked into the camp one day with her chest all puffed up and her black hair flowing like she was in the middle of her own personal tornado and started talking about mass murder. We paid little attention to her after that. My father and I didn't want any part of another war. But it seems we're stuck in the middle of one anyway."

Maya turned in her seat. "She resurrected Aquaria, who has the power to summon the Hound of the Ocean."

"But why?" I asked. "If Sean Wilson is doing her job for her."

"Because she's a bitch," Dylan said simply.

Christina heaved a sigh. "Because she's a selachii scorned."

"And she handed over Jordan willingly," I said, my anger sparking, my fingers glowing with heat. I stuck my hands under my arms and willed the fire away. "How many Atlanteans has Sean captured?"

"And what will they do to them?" Christina added, sharing a concerned look with me.

Wade. Where are you now? Please be okay. Every time I thought his name, imagined his handsome face, remembered the feel of his touch, my heart rate kicked up into an uncomfortable pace and my fingers heated. And part of me was furious with him for walking away without something as simple as a discussion, let alone a plan of action. We had promised each other we would fight together, that we wouldn't separate, but Wade's guilt over the fate of our people had led him to a reckless act. I understood it, but I was still furious. And terrified.

"Altogether? I don't know," Babette replied. "So far, my father has freed five merfolk from Sean's camp. But countless came ashore tonight. I'm not sure how we can launch a rescue on such a scale."

"Maybe I should have stayed on the mainland," Raina muttered.

I looked at my sister. "But then you'd be dead. And I would never have known you."

"I've never been in a war before," she said. "I've reported from the front lines, but never have I had to fight."

I had no words of comfort to offer her, so I held her hand, even though fear was building a block in my stomach.

"What will they do to them?" Christina asked.

I caught Babette's wary look in the rearview. "Kill them."

Pain exploded in my chest. Were Wade and Trent and Ford still alive? A landslide of grief overwhelmed my thoughts. The last year on Atlantis had been so blissful, I'd believed nothing bad would happen to us again. How foolish I'd been. Where merfolk and selachii were concerned, there would always be battles. Always an enemy to defeat. But they kept getting harder. The cost too much to pay. My mother's deathly pallor was impossible to deny. Wade was gone, among many others. How could we come back from this?

Maya refused to speak of the worst prophecies, but she held them in her head. Were we still careening down a tragic route?

To save Atlantis, the royal couple must unite with a third, the one who died and lives again. Family is important.

The words formed a jigsaw in my mind, falling into their correct places, making their meaning more apparent.

If Babette was to unite with Wade and me, he had to still be alive, or the prophecy would never have existed. Yes, we needed to make sure Babette was the correct candidate, to delve into her past and the way she had died. Family was important, but whose family? And what constituted a family? Maya and Trent weren't related to me by blood, but I considered them my family.

"We're here," Babette said, turning onto an unpaved road. Tents rose out of the ground like the jaws of a blunted saw, and lanterns glowed every so often, eating away at handfuls of darkness like the insistent chomping of a Pacman mouth. Men huddled in groups around fires, while others, with automatic weapons resting on their shoulders, walked a perimeter patrol around the camp. "This is base camp."

CHAPTER SIXTEEN

Soldiers swarmed the car before Babette turned off the ignition. Maya and I both threw our hands in the air, afraid we would be accosted, arrested, or something worse.

Babette laughed. "Relax. They're friendlies."

Christina raised an eyebrow. "I'm glad they're on our side."

Most of the soldiers were dressed in fatigues, but others wore ordinary sweatpants and T-shirts or hoodies. All of them carried dangerous looking weapons. Babette hopped out of the car and engaged in a rapid-fire conversation with a soldier in a foreign language I couldn't understand.

The soldier turned toward me and gestured for us to climb from the jeep, instructing us in the same foreign language. When we didn't immediately follow the instructions, they attempted to speak to us in broken English.

"It's okay. We friendly. We help nice lady." One pointed at my mother, holstering his automatic weapon.

"They're refugees from the war," Babette explained. "Some of them gathered here in America after the bombs thinking this once great nation could protect them or offer shelter." She rolled her eyes sarcastically.

One of the guards took my mother from Dylan's arms. He walked away with her into the darkness, circumnavigating the edge of the camp.

"Hey! Wait!" Raina called after him.

"It's okay," Babette said. "He's taking her to the medical tent."

My chest squeezed painfully as I let her go. A burgeoning sense of panic spread through my limbs and scattered my thoughts. Wade was captured, my mother was injured, and I had no idea where my dad was...tears prickled. *Not now, Cordelia.*

We followed Babette and a second soldier along a winding path through the tents, reminding me of old-fashioned war encampments of long ago. Memories of Gal filled my head. He'd experienced wars like this before he'd become a High Council member. What I would give to have him by my side now.

"Babette?" I drew level with her. "Did you die when you were a kid? I heard a story about you drowning or something?"

She halted ever so briefly before continuing along the path. "No, but I came close. I didn't know anyone knew that."

No? How could it be *no?* Was she not to be our united third? Part of me was relieved, but the other part knew I would still need to find that third person. I wasn't sure which was worse.

She shivered, even though the night was warm. "I don't talk about it, but I remember every freaking detail."

"I'm sorry."

She shrugged, her shoulders high and defensive. "I think that's why I was always a little jealous of you and Wade. How easily you both took to water. Me? I wanted nothing to do with it."

"I get that," I said. "Do you want to talk about it now?"

She gave me a sidelong glance. "Why do I get the feeling you're going to pester me until I've told you?"

"It could be important."

"How?"

"Something to do with a prophecy."

"Uh-huh."

"I'm serious."

"Harry Potter is just a book."

"I'm no Harry Potter."

She smirked. "You got that right."

"So?" I asked.

"Trauma sucks."

"I'm with you there." I'll never forget the day my mother and Dylan were taken by Zale. Despite the miracle of them coming back to me, I was terrified of losing them again. I glanced at Dylan as we walked through the tents. Trauma had been hard on him too.

"I drowned in the ocean," Babette said.

"I'm sorry."

"I remember taking my first breath of salt water, and when it flooded my lungs."

Although water was the place I felt most at home, drowning was an awful fate for a human or an ocean shifter.

"I ran out of air, ran out of light. I sank like a stone."

"I almost died once too," I said, thinking of the battle with the ice demons at Mount Rainier. One of them had sliced my stomach open with a deadly claw. Gal had saved me. Both Wade and I, then given us the Power of the Sea to restore our health. But it gave us extra gifts too. Flames for me, strength for Wade.

"So, yeah, not so tempted to come and visit your little island," Babette said.

"Who saved you?" I asked.

"My father pulled me from the water," Babette replied. *Family is important.* Her father saved her. Maybe all the pieces did fit. Maybe. "And here, you can meet him now." She stopped outside a large once-white tent, the obvious headquarters. Soldiers rushed in and out, speaking into walkies, carrying paperwork or weapons, all with a purpose to their steps.

"I think you're right about her," I whispered to Maya. "Now we need to get Wade back before the Hound of the Ocean makes an appearance."

"And Trent and Ford."

"Of course."

Babette ushered us inside the tent.

"Dad," Babette greeted her father.

A man sitting at a portable table looked up. He had a serious face, seamed with worry. But he had the same blue eyes as his daughter. His were older and wiser, but not without a hint of kindness. He stood and came around the side of the table, giving us brief nods of acknowledgement.

"Babette." He embraced his daughter, his long arms wrapping around her and almost taking her off her feet. She barely made it up to his shoulder. How it made me crave a hug from one of my parents.

He turned to take us all in. "And who do we have here? More refugees from Sean's camp?"

"No, Dad, these are Atlanteans," Babette replied. "And old friends. And we need to help them."

"Atlanteans?" Babette's father raised an eyebrow. "That means you're all...merfolk..." he stumbled over the word as if he wasn't sure we really existed.

"And selachii," Christina added.

There was a pause as he took a second look at us all.

"Cordelia's mother was injured, so I've had her taken to the medical tent," Babette said. "She needs IV anti-biotics."

Babette's father nodded, still examining us from our heads to our feet, perhaps looking for a gill or a scale.

"Of course," he said to his daughter. "Rob Jones." He stuck a hand in Christina's direction. "Excuse my manners. I'm a little bewildered. I've rescued a few of your kind from the other camp, but I've never had the opportunity for a chat."

"...could you get your bloody hands off me...I'm free to roam about here as I please..." a loud, disgruntled voice shouted from beyond the tent walls.

Rob sighed. "You might be able to help us with this."

Without warning, the tent flaps flung open and a wall of

bristling indignation bore down on us, followed by three frowning soldiers.

"Jordan!" Christina said, rushing to his side. "I thought they'd captured you."

"I *have* been captured!" he snapped, glaring at Rob and Babette.

"We rescued this young man from Sean's camp," Rob explained in a rush of words. "He's refused to tell us his name or communicate with us. We've been trying to impress upon him that he should remain here where he'll be safe, but he seems hell bent on seeking his revenge against Stephanie. I've arranged bodyguards for him in the meantime until he comes to his senses."

Jordan shrugged off the guards at his side. "I will get my payback."

Rob ran a hand through his thinning hair. His blue eyes, although bright, were bloodshot and ringed with dark circles. Fatigue rolled off him in heavy waves. "That's what got us into this whole mess to begin with. People blaming people, pointing fingers, throwing knives and shooting guns."

"And then the bombs," Babette added.

"Yes, and then the bombs," Rob said.

"Jordan," Christina said sharply. "Rob is right. The humans are on Atlantis."

"Soon to be followed by Sean's army," Rob said.

"All because of her," Jordan snarled. "We need to find her."

"Our priority is our people," I said.

"Our injured people, especially," Raina added.

Jordan thrust a tattooed arm at us. "So we take them back to Atlantis and use the Fountain of Youth."

"The Fountain of Youth is tainted," Christina said. "The land will quickly fall to ruin without its power working. They'll soon realize there's nothing there for them."

"Shit," Jordan replied, his black selachii eyes flashing. "I will find her, and I will make her pay." He swiveled on the ball of his foot and stormed out of the tent.

Christina sighed. "That line of the family has always been a little dramatic."

"Funny, considering his uncle never says a word," I said. Wade's father was monosyllabic at best.

Christina frowned at me but didn't reply.

"At least we know he's safe," Dylan said, as the tent flaps eased back into position. "For now."

"He'll get his chance soon enough," Babette said. "When we storm the camp and rescue the rest of your people."

Rob looked his daughter up and down. "We will storm the camp and we will rescue the captured Atlanteans, but you, Babette," he raised a hand as she interrupted, "will not be going with us. You will stay here where I know you're safe."

Babette clenched her fists. "Like hell I will!" That was the fiery Babette I remembered. It's probably what had kept her alive.

"This is not a good life for you." Rob crossed his arms. "All this violence and death."

"It's the only life I have," Babette said.

Rob shook his head. "I want you to be safe."

"Dad..." Babette paced a small line in front of him. "Like

it or not, this is my world now and I intend to defend it with every cell of my being. If I die in an honorable battle, then so be it. It's the way life is now, and I could never walk away from my responsibilities. I could never live with myself if I hid away while others died."

Maya raised an eyebrow at me. Dylan gave me an "I told you so" look.

It was clear Babette had changed. My guard was falling, and I hoped I wasn't being gullible. We needed her. And maybe she needed us too.

"God, you sound just like your mother," Rob remarked.

Babette managed a weak half smile.

"Besides..." Maya approached the pair. "We need Babette. With all due respect, Rob, Babette is part of a prophecy, and we need her to fulfill it."

Father and daughter startled, their heads snapping toward Maya, their mouths dropping open.

"Excuse me?" Rob asked. "What exactly do you mean by a *prophecy?*"

Maya was forced to explain the existence of *The Mermaid Chronicles* and the list of prophecies that appeared when they became relevant.

"*To save Atlantis, the royal couple must unite with a third, the one who died and lives again. Family is important,*" Maya quoted the most recent prophecy.

"How accurate do these prophecies need to be?" Raina asked, turning at a burst of noise outside the tent flaps.

"Did Babette die when she was little, when she drowned?" I asked.

"You were only out for a few seconds," Rob said, running

a hand over his military haircut. "I pulled you from the water. But it was the lifeguard who gave you mouth to mouth."

"You played an integral role in saving her life," Maya said.

"But I never actually died," Babette said.

"Maybe you did," Rob said. "You were blue when I dragged you onto the beach. Not breathing. The lifeguard acted quickly. Brought you back to me."

"Family is important," Maya said. "Rob, you played a role in keeping your daughter alive. So she could fulfill her destiny. I think it's safe to assume Babette is the human we need."

Babette's eyes shined with new purpose. "See, Dad? It's my *destiny*."

Rob considered, stared at his daughter, swept a scrutinizing gaze over all of us, muttered a few indecipherables. He jabbed a finger at Babette. "Stay with me at all times. And you will be armed to the teeth."

"Of course." Babette patted a pistol on her hip.

"And Stephanie?" Christina asked. "What do you know of her?"

"Not as much as I'd like, in retrospect," Rob replied. He gestured to a guard to fetch bottles of water from a cooler in the corner, and they were handed out to us.

"Anything stronger?" Dylan asked as a guard placed a bottle in his hand.

I glared at him.

"Kidding," he muttered at me.

Rob gestured to a ring of plastic garden chairs, then sat himself and propped an ankle across the thigh of his opposite leg. "Stephanie came blazing in here one day asking if I wanted to be the king of the world. Or the next president, or emperor of the universe, or some other such nonsense. She had a tale about a sea witch from the deep, and a terrible monster." He rubbed the bridge of his nose. "I thought she was a little...unstable—"

"Batshit crazy," Babette muttered.

Rob acknowledged Babette's comment with two raised eyebrows. "With the storming of your island, I'm beginning to see her words weren't just wild threats, they were promises, and I wished I'd paid more attention. But I sent her out of here and told her I wasn't interested in more war. I am fighting for peace, as oxymoronic as that sounds, but someone has to stand up for those who can't, and someone has to restore order to this forsaken country." Rob swept a hand around the tent, encompassing the small crew of military personnel huddled around a folding table in whispered conversation, maps spread out across tables, boxes of rations stocked along one wall.

"Where is Stephanie now?" Christina asked.

"She can't be too far," Raina said, tapping her chin. "If I were Stephanie, I'd want to witness the destruction I'd caused."

"You're probably right," Christina said, glancing at the narrow gap in the tent flaps. "I should have kept a closer eye on her."

"We all thought she was happy in Jordan's company," I said.

"I don't know where she is," Rob said. "When I rejected her alliance, she said she would go to the other camp, but that she would be back to deal with anyone who had snubbed her. I got the feeling I wasn't the first on her list."

"You're not," I said. "Wade is. Wade and me."

"Who is Wade?" Rob asked.

"My husband," I replied.

Rob glanced at the rings on my finger.

"What Cordelia is forgetting to mention, because of her rather charming modesty, is that she and my son are the King and Queen of Atlantis," Christina said. I blushed. The last year on Atlantis had been a bubble. Kings and queens and senates and magical water that restored any injury or disease. Hearing it all said out loud, it now felt...irrelevant. While Wade and I had been playing king and queen, a nuclear war was being fought. How could I have turned my back on the mainland so easily? "Stephanie was in love with Wade. No, that's not right. It would be more accurate to say Wade is her obsession. She is a selachii scorned and will stop at nothing until she is avenged."

She didn't mention her part in encouraging Stephanie. Typical Christina.

"I see," Rob said. "And where is Wade now?"

"He is a prisoner at Sean's camp," Babette replied.

"I guess we'd better rescue him before Stephanie has the opportunity to get her hands on him," Rob said, walking to one of the open maps. "Intel informs me a large section of their army is heading to Atlantis right now. They've executed their initial wave of attack with zealous civilians. Now he plans to send in his trained army," Rob glanced at his watch, "very shortly. We'll be able to rescue Wade—"

"And Trent, and Ford, and all the others," Maya said. "Half of the population of Atlantis is over there."

"And Trent and Ford and all the others," Rob repeated. "We can do it at first light, before people rouse. I have a handful of special ops here, trusted men, and we might be able to exact the rescue with minimal fighting and loss of life."

Loss of life. Pain lodged in my chest.

"Agreed," Christina said.

"A few of us here will want to come," I said. "And I have a unique ability which might help."

Rob gave me another cursory examination and I knew he was wondering what, beneath my wild red hair and translucent skin, I could possibly offer. I took a breath and closed my eyes, praying the small signals I had experienced in Babette's jeep were a sign my power was working again. I smiled when each of my fingernails lit up in tiny, red flames.

"What is that?" Rob asked, leaning closer to inspect my hands.

"My fire power," I replied, as the flames grew to an inch in length.

Cautiously, Rob touched one, then snapped his finger away with an "ouch."

The rest of the group laughed, and the band of tension loosened.

Babette watched my flames, a small muscle in her jaw pulsing, but she didn't speak, and I couldn't tell what she was thinking. I'd never been good at reading her expressions.

"What does it do?" Babette said, raising her eyes to meet mine.

Dylan answered for me. "She took out the entire race of dragon kings with her fire power. Comes out of her mouth, nose, and eyes too. Decimates anything that needs destroying." He withdrew a cigarette from Babette's stash and lit it on one of my fingers.

Babette's expression didn't change. "I see."

"I only used it like that the one time," I said, sensing her hesitancy. "To save my people. We lost so many that day."

Gal. How was it that the pain of his loss had only worsened?

"I'd give you an example," I said. "But I can see you're already freaked out."

"Just a little," Rob said, a bottle of water at the ready.

"Not me," Babette said, her voice and face as hard as stone.

"Still trying to wrap my head around the idea that the monsters in my favorite childhood books could be real," Rob said. "I've been recalling the tales of my youth with new appreciation."

"Vampires and werewolves aren't real," Maya said. "Just in case you were wondering. But ghost pirates—"

I raised a palm. "One thing at a time."

The others were quick to fill in the stories of previous battles and of how we defeated the dragon kings.

Babette approached and crouched by my chair. "I'm glad you're on our side." She gestured to my fingers, now unlit. "This could get really ugly."

"Yes, and yes," I agreed. "We need to be united. I'm glad you're on *our* side."

"What does that mean, exactly?" She tilted her head. "All

these stories of you and Wade being united, being in love...I don't understand where I fit...if I have to become part of some weird threesome..."

Dylan chuckled, stamped his cigarette out on the ground, and leaned toward Babette. "It's not like that, Bette. While *I'm* not opposed to a good old-fashioned threesome, you don't have to spend a night in the royal bed." He smiled at her. Turning his chair around, he straddled it and took her hand. "But if you do fancy being united, in the purest of physical terms, I could offer my services." His grin turned mischievous.

I socked him on the shoulder. "Time and place, bro."

Babette laughed, then winked at Dylan. "I'll think on that."

"Prophecies are not about threesomes," Maya said in her schoolteacher voice. It reminded me of the days when she dreamed of attending Harvard. "Being united means the three of you must stand together against our mutual enemies. You must believe in the cause, the future of Atlantis, humanity, *and* believe they can exist side by side, in peace."

"I see." Babette's expression hardened, the smile slipping away too quick. "Cordelia can shoot flames from her body. Wade can lift an armored tank with one hand. I don't have a problem fighting when the playing field is even, but I don't have a power. I only have a gun. You mentioned a sea witch and the Hound of the Ocean. Tell me, how am I supposed to fight that?"

Behind her, Rob paled. "Maybe this isn't such a good idea—"

"You won't be fighting against us," I said. "You'll be

fighting *with* us. Wade and I can protect you when the time comes."

"Against a murderous psycho bitch? No wait, make that two if we want to count Sean. And then there's a sea witch and a sea monster?" Babette didn't bother masking her sarcasm. "I like that we're getting on again, Cordy, but I prefer to be responsible for my own life."

"I get that," I said. "And I get that you've got no love for Atlantis. But if humans, merfolk, and selachii are meant to be united, I have a feeling we're supposed to be on Atlantis, away from this nuclear wasteland. If we don't get control of the island, there'll be nowhere for us to go."

"I don't like it," Babette said.

"There's nothing about war to like," Raina said, coming to my side.

"There certainly isn't," I replied. "It's not an easy path. But no matter what we choose, Stephanie and the Hound of the Ocean are coming. I'd like us to be prepared. To be as united as we can be. Maybe then we stand a chance."

Dylan clapped. "Nice speech, sis."

"Maybe you could be helpful for once," I snapped at him.

He raised both palms. "I meant that genuinely."

"Well, thank you," I said, still bristling.

"Let's get to it," Rob said, then began barking orders at his soldiers.

Babette stared at me, then flicked her eyes to my fingers. "United. Okay then." She nodded curtly, pushed out of her chair and left the tent, leaving me staring after her.

United. That was the key. It was always the key. I glanced at my fingers again and examined the tips where the flames liked to play. The LED lights of the lanterns washed over my rings, picking out the sparkling diamonds. But it was the pearl in my engagement ring which captured my attention. It was different, brighter somehow. Pearls were important to Atlantis, often providing a key to a portal or a way to summon The High Council. Could it be my ring, the very ring that had been passed down Wade's family for generations, held its own mystery?

Dylan followed Babette out of the tent, causing a gust of humid air to blow inside. The hairs at the nape of my neck were damp and stuck to my skin. Sweat beaded on my forehead and gathered under my arms. It wasn't just the heat. It was war.

Rob poured over his strategy map with Maya, Raina, and Christina. I couldn't summon the energy to join them, and instead glugged on the bottle of water the soldier had handed me earlier. Another soldier entered through the back entrance of the tent and whispered in Rob's ear.

"Cordelia, Raina, Dylan, your mother has been treated," Rob said. "The IV antibiotics are working, and her shoulder wound has been tended. I'll take you there now."

Even though I was sitting, my knees trembled. I'd been trying not to think about my mother, but now that good news was here, the tension I'd been carrying evaporated. At least the tension that concerned my mother, anyway. Wade and my father were two other lumps lodged firmly in my throat.

After Christina was taken to visit Jordan, Rob led Raina, Maya, Dylan, and me through the back entrance, weaving a path through campfires and tents, soldiers drinking and telling stories, kids running between the flaps.

Fires burned periodically. Some gathered around them, cooking food. Others wandered the pathways alert for danger. Humidity pressed in, bringing with it a swarm of insects and the chirp of cicadas hiding in the scrub grass. The gravelly ground was harsh under my feet, and despite going barefoot for the last year, I winced as I stepped on sharp stones.

When we arrived at the medical tents, a deathly hush eased through the open flap of the nearest one. The tents were as large as big tops; the tips rising to meet the muted stars, the silence within more ominous than screams of pain and death.

"It's so quiet," Raina said, clutching my hand.

"Most of the people in these tents have radiation poisoning," Rob said. "They're near the end." He indicated the tent holding my mother and ushered us toward it.

Raina ducked through the flap with him, but Maya laid a hand on my arm and held me outside the entrance. "I want to talk about Babette."

My shoulders stiffened as a blustery wind tunneled down the pathway. I toyed with the necklace at my throat. "There's no denying she's our third."

"Yeah."

I circled my tense shoulders, trying to get myself to relax, to accept that which was not in my control. "Weird, isn't it?"

Maya scanned the smaller tents lining the path we'd walked along. "So weird."

Dylan frowned. "Bette's not weird."

"You didn't know her like I did," I said.

Dylan crossed his arms. "She was always nice to me. And

you never know what's going on in someone else's life, Cordy. A little kindness goes a long way."

I seethed. "You can tell her that too."

He rolled his eyes.

"*But*, I agree," I said. "She does appear to have changed. I don't know if she's hiding something, but maybe we should give her a chance."

"Agreed," Maya replied.

I glanced at the pearl on my ring again. Was it weird that it had shone in Babette's presence? Just as she agreed to be part of it all? Was it a coincidence?

"I thought we'd have to spend more time convincing her," I said.

"So much has happened," Maya said.

"You know, not so long ago I would have said she and Stephanie would have gotten on like a house on fire."

Maya frowned. "I know, right?"

"So, we'll be united, but also keep an eye on her."

"You don't need to keep an eye on her," Dylan said. "Or how about this; *I'll* keep the eye on her?"

"Not a bad idea," I said. "If you can stay sober long enough."

"Oh, fuck off, Cordelia," Dylan said, and stormed into the tent.

Maya gaped after him. "What's going on with you two?"

"I shouldn't have poked the bear."

"Family is important, remember?" Maya nudged me with an elbow. "You two need to stay on side."

I dipped my chin. "I'm sorry. You're right. I'll apologize. I just get...frustrated, you know? Getting him back was a miracle, but it's not how I thought it would be. He's not who I remember."

"None of us are," Maya said kindly. "We've all changed. Life, you know?"

"I know." I sighed, staring at the dark opening of the tent, hoping Dylan had cooled off enough to allow me to apologize. "So, united. Do we need to get Babette to sign a contract, or something?"

Maya chewed off a hangnail. "I don't think it's as easy as that. I think we have to feel truly united. Like you and Wade using the pearl that first time."

"For fuck's sake."

She slung an arm around my shoulder. "We'll get there."

I looked at the sky and the stars and the medical tent, and then at my dusty feet. "I hope so."

CHAPTER SEVENTEEN

My mother sat up in a hospital bed under a thin blanket with an IV tube trailing out of her arm. Her eyes contained a hint of their old sparkle and color bloomed in her cheeks. A screen gave her privacy from the rest of the dying patients. The air filled with the reek of stale body odor, urine and bleach, a nausea inducing combination.

"Thank God," I said, rushing to her side. I eased myself onto the narrow bed and hugged her as best I could around her bandaged shoulder and IV line.

"I'm okay," she said. "Thanks to all of you."

Dylan and Raina sat on chairs either side of her, while Maya hovered at the foot of her bed. I caught sight of Babette's blonde hair in the distance as she brought water to the patients and helped them to drink.

"Raina has filled me in on the rescue mission," Mom said. "I wish I could come with you." She gestured helplessly to her IV line and bandaged shoulder. "But I don't think I'll be much use."

"You stay here, where it's safe," Dylan said.

"I'll stay with you," Raina said. "I have no experience with war, with Atlanteans, with sea witches. I'm afraid I'd be a liability."

I squeezed my sister's hand. "Look after our mother."

"Of course."

Mom sighed and leaned back against the pillows. She winced as she eased herself down and held onto her shoulder with her good hand.

We had a few hours to kill until we needed to leave for Sean Wilson's camp. The four of us surrounded my mother, watching the healing drip of the IV flow into her arm. When I thought she was asleep, I rose.

"Cordy." Mom's voice halted my footsteps. Her eyes remained closed. "Be careful."

"I will, Mom." I leaned down and kissed her cheek.

Before I left the medical tent, Babette appeared. She halted me with a hand on my arm. "I could use some help."

I looked beyond her to the rows of dying patients. The ones with radiation sickness. Lines of camp beds and white sheets stretched on like the rows of headstones in Arlington cemetery. The sight of so many dying was grim. Everything about the tent was grim. "There's so many of them."

"There are." Her gaze passed over each restless soul. "This tent used to be a dormitory. Then we realized we had more sick than healthy. No one here will make it." She dipped her chin. "But they still need help eating and drinking. And a kind word or two."

If only the Fountain of Youth could cure humans. "How did you escape?"

"I was traveling with my father." Babette kept her voice low. There wasn't a hint of emotion in her words, as if she were retelling a story for the hundredth time. "We were in Hawaii on one of his business trips. He was examining the damage left by a tsunami. Hawaii wasn't hit by a nuke, just by regular missiles. We had enough time to get to a shelter. We stayed in it for a month with two hundred others, just in case, until our drinking water ran out. Then we braved the elements. We made our way back to San Diego. The radiation clouds had dissipated. The bombs were apparently clean, built with isotopes with short half-lives. That's the rumor anyway. But I might still get sick." She shrugged, as if the thought of dying prematurely was of little consequence. "Time will tell. Until then, we have people to help and a war to fight."

"You've got some balls."

"So do you." She faced me. "United, huh?"

"I guess there's a reason it's you."

"We need to get started." She gestured for me to follow her.

"We'll all help." Dylan, Maya, and Raina joined us. "Tell us what to do."

Babette led us to a couple of water dispensers on the other side of the tent. "It's time to hydrate them. We go around every hour. A few are on IVs, but we don't have enough for everyone. Some of the worst are using up our morphine reserves."

"Where do you get it from?" I asked.

"We have scout groups scouring the country and raiding pharmacies. Hopefully, we'll find enough. And if we don't, we'll cross that bridge when we get to it," she said as she thrust a jug of water into one of my hands and a stack of plastic cups in the other. "Now please help."

For the next three hours, the five of us walked up and down the rows of patients, rousing those who slept to make them drink through cracked lips lined with oozing ulcers. Many needed a straw, several more could only manage one or two sips. There was a bucket by each bed for vomiting or relieving themselves. We emptied all of those that needed it in the ditch beyond the boundary of the camp and brought them back rinsed.

The smell was the worst of it. A devilish perfume of stale body odor, piss and shit and vomit, laced through with a heavy dose of despair. It was the smell of hell, the smell of damnation, the smell of death.

More than a few of them were bald or only had sparse patches of hair. The more severe cases revealed large, angry swellings on their faces and necks. A couple needed sheets changed after an episode of bloody diarrhea.

Babette caught me staring at a few with bandages around their faces. "Trust me, you don't want to see."

I took her word for it.

Babette tied a handkerchief around my nose and mouth. It was such a simple thing, a piece of cloth between mouth and the reek of the dying, but it made a difference. After that I could breathe without my eyes watering, but every half hour or so I stepped outside to take a gulp of fresh air. I yearned for the cleansing feel of the ocean, so many miles away. This far into the desert, we weren't near a single body of water. There were no smells in the ocean, not underwater.

I didn't need to breathe. My gills did the work for me and never did they pass along anything so wretched. It was just blue and salt and the feel of my limbs as they carved through the waves. I longed for it now. Instead, I took my lungful of air and returned to the tent and the patients.

"Thank you, all of you," Babette said a couple hours later. "We've got time for a couple hours of sleep before the rescue. I'll show you where."

Raina stayed with our mother and a cot was brought in for her. Dylan, Maya, and I followed Babette to a vacant tent, trudging through the drifting sand. There were sleeping bags stacked along one wall.

"Grab one of those," she said. "And hunker down for a while. I'll come get you when it's time."

"Thanks, Bette," Dylan said, his hand grazing hers.

She nodded and left the three of us alone. Dylan fetched three sleeping bags and unrolled them on the canvas floor.

Dylan snuggled into his and faced the wall. I doubted he would sleep. He wasn't good at it at the best of times. But he clearly needed to be alone with his thoughts.

"Goodnight, bro," I whispered as I settled into my sleeping bag.

"Goodnight, sis," he whispered back.

Maya lay on her back next to me and sought my hand. "Only a few hours until we get them back."

I didn't reply. I couldn't. The possibilities were endless, and many of them devastating.

I expected to lie there all night, staring at the canvas ceiling, swatting insects away, itching at the spots of heat turning to eczema on my skin. But sleep came, heavier than a sledgehammer, and took me to a battle-filled world. A camp was invaded by horses and swords. Fire and smoke poured from every opening. Screams lit the air with terror. The sky and the ground turned red, the dying and injured left untended, and a stench permeated the battleground. Someone grabbed my shoulder.

"It's time," Babette said, her hand on my shoulder.

We rose silently and dressing in camouflage clothing, donned heavy combat boots, then followed Babette to the jeeps. Dawn smudged a corner of the night.

Dylan climbed into a jeep next to Babette and gently squeezed her shoulder. "It's going to be okay Bette."

A ghost of a smile passed across her lips. "Thanks, Jared. Sorry, Dylan. I have to get used to that."

"As long as you do," Dylan replied, trying on a smile of his own. It was a smile I hadn't seen in some time, not since we'd first been reunited. Hope bloomed. It wasn't too late for him. As long as Babette didn't screw it up.

Babette gunned the engine and reversed onto the dirt road. I climbed into another jeep with Maya, Rob, Christina, and a subdued Jordan. But his hands were fisted and his jaw tight. It wouldn't take much to set him off again.

The convoy consisted of six jeeps. We bounced over the uneven ground, kicking up dust into the lightening sky. I kept the bandana Babette had given me over my mouth and nose.

As fingers of light streaked across the sky, we drove through a forest and arrived at Sean Wilson's camp. I could feel Wade's presence. My limbs turned to liquid. I had a strong conversation with my fingers, making sure they understood it was time to act.

Rob jumped out of the jeep. "We're here."

We hovered at the edge of the forest. Rob's special ops team, dressed from head to foot in black, led the way. They unholstered their weapons and weaved around trees and bushes. Babette held her pistol in a two-handed grip, aimed at the ground, her finger hovering on the safety button.

Vast fields of flat land rolled from the forest all the way to Sean Wilson's camp. It didn't look much different from the one we'd left behind; towering tents and the flicker of camp-fires. The stench of smoke reached me, and the odd caw of a bird. The occasional shout made my skin tingle with apprehension.

As we cowered behind the last line of trees, someone passed a pair of binoculars around.

"Looks like we missed the start," Rob said.

I grabbed the binoculars from him. I spotted jerky movement. Flames. Big, bright, bullying flames consuming the camp.

"Holy shit," I said. "It's on fire."

Rob snatched the binoculars. "Maybe someone has done our job for us."

"Don't start celebrating yet," Dylan said. "It could be Stephanie or Aquaria."

"They don't have the power of fire," I said.

"It only takes a match to light a fire," Jordan said. "Why didn't I think of that?"

Thick tendrils of black smoke snaked into the sky, clouding my vision of the camp. Enemy soldiers ran in random directions, some yelling over their shoulders, others crying out as flames licked at their limbs and melded their uniforms to their bodies. I caught sight of Wade, shirtless and blackened by smoke.

Wade.

My heart raced and I could only hear my rushing pulse in my ears. Wade heaved boulders over his head and hurled them at the soldiers. Ford and Trent flanked him.

Maya grabbed my hand. "Thank God they're okay."

Hordes of Atlanteans ran through the camp, making a beeline for the fields. As they reached us and the trees, they doubled over, some panting, others yelling explanations I couldn't follow.

"But where is Stephanie?" Jordan asked each one of them, gripping their shoulders, turning their chins.

A barrel of ammunition exploded. I clamped my hands over my ears as ringing tore through my hearing. The world tilted, the ground rushing up to meet me. I swiped a bead of blood away from my ear and staggered toward a tree for support.

Smoke turned the world a toxic gray. With my hands still covering my ears, I ran toward the warring battle. Babette came after me, one hand flicking off the safety on her pistol. Dylan followed behind her. We stumbled over the uneven ground, twisting ankles in rabbit burrows, choking on the toxic fumes. Rob and the special ops team surrounded us, throwing themselves into combat.

"What's going on?" Dylan yelled when we reached the first line of tents. Flames crackled and spat. People ran and yelled. Gunfire surrounded us.

"That's what's going on." I pointed at a figure hovering in the sky, a figure I never thought I'd see again. "There's a dragon king."

"I thought they were all dead," Babette said, coming to a sudden stop, her wide eyes taking in the massive creature.

"I did too," Dylan said.

Fire flamed on my fingertips. If a dragon king was behind everything, wanting to take Atlantis back, they had another thing coming.

The dragon king appeared in its full dragon form. It held its massive wings wide while its tail whipped from side to side. Fire spewed from its mouth, showering victims with a burning rain. The tent beneath it caught fire, collapsing and melting, obliterated from existence in an instant.

The fiery creature flapped its powerful wings and hovered majestically in the air. Fire made its skin shimmer and menacing shadows of black smoke rippled along its flanks. It turned its head. Looked at me. Familiarity blazed through me. A face so like another. Its eyes rolled over our group and a small flame burst from its nostrils, licking its way through the camp.

"Cordy," Babette whispered. "Can you kill it?" She took one hesitant step toward the dragon king and raised her pistol.

"No," I replied, smiling. "We don't need to. He's on our side."

The dragon king nodded at me before directing its gaze into the battle beneath it. It shot fire from its mouth around Wade, and I momentarily lost him in a cloud of smoke. My heart seized, doubting my instincts. But when the smoke dissipated, I saw Wade was unharmed. The soldiers who had been bearing down on him lay burned and dead at his feet.

"I don't know who he is or where he's come from," I said. "But I do know he's here to help."

"It's a he?" Babette questioned. "How do you know?"

"I just do," I replied, and marched into the battle. We would win.

As we wound deeper into the camp, Jordan and Maya caught up with us. Another group of our imprisoned people ran through the pathways. I directed them to the treeline where the others waited and a medic crew stabilized injuries.

I reached for Wade. He wrapped his arms around me and whispered to me. With the ringing in my ears, I relied on our telepathy to hear him.

"I am furious with you," I said.

"I'm sorry."

And it was as simple as that. All the anger drained out of me. We were together again. My friends were together again. Wade, Trent, Ford, Maya, Dylan, Babette, and me. I scanned the destroyed camp, spotting soldiers on both sides, but no sign of Sean Wilson himself. Rob said he'd gone to Atlantis. He would pay for his sins another day.

Jordan charged past us, screaming Stephanie's name, dodging and ducking bullets as he careened around a corner.

A soldier ran at Wade. Wade sent him spirally through the air with one punch of his fist. A bullet sped by my ear. My flames blazed with a new ferocity, streaking from my fingertips, looking for enemy targets.

Machine gunfire came from the right. We dropped to the mud floor. Maya covered her ears. Smoked curled around us. People lay wounded, covered in mud and blood, screaming. My flames streaked through the camp, finding their own targets, every one of them a member of Sean Wilson's nefarious army. I prayed for mercy. I prayed they had quick deaths, because when my flames were involved, death was unavoidable.

The air heated, my scalp burned, and my ears rung. My friends gathered behind me. A hushed silence descended. All I could hear was the crackle of fire.

Wade helped me to my feet. "It's over."

I retched into the ground, but my stomach was empty. My eyes stung and my chest heaved with the guilt of so much death. The campsite was a mass grave. I tried not to look, tried not to take it in, tried not to see the charred remains of so many.

"You okay?" Wade asked, his arm around my waist.

"I will be."

We had rescued our people. I had my husband back in one piece. But we were no closer to finding Stephanie. Or defeating Aquaria and the Hound of the Ocean. Exhaustion weighted my limbs, but I couldn't give in to it now.

"Shit!" Dylan screamed, sliding to his knees. He huddled over an inert figure.

"What's wrong?" I asked.

"It's Bette."

My thoughts slowed, as if the smoke affected my logic. How could the prophecy be so wrong?

Maya crouched by his side. "What's wrong with her?"

"She's been shot," Dylan said. "She's not breathing! She's got no pulse!"

He rolled her onto her back. A large, red stain bloomed below her collarbone. Dylan covered her mouth with his own, gave two quick breaths, and began chest compressions.

"Let me help," Wade said, crouching beside him.

Dylan shook his head. "You might break her ribs."

Wade backed off. It was true. With his increased strength, sometimes he was unaware of how to deliver a delicate touch.

"Come on, Bette," Dylan said, hands planted in the middle of her chest.

Her eyes fluttered open, and she inhaled a weak breath.

"That's my girl!" Dylan said. The relief in his eyes was painful to witness.

But the red stain continued to spread. Babette couldn't keep her eyes open. Her features contorted and she screamed. The color drained from her face.

"That *hurts*," she mumbled, then passed out.

Trent kneeled on the ground, hands searching Babette's shoulder. "We need to find the bullet and stop the bleeding."

But Dylan was already on it. He had a finger halfway into Babette's wound, feeling around for the metal object.

"I can feel it," he grunted. "I just need to get to it."

He looked wildly about, and seeing nothing, dug a second finger into the wound. Babette was unresponsive. Unconscious and barely breathing. But she wouldn't want to be awake for this. The rest of us crowded around. Maya supported her head. I did my best to mop up the pooling blood.

"Got it!" Dylan declared and removed the bent, lead bullet from Babette's chest.

A gush of blood oozed from the wound.

"Get me something to stop the bleeding," Dylan said,

throwing a bloody hand at us.

Maya and I shot to our feet and scoured the camp. After a couple of minutes, we found a tent filled with sleeping bags and towels. We grabbed a couple of both. When we returned, I tossed Dylan a towel, and he pushed it against Babette's chest. Maya maneuvered one of the sleeping bags under Babette's head.

Jordan and Rob rounded the corner.

"No!" Rob yelled, dashing to Babette's side. He held a first aid kit in his hands, flicked the lid open, and spilled the contents on the dusty ground.

Jordan left, tearing through the camp, overturning anything that wasn't already destroyed, continuing to scream Stephanie's name.

Together, Rob and Dylan cleaned and packed Babette's wound. I cauterized it with my fire power and Dylan, with surprisingly steady fingers, sewed it shut. Babette remained unconscious through it all.

"I can get her antibiotics and an IV back at our camp," Rob said.

Dylan lifted her in his arms and carried her to the jeep.

"Thank you," Rob said to Dylan. "For saving her life."

With my hand tucked in Wade's, I took two steps toward our people where they'd gathered in the trees before I swiveled on my heel. Where was he?

I scanned the burning camp, peered through the dark smoke, until my eyes rested on his shadowy form. A man wearing only leather straps for clothing, his skin slick with sweat and blood. He was tall and muscular, his chest as broad and powerful as Wade's. His hair was dark and clipped shorter than the others I'd seen before, but I knew it was the dragon king in his human form.

We stared at each other across the burning bodies and through the dissipating smoke. We stared until our breathing became even and rhythmical and followed the same pattern. Wade remained by my side, holding my hand.

"That's Blaze," Wade said.

At the mention of his name, Blaze approached. He offered a hand in greeting. Wade took it and thanked him for his help.

"Blaze was responsible for setting us free," Wade said, a fist curled against his chest in a symbol of thanks.

Blaze and I looked each other up and down once more. I ignored his outstretched hand and wrapped my arms around his neck instead. I pecked a kiss on his cheek and inhaled the smell that was so familiar to me, but also altered, like a favorite pillow turned the wrong way around. Gal never told me he had a son, but I knew this man before me was his.

"You don't know me," I said.

Blaze shook his head, his expression softening. "But I've heard stories."

"Why didn't your father tell me about you?" I asked.

Blaze's smile faltered. "I have only seen my father once in the last twenty years."

"But he told you of me."

"He did," Blaze replied.

"What's going on? Who's your father?" Wade asked.

"Isn't it obvious?" I replied. "Gal is his father."

"Gal is your father?" Wade stared at our new friend, assessing his appearance, examining him for similarities.

"He is," Blaze replied. "Was."

"How were you not on Atlantis with the others? How are you still here?" Wade asked.

"My mother—"

A loud jeep horn drowned the rest of his words. Dylan gestured for us to hurry.

"Later," I said.

The three of us jogged to the jeeps. Our people had been loaded into transport trucks. We would take them back to the ocean where they could stay at Mermaid Lagoon until the battle for Atlantis was over. They would be safe there. I hoped.

Wearily, I climbed into an empty seat next to Maya. We pulled away from the burning camp and followed the road to the ocean. She stared out of the window as we drove, a frown creasing her forehead.

"What's wrong?" I asked.

"The prophecy," she replied, turning toward me. "I clearly got it wrong."

It had never occurred to me to question Maya's wisdom. I understood the prophecies weren't always clear, that they could be interpreted in a multitude of different ways, or that they took time to reveal their complete message, but until now, Maya had experienced an almost supernatural intuition in deciphering their meaning. That was why she was the oracle.

Noxious tendrils roiled in my stomach, aided by the jostling of the jeep over uneven ground. How could she have gotten it wrong?

"Wrong?" I asked. "Which part?"

"Relax," she said, taking in my anxious expression. "It's okay now."

"Care to explain?"

"Babette may or may not have died when she was a kid."

"And that's not a problem? It's supposed to be *the one who died and lives again.*"

"Not a problem," Maya said. "Because the prophecy wasn't

referring to that experience. It was referring to the fight at the camp. The death that hadn't happened yet. Family is important because it was Dylan who saved her. *Your* brother. *Your* family."

"But you're my family too," I said.

Maya smiled. "Right back at you, but that's not how the book works."

"That book is way too vague."

A frown flickered across Maya's forehead. "I need to get better at it."

I nudged her side. "You're doing fine."

"It's curious though," Maya said. "The fact that Babette drowned in the ocean when she was a kid was coincidental. I wonder..." she paused, tapping a finger against her jaw, her lips pursed to the side.

"Wonder...?"

She shook her head. "It doesn't matter. *The Mermaid Chronicles* is still on Atlantis. I've no chance of reading it. We're on our own for now."

"We could use some help from the Power of the Sea too," I said, as I braced myself for a large bump in the road. "What will happen if the humans get hold if it?"

"They won't," Maya said. "It's like the Fountain of Youth. Doesn't work for humans."

"That's one weight off my mind." A flicker of light distracted me. I glanced at my ring. The pearl was shining again. "But we still need to deal with Aquaria, Stephanie, and the Hound of the Ocean."

"We'll get there," Maya replied.

Surprised to hear a lightness in her tone, I looked at my

best friend. "I thought you said if Trent went to the mainland, the future looked very difficult?"

"It did, it does, but we've fulfilled the prophecy. Dylan rescued Babette. Wade, you, and Babette are all together. We're prepared. We're exactly where we should be."

"Babette's not out of the woods yet," I cautioned.

"She'll be fine." Maya patted my hand.

"Hon, I love your optimism, but if there's anything I've learned about being a mermaid, it's that life doesn't always run smooth, there are always snags."

"True," Maya said, "But sometimes when you've dealt with a few snags, life runs smoothly again."

"I hope you're right."

Back at Rob's camp, Dylan carried Babette to the medical tent and put her in a bed next to my mother. I gave Raina a hug, and she reported that our mother had slept the whole time we'd been gone. An IV was set up for Babette, and Dylan insisted on remaining by her side. Rob gave his daughter a cursory examination and agreed to leave her in Dylan's care.

"We could use that mythical Fountain of Youth of yours," Rob said as we left the medical tent.

"It's not mythical," Wade said.

Rob raised an eyebrow.

"But it's not working right now." I looked toward the horizon where I knew the ocean existed beyond the limit of my eyesight. I yearned to be in the water. I felt a stronger pull to be back on Atlantis defending my island from Sean Wilson's tyrannical army. "And it doesn't work on humans either." If only it did, it could cure all those suffering behind me.

"What a shame." Rob sighed. "I know you're exhausted. Let's get some food."

He led the way to his headquarters. Once inside, Wade, Ford, Trent, Maya, Blaze, Rob, and I sat in the plastic chairs and contemplated the food in front of us. Some kind soul had made a platter of crackers with peanut butter and jelly. There were a few bags of Doritos chips and a selection of canned fruit as accompaniments. Rob poured water into plastic cups for us all. We spoke of the battle, spreading the horror a little thinner.

"Fresh stuff has gone to waste." Rob indicated the canned and packaged food. "We send raids out regularly to stock up on canned goods from the grocery stores and warehouses around. But it will run out eventually. Before we can grow healthy crops again."

The nuclear bombs weren't the worst of it. Surviving in this apocalyptic aftermath was much harder. I didn't envy the humans on the mainland.

Shirtless and wearing only his leather straps, Blaze paced the length of the tent, hands on hips, swiveling jaggedly to change direction. "We need to do something about this prophecy."

Wade and I shared a look.

"We need Babette," Ford said.

"My daughter is incapacitated," Rob said. "She can't fight."

"With Sean Wilson's army on their way to Atlantis, Stephanie and Aquaria will use the opportunity to launch their next attack. They won't wait for Babette to recover," Wade said.

Rob glared at Wade. "I think we can spare one night."

"Wade is right." I took my husband's hand. "But maybe we can let Babette rest tonight."

"Tomorrow morning, we will take our people back to the ocean," Wade said. "And Babette, Cordy and I need to be ready to face Aquaria and the hound."

"God have mercy on us." Rob dropped his face into his hands and contemplated the bottom of his cup.

"I'll help." Blaze stopped pacing and planted his feet. "In any way I can."

"We're going to win," Maya said.

"Is that something you know? Or something you hope?" I asked.

"I feel it," she replied.

Rob dropped his cup. "It's all right for all of you, the merfolk, the selachii, and the dragon whatevers—"

"Dragon kings," Blaze said.

"Whatever," Rob said. "You can return to your precious island. Us humans are stuck here, dying from radiation poisoning."

"We need to be united," I said.

Rob stared at me. "To what end?" He didn't wait for an answer, but instead walked to the back of the tent muttering something that sounded like the Lord's Prayer.

I left the group and approached him. "If we win this battle, we'll have you on Atlantis. You'll always have a home there."

"I appreciate that." Rob passed a weary hand over his

face. Wade joined us. "While you and my daughter are battling monsters, I plan on going after Sean. We have unfinished business, and I will not let him claim Atlantis as his own. I will not let him inflict on your people what he did to us."

"Thank you," Wade replied. "I appreciate your help. And if there's anything we can do in return—"

"Just keep my daughter safe."

Wade nodded but made no promises. "We need to get some rest. Most of us have been awake for forty-eight hours. We're in no condition to fight."

Rob led us to the dormitory tents. He indicated a row of spare bunks. Jordan was there already, with an arm across his eyes to block out the world. Rob located more appropriate clothing for Blaze.

Wade pulled me close against his side. I laid my head across his chest and listened to the reassuring rhythm of his heartbeat. It was the first chance at aloneness we'd had since we'd been reunited.

"I'm so glad you're safe," I whispered. "When you stormed up the beach to fight the army, part of me thought I'd never see you again."

"Shh," he whispered into my ear. He turned onto his side and cupped my cheek in his hand. He kissed my nose, my eyes, and then my lips. "Everything's okay now."

"I don't think I can sleep." I rested a hand on my fluttering stomach.

"I know."

"So much has happened."

He swept a hand through my hair, which still reeked of smoke and rotten flesh. "So, we'll rest."

I nestled closer. "Can you believe Babette?"

He smiled. "She really came through for us."

"She's changed."

"Agreed."

"So has Stephanie."

"Also agreed."

"And not in a good way."

"I realize that too, Cordelia."

"Your mother thinks she can reason with her."

"It's too late for that," Wade said.

"I'm glad you see that." I shifted onto an elbow. "What are we going to do about her?"

"I don't know," he replied.

"Does Atlantis have a jail?"

"We've never needed one before."

He kissed my cheek again and stroked my arm gently until desire flamed. I craved his touch and yearned to be alone with him.

"Do you really think Rob will help us?" I asked.

"He said he would, and I've no reason to doubt him."

I thought of Atlantis and all it meant to me. "My father is still there."

"And mine. My sister too."

We fell silent. I closed my eyes and listened to him breathe. His hands went to my hair, and he wound it around his fingers, pulling gently in the way he knew I liked.

"Wade?"

"Shh, rest now."

"But there's something I need to tell you." My eyelids drooped.

"Later."

I opened my mouth so speak, but the aftermath of the battle took effect. I was too tired to talk.

A muted gray dawn crept into the tent, highlighting the shifting bodies and whispered conversations. Not many of us were sleeping. Images of the battle filled my mind, images I couldn't squeeze out by closing my eyes, like a nightmare that refused to be forgotten. The stench of the toxic smoke and the sound of pain-filled screams overwhelmed my senses. There had been so much death when I had arrived at the scene, but my flames had caused so much more. The responsibility that came with the power rested uneasily on my shoulders. I wished it wasn't so hard to use, but the day it became easy brought other concerns. Warmth bloomed on my fingers. Clenching my fists, I cradled them against my chest and held my flames inside. A strange fatigue stole over me. I fell asleep against Wade's chest, the only place I ever felt safe.

I woke to Maya's voice in my ear. "It's time to go, Cordy."

I reached for Wade, but the space he had occupied beside me was now empty.

"Wade is talking with Rob. They're making the final preparations for Rob's attack on Atlantis." She handed me a bottle of water. "There's breakfast in the food tent."

We walked to headquarters, making a quick detour via the food tent to pick up crackers and cheese, something that would settle my stomach. I ate on the go. When we arrived at Rob's headquarters, Babette was there. She was on her feet, dressed in fresh army fatigues, her hair tied into the ponytail she'd worn through high school, her eyes bright with resolve. She rested a hand on Dylan's shoulder. I tried not to see the tremor in her arm.

"How are you feeling?" I asked.

"Hurts like a bitch," she replied. "But pain is good for fueling my anger."

"Be careful," Wade said.

Babette's eyes narrowed to pinpricks. "We're in this together, right?"

"Right," I replied.

"So have my back, okay?"

"Okay," Wade said.

"We're all in this together," Dylan said. "It's not just you three."

"You're right," I said.

Blaze stood in the entrance, his hands on his hips, the joints in his wings threatening to rise. "Let's get going."

Rob raised a hand. "One minute, I'd like a word with my daughter." He looked at Babette. "Are you sure about this?"

Babette planted her booted feet. "Absolutely."

Rob scanned our small group. "Please take care of her. She's all I have left."

"I'll make sure she's safe," Blaze said, sprouting his wings. Rob visibly relaxed.

"See?" Babette said. "I have my own dragon king to keep me safe."

Father hugged daughter. "Stay alive."

"You too," she replied.

Rob left with the bulk of his army and half my heart. I

stood outside the tent with Blaze and watched them drive away. The fate of Atlantis was in his hands. Now it was time to face Aquaria and Stephanie.

We were a small army, but a courageous one. Wade, Trent, Ford, Raina, Blaze, Dylan, Babette, Maya, Christina, Jordan, my mother, and me. Twelve people to defeat a centuries old sea witch and a monster none of us had ever met. And we would bring Stephanie to justice.

As we followed behind Rob's jeeps in the direction of the ocean, I pictured the Power of the Sea and *The Mermaid Chronicles* on Atlantis. We had no way of knowing if we were doing the right thing, if the prophecy had changed, if our mission had a chance. We could only keep pushing forward and hope that staying united would bring us a future.

As I caught my first sight of the ocean, Rob's convoy peeled off toward the docks. It had been a few days since I'd seen the ocean, and the pull it evoked was almost irresistible. But I would be in the water soon enough.

When we arrived at Ocean Beach, a bright sun stole the clouds from the sky. The ocean barely rippled, hiding its secrets in its depths. Seagulls dipped and dived and shot through the columns of the pier, mimicking the dangerous surfing trick Trent had loved to scare us with. The town behind us lay in ruin, but the beach and water would always be perfect.

Those who hadn't sought refuge in Mermaid Lagoon disembarked from the remaining jeeps and waded through the shallows. I stood in the pier's shadow, the water lapping over my feet, taking a moment to relish what was mine. Wade called to our people, urging them deeper into the water. Little white crested waves broke against them.

Blaze stood with his wings unfurled, one of them hovering over Raina and my mother, offering them protection from the sun. Maya and Trent approached the shallows. Dylan remained glued to Babette's side.

Without warning, the sky turned gray, swallowing the sun and our blossoming hope. The waves whipped up and the temperature dropped. Salt stung my skin and gulls dived dangerously close to the ground.

I looked for Wade, found him along the beach where he was directing our people into the water. He locked his eyes on me. We stared at each other, unmoving, knowing without a trace of doubt, the next thing was about to happen.

Blaze shot into the sky, small flames licking from his mouth and nostrils.

"What is it?" Raina called.

Our people stalled in the shallows, looking for encouragement, or a reason to run the other way.

Babette unholstered her pistol. Trent and Maya dashed up the beach, tugging Raina and my mother with them. Christina ran to Wade's side, yanked on his arm, trying to get him out of the water.

A couple of Blaze's flames scorched potholes into the surface of the pier.

"What is it?" Raina called again, caught halfway between running in my direction and dashing after the others. She scanned the water, her eyes flicking across the length of the horizon.

I examined the sky, then the ocean.

Twin holes of nothing appeared in the ocean halfway along the length of the pier.

"There!" someone shouted.

Our people crept out of the shallows, backed up the beach, their eyes fixed on two growing whirlpools.

I raised my hands, called to my flames. Whatever emerged from those whirlpools was going to get a rude awakening. My heart beat recklessly against my ribs and my breath came in short pants. I would have preferred to be in the water, but prudence suggested distance from the growing and seething masses.

Wade jogged along the beach to stand by my side. The others in our small army gathered around me. Maya and Ford to my right, Blaze hovering overhead in his human form but his wings outstretched. They beat powerful strokes in the air, lifting my hair and whipping it across my face. They stirred the flames on my fingers higher. Babette stood to my left, her pistol trained on the water with one hand, the other gripping Dylan's arm. There was no color in her face. Had we brought her here just for her to die?

Jordan stalked the shallows, scowling at the water. He was shirtless, his tattoo twisting angrily with every jerky step. Christina kept pace with him, one eye on her nephew, the other on the ocean.

"Are we ready?" Wade called.

"As ready as we're ever going to be," Dylan replied.

"Fuck me, I'm actually scared," Babette said.

"I got you," Dylan said.

"We got each other," I said, as flames licked out of my nostrils.

Blaze gave me a small nod of encouragement. I wasn't the only one with a devastating power. We would bear the responsibility together.

"That's one badass power you got there," Babette said to me.

I narrowed my eyes at the swirling mass. "You haven't seen anything yet."

Two figures emerged from the whirlpools. Dark shapes writhing with unholiness.

"What's the plan?" Babette asked. "Do we have a plan? What do we have to do, *exactly*?"

"Stand united," Dylan answered, supporting her injured arm.

Babette flicked her safety off.

"And fight," Ford said, narrowing his focus on the two figures, his short swords unsheathed.

"Message received." Babette checked the bullets in the clip. Satisfied, she slammed the clip back in the gun and rested her finger on the trigger. She seemed to draw reassurance from the modern weapon, and I was glad, because when it came down to it, I didn't think it would be much good against a sea witch and a monster. But I didn't want to tell her that.

The two figures hovered over the water. Their identity was no surprise. Aquaria looked exactly the same; her wide slash of a mouth, her wriggling snake hair, her blank black eyes. But Stephanie was completely altered.

Gone was the blonde hair, the charming smile, the hint of dimples. Instead, her eyes were black and blank, like Aquaria's. Her hair was darker than midnight, cascading to her feet, but also no longer hair. The snakes making up her headpiece weren't as thick as Aquaria's, but they were long and equally deadly.

They both wore long purple dresses with corset waists. Seaweed trailed from their limbs and barnacles adhered to their chests. Worms and eels slithered across their bodies, giving the effect they were constantly moving.

"That. Is. Gross," Babette muttered.

"You get down here where I can talk to you," Jordan screamed at Stephanie, his neck taut, his words carrying in the wind. She only smiled, revealing a mouth of jaggedly sharp teeth. Three lines of them, like a shark.

"Stephanie!" Christina called, daring a few steps into the water.

The whirlpools beneath Stephanie and Aquaria ceased their tumultuous movement and closed. The wind calmed, and a deadly stench poisoned the air.

"Stephanie!" Christina called again, her stature as incensed as her nephew. "This must stop. Now!"

Stephanie's black eyes focused on Wade's mother. She pointed one long finger in her direction, trailing seaweed and kelp across the surface of the water.

"Save it, Christina," Stephanie said. "There's nothing you can say to change your destiny."

"Stephanie!" Christina yelled, wringing her hands. "Stephanie! Does our relationship mean nothing to you?"

"What relationship?" Stephanie laughed. One, lone, poisonous snake erupted from her skull and shot toward Christina. Christina ducked, throwing her hands over her face. Blaze and I both released a tendril of fire, but we were too late, the snake moving much faster than I anticipated. The snake dug its venomous fangs into the smooth flesh of Christina's cheek, the small fireballs flying harmlessly to land in the water with a hiss.

"You fucking bitch!" Jordan screamed.

"Please, Stephanie," Christina cried, pulling on the end of the snake. "It doesn't have to be like this."

"Mom!" Wade dashed down the beach to his mother's side.

"Are we supposed to do something now?" Babette said, closing one eye to sight. "I think I can take one of them out from here."

"It's a risky shot," Dylan said. "They're playing it smart, staying on the ocean out of reach."

Wade reached his mother, grabbed the snake and twisted its neck. It hung limply from Christina's face. Wade widened its jaws until it released his mother's cheek.

"I'm okay," Christina said, sinking to her knees. "I'm okay." Her eyes rolled into the back of her head. She faced planted the sand and her body was struck by a series of violent convulsions. A sickening yellow froth poured out of her mouth.

I hurried to her side. Wade searched for a pulse.

"We can't even do CPR," Wade said, fear running through his black selachii eyes. "She's still vomiting froth."

"They want us distracted," I said, keeping one eye on the murderous sea witches.

"Job done," Wade snarled.

The veins in Christina's face turned black and rose to the surface like smaller versions of the snake that had attacked her. Her eyes bulged, her tongue swelled, and her cheeks bloated.

"Fuck!" Wade screamed at the sky.

Jordan kicked at the water, hurling obscenities at Stephanie, who only laughed.

"She always was a pain in the ass," Stephanie sneered.

Jordan dove into the water, his blue shark tail emerging immediately, quickly transitioning to full shark. I lost sight of his shape under the waves.

With one final, horrifying look, Christina opened her eyes. But there was nothing but red. Her eyes bled. Her nose bled, and the yellow froth turned red. She clutched her throat. Her back arched impossibly high, holding a contortionist's position before she collapsed.

"Oh, Mom," Wade said.

I put a hand on my husband. "She's gone."

Wade pounded the ground and sent a small cyclone of sand rising around our heads.

"Wade..." Words weren't adequate. He had lost his mother once before. But there was no coming back from this.

Wade allowed a single tear to escape before he wiped it furiously away. His jaw hardened, the look in his eyes hardened, and his fists hardened. A ferocity I'd never seen before whipped through his body. He flexed his muscles, exhibiting his strength. There was no holding him back now. Wade was King of Atlantis. He was a kind king, a good king, a beloved king, but now he was an angry king seeking retribution. He would still be loved, but he would also be avenged.

Wade marched toward the ocean, keeping his glowering

eyes trained on Stephanie's shifting form. I readied my flames.

Our people huddled further up the beach. Babette kept her gun trained on the evil sea witches. Blaze flew along the line where the water met the sand, small fireballs gusting from his mouth.

"Not so fast." Stephanie raised a halting finger. "Unless you want me to release the snakes on the rest of your people."

"You wouldn't dare," Wade hissed.

"Try me," she challenged.

Wade dug his feet into the sand. Babette let off a shot. The bullet pierced a hole in Aquaria's palm, which healed instantly.

"How is that possible?" Babette lowered the gun.

"That's not her weak spot," Dylan replied. "You need to aim for the heart."

"Noted," Babette replied, lining up her sight.

Another of Stephanie's snakes streaked through the air, brushed past my cheek, and sank its teeth into an Atlantean further up the beach. The young man was dead in seconds, just like Christina.

Aquaria began a chant. One I had heard before. She raised her arms skyward and thrust her face up to the clouds. Words tumbled from her lips. A spell. An incantation. The Hound of the Ocean was coming.

"Stop it!" Wade yelled.

"Then stop shooting at us," Stephanie replied.

Before Babette could squeeze off another shot, a third whirlpool formed beyond Stephanie and Aquaria.

"The Hound of the Ocean," Maya murmured.

This is what I had been waiting to use my flames for. I looked at Blaze, seeking reassurance, but his eyes were locked on Aquaria.

As the whirlpool widened and the waves thrashed, rain slashed the sky into a million pieces. A couple of brave Atlanteans dashed into the water, their tales emerging, only to be attacked by Stephanie's snakes. I caught no sign of Jordan.

"Mother, no!" Blaze yelled, his face filled with a fiery fury, his eyes revealing nothing but disappointment. "You don't have to do this."

Mother? The final truth of his parentage hit me. I had known Gal was his father; I had sensed the truth of it. But Aquaria was his mother. I should have known; Gal had alluded to it before.

"I see you've chosen your side, son," Aquaria replied. "Now you can reap the consequences."

There were no more shouts or pleas for mercy. The battle began, and we fought for our lives, our people, and our island.

CHAPTER NINETEEN

My stomach chose that moment to hit me with an attack of nausea. As Stephanie and Aquaria's snakes shot from their scalps and streaked through the sky, my knees buckled and I retched into the sand. My flames winked out. The hiss of snakes skimmed past my head, narrowly missing my exposed skin.

Babette's gun went off, Blaze's fire heated the water, and the third whirlpool seethed with life.

Christina lay at my feet, altered in the way only death can alter a person. She had gone to another place. Whether it was Heaven or Hell or the air around us, I didn't know, but I could do nothing more for her.

Wade offered me his hand and I staggered to my feet. He held me close, supporting me against his side.

"Are you okay?" he asked, his voice desperate.

"I don't know." I urged heat back to my fingers, but my flames stubbornly refused to appear.

"We need that power of yours."

Panic almost sliced me in half. "I'm trying..."

The snakes swarmed through our ranks, latching on to any Atlantean who was unlucky enough to be in the way. Anguished screams ricocheted along the beach as, one by one, our people succumbed to the poison.

Black lightning flashed in the sky. The clouds whirled with an unseen presence, and the angry waves whipped even higher.

"Is this hell?" I heard Babette ask.

"I damn well hope not," Dylan replied, helping her to reload her clip.

Our army gathered, our strongest members to face the mounting threats. Although her breaths came in nervous pants, Babette planted her feet and didn't shy away from the devastating enemies. She had balls, I'd give her that.

No one ran. I was proud of our people. Terrified, but bravely facing our fate. Together. United. If only my flames would protect them. What the hell was going on with my power?

Babette annihilated a couple of snakes who ventured too near, proving she was more than target practice and ponytails.

Stephanie's voice boomed over the ocean. She uttered no words, merely laughed at us as though our fates were already sealed. Her attitude drove a violent rage through my veins, evoking my flames once again. This was the last time Stephanie would be an obstacle in my life. I narrowed my eyes and finally, my fire burned. I directed my power at the snakes, taking out over a dozen of her poisonous weapons.

"I'm out of bullets," Babette said, frantically searching the beach. "And there's still something coming out of that whirlpool. What now, Cordy?"

An unnatural light bloomed in the sky. A light that emanated goodness and hope. I didn't have time to question it as Aquaria shot another army of snakes in our direction. Blaze and I aimed our fireballs, their evil-seeking power targeting the snakes as they weaved through our people.

The strange light brightened, forming into a shape. A cone of light surrounded the Atlanteans.

"What's going on?" Dylan asked.

Maya only smiled.

"Maya?" I asked.

"You'll see."

The strange light didn't extend to cover the snakes, Aquaria, or Stephanie. I followed the path of one of my fireballs as it tailed a snake, only to see the serpent arrive at the wall of light and then drop inexplicably to the ground, dead.

More snakes followed, with wide jaws and needle-like fangs. Their black eyes rolled from within blacker bodies, seeking soft flesh to sink their teeth into. But they met only the light and their death.

"Holy cow!" Dylan slapped his thigh. "We may not have the Power of the Sea, but we have a goddamn force field."

"We do?" Wade asked.

I searched the area for the source. "Where did it come from?"

"No freaking idea," Trent said, watching a snake sizzle to death at his feet.

I glanced at my hands, not at my flames, but at the pulsating pearl in my ring. It was the source of light.

"Did you know?" I asked Wade as I raised my hand aloft.

He shook his head. "At least we can keep our people safe."

"Maybe from the snakes," Ford said, ducking inside the light's protection. "But there's still Aquaria and Stephanie and..."

"The Hound of the Ocean," Babette finished. She waved at the cowering crowds to take cover with us under the cone of light.

I didn't know how long the force field would last. How strong it might be. And I didn't have time to question it. I could only pray it lasted long enough.

I looked at Babette. She grinned at me. I held my hand high to allow the ring to shine its protective light over our people. Blaze hovered above my head. He spewed fiery tendrils and burned the remainder of the snakes before they could arrive. Then he focused his unforgiving gaze on his mother.

Stephanie's black eyes seethed. Did she think she could defeat us so easily? She dropped silently into the ocean. A shark leaped out of the water, narrowly missing Stephanie's transitioning black tail. Jordan.

Aquaria held strong. The waves surged. The third whirlpool was large enough to contain the entire town of Ocean Beach. I kept my hand high, despite fatigue shooting through my limbs. Heat from my flames and the pressing crowds sent a cold sweat coating my skin. My lips trembled.

"Cordelia?" Wade questioned, taking in my faltering appearance.

"I'm okay." I didn't know if that was true, but I wouldn't give up. "Can you see my Mom? Raina?"

He craned his neck to look at the people gathered behind us. "They're safe."

Blaze hovered above the rioting waves, facing his mother.

"You wouldn't dare," Aquaria hissed.

Blaze didn't wait for an evil diatribe. He didn't wait for forgiveness. He didn't wait for an apology. He sent one powerful flame streaking from his mouth. It swallowed Aquaria whole. She didn't scream. She was burned too quickly, turning to ash that disappeared into the warring water.

"I thought you had to shoot her heart," Babette said.

"I'd say burning it to a crisp works just as well," Dylan replied.

Blaze landed by my side, under the protection of my light. "I'm not like my father."

"I can see that," I said.

"There was no good left in her." Flames licked out of his nostrils. "I don't believe in second chances."

Blaze squared his shoulders and lifted his chin, but I caught the flash of sadness in his dragon king eyes.

The whirlpool swarmed onto the beach, so large now I couldn't see the other side of it. But before anything could emerge, the beach was unexpectedly filled with people. Transported from another place.

"What the...?" Babette's mouth hung open.

There were many mysteries to Atlantis I hadn't yet discovered: the power it contained, the secrets it kept hidden. It was alive in its own right, only revealing parts of itself when necessary, or when we were ready for it. The people on the beach were not Atlanteans, but humans. I assumed the humans who'd been on Atlantis had been transported here. Perhaps the veil had been raised once again.

I caught sight of a familiar face running through the crowd, turning people to face them, scanning the crowds. Rob. Our eyes met. He strode up the beach toward us, elbowing his way through the shifting crowd, then hugged Babette, who winced under his embrace.

"Sorry," Rob said.

"What happened?" Wade asked, cupping my elbow and helping me to keep my ring high. "Why are you here?"

"I have no idea," Rob replied. "One minute I was hand to hand with Sean Wilson. The next I was standing on this beach. And it's a good thing too, because he'd just fired in my face at point blank range."

"Oh, Dad!" Babette said.

"Where is he now?" Wade asked. "Is he here?"

"Everyone's here," Babette said, eyeing the beach. "I can see Sean over there."

We followed her pointed finger to a man sat on the beach. His elbows were draped over his knees as he watched the whirlpool expand. His hand went to the butt of the gun. The other rubbed the back of his shaved neck. He popped to his feet and released his gun from his hip.

"It's not just us three who need to be united," Babette said. "It's the entirety of our three species."

"The young woman is right," a familiar voice said from behind my right ear.

I turned to see Edward, the High Council member, his

gray hair flying in all directions. He was beaten and bloody and terribly aged, as if he had spent years outside his protective blue chamber.

"I've been on Atlantis helping your father," he said.

"He's okay?" I asked.

Edward nodded. "Marina too," he said to Wade. "And your father."

Wade closed his eyes briefly.

"The hound will be upon us shortly," Edward said, fiddling with a jewel hanging around his neck. "I came to help you. I didn't have time to reach the Power of the Sea, but I always carry this on me." He pointed to the jewel at his neck, a tiny swirling speck of Atlantis' magical power.

"Thank you. You didn't have to," I replied. "I know what it means for you."

"I think my time will be here sooner rather than later." Edward cast a loving gaze over the beach. "I couldn't imagine a better cause to die for, or a better way to die, than helping you, Cordelia. You've always been special to the High Council. I couldn't let you fight this alone."

"I'm not alone."

"I see that." He smiled. "The united three. Your union has also brought back the veil on Atlantis. That's why the humans were expelled. That, and because you are standing together. All of you. Here it comes now."

Wind whisked along the beach, kicking up sand which stung my skin. The whirlpool frothed and foamed. The waves raged. Gulls squawked in the air, flying wide circles around the widening whirlpool. The water thrummed with impending menace.

"It's coming," I said to Wade, to my friends.

"I love you, Cordelia Blue," Wade said

"Don't you start with that." I looked at my husband. "But I love you too."

An enormous snout emerged from the whirlpool. It was every bit the picture Esmerelda had shown us within the Power of the Sea. A tremor of fear rippled through me, and my legs trembled. Babette stood to one side of me with her father and Wade on the other. I pushed my hand high and the brilliant white light shone from the ring. But it didn't extent to protect the humans. It wasn't enough.

The hound had to be destroyed. We needed an offensive power. Blaze's fire. Wade's strength. My flames. The coming together of three species in a unified fight. And then there was Edward, who carried a tiny portion of the Power of the Sea on a chain around his neck.

I caught a look from Blaze. He flew above the white protection of the ring and blew his fiery breaths at the ocean and the hound. Fire burned on the water, fighting against the foaming crests, bullying them into submission. But still the monster came.

The hound poked its muscular neck above the waves, sniffed at the air, and released a cloud of thick, yellow fumes. A noxious scent of sulfur drifted to the beach. The rest of its body followed. Its long mouth was lined with numerous rows of sharp teeth, its scaled brown skin glistened with salt, and dark purple spikes ran the length of its tremendous spine. Each spike sported several foot-long claws, and the beast itself seemed to stretch from one side of the ocean to the other. Enormous. We didn't stand a chance.

"Holy mother of God and all things sacred," Trent said. "That thing is freaking huge."

Maya clenched her hands. "It's bigger than I thought."

A warm flush spread through me, anxiety warning me to turn and run. But my planted feet refused to move. I couldn't desert my people, my family, my friends. Wade. No matter how terrified I was. I rubbed a hand across my stomach and prayed for strength.

With its impressive arrival, the whirlpool abated, and the ocean calmed for a brief interlude. Blaze's flames skipped across the surface, then went out. The beast paddled through the water, its large, reptilian eyes roving up and down the beach, taking in the horde of hapless victims. Its nostrils flared, snorting new clouds of noxious fumes. Faint swirls of yellow drifted over the water. More gas than smoke. More acid than fire.

With each forward stroke, the hound shortened the distance between us, and its toxic breath thickened. The stench filled my nostrils and pushed an overwhelming pressure into my head. Atlanteans and humans all took a collective step backward. Many more scurried under my protective light.

"I'm scared." Raina crowded close to me. "I want to go back to Kansas."

Mom took her hand. "We're together now. That's all that matters."

The hound's eyes were its most unsettling feature. They were nothing more than one-dimensional reptilian slits, but a baleful intelligence hovered there. It wouldn't be reasoned with. It was only here to hunt, to feed, to survive.

"Are your flames working, Cordy?" Wade said in my ear.

"I think so," I whispered back, showing him the fiery tips of my fingers.

The hound's acid breath wouldn't be its only weapon. I scanned the crowd for my family. Locked eyes with my mother and sister, shared a look with Maya and Trent, spotted the distant figure of my father. Dylan gave me a short nod of acknowledgement. Babette and her father stayed close to him. Ford and Blaze stared fixedly at the hound. Edward clutched his necklace, the small orb of the Power of the Sea. Wade squeezed my burning hand.

The hound arrived in the shallows and prowled the coastline. Stephanie had not stayed to witness her apparent victory. She had fled. Perhaps she was afraid. Perhaps she was overconfident. We would find her another day.

I gritted my teeth and held my ring high, my fire licking the sky. Sean Wilson ran to the water. He splashed through the shallows, aiming his gun at the beast's chest. The hound blew its noxious breath toward him. Sean screamed, but he didn't stop running. He released a stricken war cry as he emptied his clip. The sound of the bullets slammed into the sky. When they were spent, he dropped the gun in the water, his skin sloughing from his bones. He had caused so much pain. Killed so many of our people. And his death had come so easily. He was the first fallen in a united fight.

Humans and Atlanteans waded into the water, carrying guns and spears and whatever else they could lay their hands on. They stood tall, lifting their chins and squaring their shoulders. They were my people, both the humans and the Atlanteans. I was proud to call myself both.

The hound blew a second breath at our defensive gathering. I shielded a large number from the fumes with the power of the ring, but the light could not protect the humans, or those who had waded out of its reach.

"If we're going to be united," Babette hissed. "Why doesn't your ring work for everyone?"

"I don't know," I said. "I wish it did."

"Convenient," she said. "That it's only my people who are dying."

"It's not Cordy's fault," Dylan said.

I pushed a challenge into my eyes. "They are *our* people."

The toxic gas washed over them, downing clumps of people with anguished screams.

But our people didn't stop fighting. They fired their guns, aimed their spears, turned to sharks in the water and attacked the monster's flanks. Wounds appeared in the beast's thick skin. Bullet holes sprayed its stomach and flanks, eliciting ribbons of blood. But still it charged at us. It was so huge; we were causing no more harm than a weaver fish.

Blaze flew above our heads. He swerved around the hound's head, avoiding its breath. Flames licked out of his mouth and nose, scorching the hound, eliciting yelps of pain.

Fire erupted from my mouth, warming the surrounding air. My flames curved toward the hound and sliced through its body, puncturing it with flaming holes. It growled and gusted a new cloud of acid breath at us. The hound was an enormous beast from a time when the oceans were one and could support such a frighteningly massive creature. And my flames, although accurate, were small. No more than a bee sting.

But I wouldn't stop. As our people fell, their screams echoing in my ears, I maintained a steady stream of fireballs. Blaze kept firing, and eventually the ribbons of blood pouring from the hound turned heavier. It staggered in the water.

"It's not enough." Dylan dashed out of my cone of light, into the water. Trent was close on his heels, and then Rob.

"No!" I yelled at them.

Dylan looked at me over his shoulder, shrugged, and turned to face the hound.

"I'll go," Wade said, dropping his hand from my wrist.

"No," I said. "I can't save you if you go out there."

"I have a power," he said. "I need to use it."

"Please, Wade. *Please* don't." My brother and Trent were already in the water ducking under the clouds of smoke. Dylan and Trent could use their gills, but Rob was vulnerable. "I can't lose you too."

"I love you, Cordelia Blue," Wade said.

My stomach flipped. "I'll come with you."

His eyes shone with the depth of his love for me. The regret that might come to pass. "You need to hold the ring."

I took the ring off my finger and handed it to Babette. It didn't stop shining during the transfer. She slipped in on her finger and held her hand in the air. The humans nearby stopped dropping under the effects of the hound's breath. Now that Babette held the power, humans were protected too.

I grabbed Wade's hand. "Were you trying to go somewhere without me?"

"I guess not." Together we strode into the ocean.

The pull of my tail struck immediately, and I quickly

transitioned. Wade and I swam together, diving deep to circle around the staggering hound.

We emerged by its rear paw. Blaze flanked us from the air. As flames seared the hound's skin, Wade and I grabbed onto the beast's sparse clumps of sharp fur, heaving ourselves up its leg. I pushed my tail away and used my legs to climb. Wade punched at the bleeding wounds as we climbed, sticking his fist into the raw injuries, making the hound jerk and snap its jaws.

"Don't get it angry," I said, eyeing its hulking mass.

The hound craned its neck toward us, glaring with primeval eyes. Wade and I cowered close to its scaled body, preparing for a noxious plume of deadly breath.

The hound regarded us with its slit green eyes, an expression of annoyance crossing its face. It shook its paw, tossing Wade and me around like seals in an orca's mouth, but we held fast to its fur. Then it shook its entire body. Nausea flooded my stomach again and I bit my tongue. Blood pooled in my mouth.

"Why doesn't it breathe on us?" Wade asked.

After one more unsuccessful attempt to dislodge us, it turned its head back to the beach.

"It's not immune to its own breath," I realized. "If it breathed on us, it would be surrounded by its fumes."

We scrambled up the massive body and picked our way across its spiked back. Occasionally, it would turn its head to check our progress and give us another shake that sent us clinging to its vicious spikes. But we managed to maintain our footing.

"We need to get to its neck," Wade called.

"Why?"

"That's what Esmeralda said. It's where a reptile's skin is thinnest."

"What if it's more dog than reptile?" I asked, navigating the narrow arch of its spine.

"Dogs are vulnerable there too. We'll go for an artery. Make it bleed out quicker. If we wait for Blaze to keep punching holes in it, too many of our people will die. They can't all fit under the light of your ring."

The hound turned its head to look at us once more, and I realized our mistake. Its infinite rows of sharp teeth loomed at us, lighting a fire of fear in my stomach.

The hound craned its neck, brought its head closer, opened its wide jaws. Blaze's fireballs zoomed into his mouth. Wade leaped as the jaws bore down on us and grabbed onto one of its elongated teeth.

"Wade," I screamed, watching my husband lifted into the air.

He hung from a tooth, his arms straining with the effort, his legs cycling in the air.

Hanging from one arm, Wade pounded his fist against a yellow tooth. A loud crack split the air as the tooth broke. Wade tumbled toward me, reaching for the hound's spinal spikes to slow his fall. The hound roared. One of the spikes sliced the length of Wade's torso, eliciting a thick line of blood. I sent fire into its mouth, searing its swollen tongue.

Blaze flew by, his fireballs singeing the ends of my hair. Human bullets whizzed past my face, tore open a wound on my shoulder, skimmed the skin of my calf. The hound snapped its head toward the young dragon king, sending a plume of poisonous breath at him. Blaze dodged it easily and managed a grin in our direction.

Wade and I rode the beast, holding fast to its spikes, avoiding the treacherous claws sprouting from the ends. My hands were cut to shreds from its needle-sharp hair, but I refused to let go, even when my grip became slick with blood. Ocean spray arced over us, causing our grip to loosen on the slick scales. Although bleeding and injured, the hound stalked the shore. Its noxious breath hung over the entire beach, burning the skin of our people, pushing them into the streets beyond.

Others rushed into the water, ducking under the poisonous fumes, aiming guns and spears at vulnerable spots on the hound. Several found their mark. More fell uselessly into the churning water.

The hound reared. Wade and I held onto each other, pinning each other to the hound's back. Wade anchoring me against the deadly beast with one powerful arm. The water was a long way down. My stomach flip-flopped. The hound's roar deafened my ringing ears. The monster placed one huge paw on the sand.

It drew up its shoulders and hunched its back, sending Wade and I scrambling in a new direction. It puffed out its jowls.

"What's it doing?" Wade yelled.

"I don't know," I replied, staring at our people on the beach. Those who remained on the sand were in the ring's protection, which Babette held high above her head. But would it be enough? They could be crushed under the hound's weight if it chose to leave the water.

A dense cloud of poison gushed from the hound's mouth. Those in the water succumbed instantly. Yellow specks danced in the air, carrying a deadly fate.

The cloud touched the beach and crept up the sand to the bordering road. Those not under the protection of the ring fell, clutching their necks, clawing their eyes, scratching their flaying skin. They vomited blood onto the sand, now pink with the evidence of the hound's success.

I locked eyes with Maya where she stood shaking next to Babette. With her face turned away from the hound's billowing breaths, Babette's arm trembled. She wouldn't be able to hold the ring much longer.

Trent wrapped his arms around Maya, his eyes fixed on the acid cloud.

"We need to do something," I said to Wade.

His expression matched the grimness in my heart.

My friends hovered on the beach, no safer than Wade and I. Jordan, Rob, Dylan, and Babette. And Edward. The High Council member stepped outside the protective shield of light and sized up the hound. How much more could we take? How much more could the hound give before it succumbed to its injuries?

A second paw plowed the beach. Blood poured from its burgeoning wounds. Its body trembled under the tight grip of my legs. It puffed out a breath, but no poison was emitted.

Edward called my name and threw his necklace into the air. It was a tiny amount of the Power of the Sea, but I would take all the help I could get. The small magical blue orb passed through Babette's protective light and flew high into the sky. Blaze and I shot our flames toward the flying necklace, melting the metal, enlarging the enchanted orb. My limbs trembled with the effort, my vision narrowed to a pinprick, and the ever-present nausea flooded my throat. But still I persisted, shooting flame after flame. The Power of the Sea was too small to cause much damage on its own, but adding mine and Blaze's power might help end this bloody battle.

Wade pounded his fist on the hound's back. The crunch of breaking bones reached my ears, the vibration shuddering under my body. The hound staggered, one of its legs buckling. Wade didn't stop.

Wade ran with the broken tooth he'd snared from the hound's mouth along its shaking spine. As the Power of the Sea, no bigger than a marble, sailed toward me, Wade leaped into the air. His hand trailed the scales, seeking purchase on the hound. He swung around its front, the tooth held in one powerful hand, and aimed at the hound's throat.

As he fell, he threw the tooth, his muscles rippling under the effort. The tooth lodged in the hound's throat. A mighty roar ripped out if its mouth, then cut off abruptly as blood poured from its terrible wound.

The flaming ball of the Power of the Sea sought the open wound like a torpedo to a boat and drilled through the hound until it stuttered one final breath. But there was no exhale and no more poisonous fumes. The hound fell. I leaped from its back as it splashed into the water, willing my tail into existence.

As I dove into the water, I searched for Wade, but I couldn't make out anything in the blood red ocean.

CHAPTER TWENTY

Wade appeared in the bloody shallows. We clutched at each other, leaning on each other for support as we staggered out of the water and onto the beach.

Babette held the ring aloft, her arm supported by Dylan, protecting everyone in its cone of light from the dissipating toxic fumes.

Wade's eyes clouded over as he surveyed the fallen and those who were broken and bloody. "We don't even have the Fountain of Youth to help them."

"Or you," I said, pressing a hand to the laceration on his side.

"We can comfort them," Babette said. "And tend their wounds as best we can." She handed me my ring and I slipped it back on my finger, its light dimming as a breeze swept the remaining fumes away. The small action caused her to wince.

"Are you hurt? Is it your arm?" I asked.

On closer inspection, I spotted the ugly yellow blisters lining her exposed skin, clustering at the corners of her mouth, creeping into the crevices around her eyes.

"The light protected everyone well," Dylan said, as Babette slumped against him. "Just not Babette."

"This is because of the hound?" Wade asked.

Babette managed a small nod.

"We need to get you help," I said.

"It's not so bad," she replied. "I'm craving water. I think that might help somehow, even though I hate the fucking ocean."

Dylan took her to the water's edge and sat her in the shallows. Gentle waves lapped over her damaged skin. Dylan cupped handfuls of water and brought them to her face. She sagged against him, her shoulders dropping, her eyes closing.

Wade took my hand and rubbed his thumb over the pearl in my ring. "I never knew this ring had such power."

"None of your family knew?" I asked.

"No one," Wade replied. "Not that they told me, anyway."

Maya joined us and wrapped an arm around each of us, causing Wade to wince. "There is a time and a place for everything."

"I'm so glad you're safe," I said.

Rob marched along the beach and drew close to our small group. "Well done, that was quite something." He offered his hand for Wade to shake. "I'm not sure I even have the words to describe what happened here today." He trudged toward his daughter and helped Dylan pull her out of the water. Her blisters had disappeared. They steadied her on the sand, and Babette wrapped her arms tightly around Dylan.

Satisfied his daughter was in good hands, Rob found members of his camp and took an inventory of injuries and worse.

A shadow loomed over our small group. I turned to see my father, who swept me into his arms and cried into my hair.

"Thank God," he said, repeating those two small words like a mantra.

My family was safe. All of them. And then I spotted Marina. She and Wade had lost their mother.

Marina approached us silently, tears streaming down her face, which she didn't bother to wipe away. Her knees buckled and Daniel Waters rushed to her side, lifted her in his arms.

They joined our growing group and we linked arms, one family. All Atlanteans.

Wade turned from his family and kneeled at his mother's side. Beside her unmoving body was another fallen victim. But this person hadn't died from the effects of the hound's noxious breath. This person had died from age.

Edward lay in the sand, a gentle breeze causing the grains to dust over his body, already interring him to the earth. I didn't see the moment he had died. But the small orb of the Power of the Sea had helped end it all.

Each member of the High Council reserved a special place in my heart. Each member had helped me in some small way become the person I was now; the girl who had conquered her fears, the fire mermaid, the curse breaker, the finder of Atlantis, the unifier of merfolk and selachii and humans. I owed them my life and my destiny.

Before I could approach Edward's body, his lingering shape dissolved. His skin, his clothes, his hair, and his bones became ash and were swept away on the wind and across the water.

The sun returned and burned evil out of the sky. A depthless blue color remained, surrounding our beach, holding us close, but also highlighting the ruined land at our backs, our trauma, and our uncertain destiny.

I stared at the blank blueness, thinking of *The Mermaid Chronicles* on Atlantis. There would always be prophecies. I knew this wasn't the end. Although it had prepared us for this fight, I didn't know if I wanted it in my life anymore. Maybe not knowing was better. I craved the oblivion of ignorance. Not that I would ever forget the possibility of future threats, but maybe during the in between times I could be happier without it.

Wade lifted his mother's body. "We need to return to Atlantis. I want to say goodbye to my mother in the traditional Atlantean way."

"We will," I replied, and kissed my husband's cheek.

"We need to take all of them," Dylan said, still cradling Babette.

"All of them," Wade echoed.

The healthy propped up the injured. Others came to help us gather our dead. We tied them together by their clothing, making long chains which we pushed into the water. We would swim them home.

"We need to leave now," I said to Babette. "And we can't

take the humans with us." The veil had risen once more. There would be no sanctuary for them on Atlantis. As much as I wanted to offer them a new home, Wade and I needed to bury our dead, take stock of our island, see if it could be repaired. Only then could we offer the humans a home, if it was even possible.

"I understand," Babette replied. "But I'm still coming with you. I need to see Atlantis for myself. I need to see if it could be a haven for my people."

"But you won't be able to set foot on the island."

She glanced at my ring, the very ring she had worn and wielded its powerful protection force. "I think I'm different."

"Perhaps you are."

"I'm not leaving her here," Dylan said.

"We need to hurry," Maya said. "Shane is holding on for us." The last living member of the High Council.

I didn't ask how she knew. "Let's go."

We entered the water. The Hound of the Ocean lay in the shallow waves, but with each tug of the gentle tide, its body was pulled out to sea. Blaze sent a fireball toward the awful corpse. Flames erupted and the body burned. We would leave it there and let nature have its way.

Atlanteans swam, with Wade still holding his mother in his arms, our subjects pulling the dead, and Dylan guiding Babette, holding her head above the surface for the duration of the long swim back to the island. Surprisingly, I could hear her thoughts. She was purely human, but her scattered thoughts as she took in our surrounds reached me through the telepathy all water species shared.

The tails are so beautiful.

How amazing it would be to be a mermaid!

Dylan is so brave.

She looked at me.

You're on fire. You look like you're on fire.

I smiled and pushed my thoughts into her head. *We are the united three.*

What will become of me? She thought.

I think we'll find answers on Atlantis. I pushed my thought at her.

A burning fullness swelled in my chest as I swam. My longing to return becoming a physical pain. As well as the grief of so many dead Atlanteans drifting in the water. My people were done paying for who they were. I would make sure of it.

My anger fueled my speed and when I staggered onto Atlantis' shore, I collapsed. But I wasn't so fatigued that I didn't take in the dismal state of the island. The sand beneath me was sludgy and coarse. Brown water trickled from the once beautiful channels. The columns surrounding the great courtyard lay in ruin, dead and withered vines choking them and tethering them to the cracked cobbles. Smoke filled the sky and flames surged across the roofs. The palace remained, but countless homes were burned and charred beyond recognition. Dylan's bar lay in a pile of wooden planks and chunks of marble.

The stench of ruin and death filled the air, suffocating me. Bodies lay strewn throughout the city. Some were recognizable as human, others were burned or maimed beyond identification. Turning my head, I squeezed my eyes shut and willed the horrific images away. I threw up into the sludgy sand, then covered the vomit with a handful of mud and pressed my face into the ground.

"Come on, Cordelia." Wade pulled me to my feet. At least his own wound had stopped bleeding. "We need to help our people."

Although we had brought back our dead, we had also brought back our injured, hoping that with the return of the veil, the power for the Fountain of Youth would also be restored.

I staggered to my feet and walked with Wade, still carrying his mother, up the cobblestone path to the Fountain of Youth. But it was as the first time I had happened upon it; brown, stagnant, and malodorous, moldering in the hazy daylight. There was no help here.

Wade released a small moan of anguish, then laid his mother on the fountain wall and slumped down beside her. As the defeat rolled off his shoulders and he covered his face with one large square palm, a building determination buoyed me. We had fought so hard to find Atlantis and make it our haven. I wouldn't let it slip between our fingers now.

"Cordelia." The voice was less than a whisper, a rasp of the dying. I turned my head, looking for the source.

"Cordelia." No stronger, but more insistent in tone.

Finally, I spotted Shane, the last remaining member of the High Council, propped up against the far side of the fountain. He was covered in blood and dirt. I hurried to his side and inspected him for injuries, but could find nothing to explain his current frailty. He had been outside the blue chamber for too long. Shane too, was dying.

"Take this." He pressed a small blue orb into my hand.

"It's what remains of the blue chamber. Put it in the fountain."

I didn't hesitate and threw it directly into the fountain. Perhaps it wouldn't be too late to save him.

When the orb hit the brown, viscous water, it bubbled with violent effervescence, as if angry we hadn't been able to maintain its beauty or magic. The rebellious foaming was short-lived. The fountain returned to its original, mesmerizing blue, and I knew our island would heal. I carried a cup of water in my hand to Shane, but he only shook his head weakly at me.

"No, Cordelia." He stayed my hand with his. "Give it to Babette."

"But she's a human," I said.

Shane locked his gaze on me, his black selachii eyes flickering with the resolve. "Give it to her."

I turned to see Dylan supporting Babette up the cobblestone path. How she had passed through the veil was a mystery. An even bigger mystery was that she healed when she sipped from the Fountain of Youth. She was the only human who could be healed by Atlantis.

When her cure was complete, her skin returned to its milky softness and her blue eyes sparkled with a new sense of wonder. The wound in her shoulder repaired itself. She stood taller and as she surveyed the land, and gasped as Atlantis was restored. I knew how she felt. Even though I had witnessed the miracle once before, it was no less bewildering the second time around, and if anything, perhaps it was more meaningful now that Atlantis was my home.

"I..." Babette turned a slow circle. "It's so beautiful."

Atlantis was a miracle. It was Paradise. A haven, a sanctuary, an asylum for the persecuted. It was the sum total of everyone's wishes and dreams and wildest fantasies. But more than that, despite the journey to find it, despite the heartache and loss, it was home.

Wade and I both sipped from the fountain. His laceration healed, the scrapes and bruises on my skin melted away, the cuts on my hands healed, and the ringing in my ears ceased.

"Cordy, Babette." Maya arrived and gestured at Shane.

His face had paled to a shade worse than white, his lips were bleached of their normal red, his bald head seemed sunken in the middle, and his once knowing eyes were dulled with the advancement of death.

"Here." He held out his arms to Babette. The main orb of the Power of the Sea rested in his hands. "I kept it safe during the battle. You are to be the next protector."

He gave one final push until Babette was forced to clutch the mysterious orb of swirling color. As her hands sank into the middle of the magical sphere, her blue eyes locked on its inner mysteries.

"It's beautiful," she murmured.

"It powers our island," I said. "Both electricity and magic."

"It keeps our oceans in balance," Maya added.

She removed her hand from the middle of the orb and balanced it on her palm. "I think I'm getting the hang of it."

"Small bits can be removed," I said, running a finger across its malleable surface and showing her a marble-sized ball of blue. "And the orb grows to replace what's been taken."

"Why me?" Babette asked, still marveling at the ball of blue.

Maya took the small orb from my fingertip and placed it back in the main sphere. "You may not be a mermaid or a selachii, but the very fact you are here on this island means you belong here. You are an Atlantean. You are the protector of the orb."

"What if I don't want it?" Babette murmured, looking at us all.

"None of us have a choice in our destiny," I said.

"I'll help her," Dylan said. I looked at my brother. Could this mission give him purpose? Would it draw him out of himself? Could Babette reach him when no one else had been able to? Even though I was grateful for Babette's central role in defeating the hound, I was more appreciative of her relationship with Dylan. She was saving my brother. And for that, I would forgive all her past mistakes.

I turned to Shane, seeking confirmation of my thoughts, but he had passed quietly away while we'd been discussing the orb.

Wade closed his eyes with two gentle fingers. But, also like Edward, the small action seemed to instigate his fading from this world. His skin turned gray, then turned to ash, then floated away.

The last High Council member. Gone.

We were on our own now, without the wisdom and knowledge of centuries of history stored in the blue chamber and in their minds. Each battle we'd endured had been facilitated by the help of a High Council member in one form or another. Could we do it without them? We no longer had a choice. Whatever prophecies *The Mermaid Chronicles* chose to impart would have to be deciphered by us, and only us.

I looked over my shoulder at the rocks where Gal had died. His voice remained strong in my head. It would have to be enough.

Blaze arrived on the beach, stretched his wings and shook off the ocean and salt from his leathery skin. He made no move to inspect the island or join our small group, but instead turned to face the ocean and sat in the yellow sand. He was not as wise as his father, and more impulsive, but I knew he would be my friend.

Wade pulled me aside, glancing at the brightening sky. "We've seen no sign of Stephanie."

"If she's smart enough, she'll stay away," I said. "If she's not, we'll deal with her."

CHAPTER TWENTY-ONE

We buried our people in the Atlantean way.

It was past midnight when Daniel Waters lay his wife atop the wooden structure of her final resting place. Dressed in a simple white sarong dress and with her features softened in death's release, Christina had never looked more elegant. Her hands were folded over her stomach. Wade and Marina covered her body in flowers, mostly the striking bird of paradise that grew throughout the island. They wove smaller calla lilies in between. My mother added baby's breath around her head and feet. Daniel kissed her forehead and descended the wooden structure. As I looked up and down the beach, I saw a hundred similar pyres.

Blaze flew in the sky, hurling his flames at the pyres as they drifted on the tides. I cast a thought to the humans on Ocean Beach, Rob and his army, how they were faring. They had no Fountain of Youth. And their medicines, since the nuclear attack, were limited. If only there was a way to have them here and protect our island at the same time.

When the crowds left, Wade and I remained on the beach.

"My mother is dead."

I took his hand. "I'm sorry."

"And my father is leaving."

"Back to fishing?"

"It's the only thing he knows," Wade said, his hand twitching in mine. "I don't know how to feel."

"There is no right way to feel."

"Everything feels so surreal." He clutched my hand with his mighty strength.

"For me too."

He looked at the palace. "All she ever wanted for me was to find Atlantis and become king."

"You did both those things."

"I never really wanted to be a king."

"But our people needed you."

"That's why I accepted it." He lifted my hand to kiss my knuckles. "And I would never have done it without you by my side."

"I'm here for you," I said.

"I know."

I held him while he cried.

We stood together for a long time. Wade's gentle exhales swept over my cheek as we thought our own thoughts, glad of the moment alone, however solemn it might be. We stood, cheek to cheek, arms around waists and breathed in each other's smells, the smells we had forgotten as battle and fear had consumed us. It was the salt and the ocean and seaweed and the musky scent I reveled in now, the smells that before I had known he was a selachii, had confounded me so. I smiled at the memories—it all seemed like a lifetime ago—and buried my face in his neck. I pulled him closer to me, my hands gripping the flesh of his back.

He pulled back, locked his gaze on me. I looked up into his eyes, those familiar eyes that had haunted my dreams and fueled my hope. They were weary, shadowed by what he had seen and done, but in them, I found a reflection of my own longing and relief. We stood there for a heartbeat, a moment stretched into eternity, absorbing the reality of each other's presence.

Wade cupped my cheek, drew my lips to his, and slipped his tongue into my mouth. Gentle and soft, his kiss was delicate, tentative, until I clung to his shoulders and pulled him against me.

The kiss deepened. It became fierce and hungry, a collision of need and love that had been held at bay for too long. His lips were warm and insistent, moving against mine with a fervor that spoke of his relief, his passion, his desperation. I responded with equal intensity, pouring all my fear, love, and longing into that single moment. It was our past, our present, and our future. All we had been through together. The separation, the battle, the death...it all came out in that kiss.

Time had no meaning. There was only the taste of him, the feel of his body against mine, the rhythm of our shared breath. It was a kiss that spoke of survival, of finding each other again amidst the chaos, of a love that had endured the unendurable. It was a kiss that promised forever, no matter what lay ahead.

Wade took my hand and led me to the shallows. "Don't transition," he said, his voice no more than a husky whisper.

He flung off his clothes, then quickly removed mine. When we stood waist deep in the gentle shallows, he placed his hands on my rear and lifted my legs so they wrapped around his waist.

We didn't kiss. We stared at each other instead. Wade slipped inside me, pushing himself deep, then withdrawing once more until he found a slow and measured rhythm. Pressure built in my core. I tipped my head back to look at the stars as I clung to his shoulders, moving my hips to take every one of his thrusts. His fingers dug into my rear, pulling me against him with each stroke, causing me to gasp with pleasure.

Wade tensed against me. The hardness inside me began to throb with a new intensity. As he thrust once more, I met him on the edge, and we fell over it together, both of us releasing the shuddering pleasure through sharp gasps and breathy moans.

When it was over, I rested my forehead on his chest. Panting, he stroked my hair and the soothing water swirled around us.

"I don't know why we've never done that in the water before." His voice caressed the shell of my ear.

I looked up at him, brushed my lips against his. "Because it's hard to refuse the transition."

"But not this time," he said.

"No," I agreed. "Not this time."

We crawled out of the water and collapsed on the sand, bundled in each other's arms. Together, we watched the moon arc across the sky. I was counting stars when I realized Wade had fallen asleep, his breaths deep and even. At last, a reprieve from his pain.

I snapped awake when dawn burst over the horizon, but it wasn't the rising sun that had woken me. It was a tingly feeling at the nape of my neck.

"Wade." I shook him awake.

"What is it?"

"I don't know." I watched the water. "We killed Aquaria and the hound. But Stephanie is the one who started this. She won't stay quiet for long."

"You're right," Wade said. "Part of me thought she'd attack during the funerals, to hit us below the belt."

"She's gone so far down this path, she won't stop now."

We hurried to the palace and located Ford.

"I want our guards on patrol, twenty-four seven, keeping their eye out for Stephanie," Wade said.

"Already on it," Ford said, keeping pace with us as we walked to the great hall. "I've had half the force on a perimeter lookout since the funeral. And along the beach. Especially as you too spent the night out there...you needed to be protected."

"Thank you," I said.

"And Maya has new information too," Ford said.

Wade shook his hand. "I knew I could rely on you. I've been so distracted."

"You had other things on your mind," Ford said. "And last night you needed a minute."

"Any sign of her?" I asked.

"Nothing so far," Ford replied.

"She'll come." Wade glanced out the window at the courtyard below. "It might not be today, or tomorrow, but she'll come."

Maya entered the room, her bare feet squeaking on the polished floor. "I've been studying the book."

"And?" I asked. "When is she coming back?"

"Doesn't say," Maya said. "But she *is* coming. I've been reading up on sea witches."

"We know they can summon the Hound of the Ocean," I said.

"Which is dead now," Ford said.

"There are other things she can summon," Maya said.

"Like what?" I asked.

"It's a long list," Maya said, beginning to tick points off on her fingers. "Ghost pirates, ashray storms, the tribe of banshee kelpies...there are so many."

I rubbed at a building headache. "What are we supposed to do with that?"

"I have a feeling she's not going to summon anything else." Maya laced her fingers together. "She tried that with the hound, the most formidable beast of the ocean, and it failed."

"Now it's personal," Wade said, his body rigid, his frown deep, his arm wrapping around me. "She'll come on her own."

"Unless she decides to free anything else from whirlpool prisons." I couldn't bring myself to say their names.

"Zale and Caol," Wade muttered, casting me a sympathetic look.

Their murderous black selachii eyes filled my head. Images of blood swarmed my mind. I had long stopped worrying over their existence, secure in the knowledge that the High Council had dealt with them. But Stephanie was capable of anything.

"She wouldn't," Wade said, his arm tightening around my waist.

Maya raised a palm. "Doesn't say she will, but we can't rule out the possibility."

"Anything else we don't know?" Wade asked.

Maya shook her head. "Her main offensive power is her snakes. We all know how they work. And her weakness is her heart—"

"Probably because she no longer has one," Ford muttered. "Poor Jordan. Unrequited love is a bitch."

"Stephanie is a bitch," I said.

"Actually, it's because sea witches are born from anger and hate, so their hearts become their weak point, their only one," Maya said.

"I'd like to see her stand trial," Wade said, fiddling with his shark tooth necklace. "Despite everything she's done, I don't wish her dead. I'm tired of all the death."

I took his hand. "We may not have a choice."

Maya approached Wade. "I know you're a good and kind person. An even better king. You want to do the right thing, but if she doesn't come willingly...force will have to be used."

Ford laced his hands behind his back. "Worst of all, she can lift the veil on Atlantis."

"No one is safe," I said. "Sean Wilson's army, or what's left of it, could invade again."

"We need to gather everyone," Ford said, marching to the doors.

An hour later, we stood on the palace steps with the population of Atlantis filling the courtyard.

"Good morning." Wade plastered a smile on his face. He wore his crown. It glinted with reflected sunlight. And he didn't let go of my hand, clutching it in a way he never had before. We were both feeling uncertain. "And welcome back to Atlantis."

Cheers rippled through the crowd, along with wolf whistles and a thunderous applause that didn't abate for a full five minutes.

Wade lifted our hands above our heads, his arm trembling. "We all saw Aquaria fall."

More cheers and claps and whistles.

"We all fought bravely against the hound, and we triumphed. But there are two people I'd like to thank, who we couldn't have done it without," Wade said. "Where is Blaze?"

Blaze rose from the middle of the crowd. His wings grew and stretched, and he hovered a few feet above the gathering.

"Please join me," Wade said to Blaze, indicating a spot on the marble steps.

Blaze flew over the crowd and landed gently on his feet next to me. He unfurled his magnificent wings, their golden speckles glimmering poetically in the sunshine.

"Thank you, Blaze." Wade extended a hand.

Blaze took it and pumped it vigorously, only enticing the crowd to louder cheers and whistles.

"And Babette," Wade said, searching the gathering. "Where is Babette?"

Babette was standing with Dylan at the side of the crowd. All eyes turned to her as she made her way to the palace steps. She walked slowly, warily, and pulled Dylan along with her, hissing at him under her breath. Typical Babette. Some things really hadn't changed.

"Our united third." Wade welcomed her to the steps.

It was the biggest round of applause yet. She smiled modestly and waved.

"But our battle is not over," Wade said, his words changing the optimistic mood. "Stephanie Bowers is the one who freed Aquaria and summoned the hound. She is now a sea witch in her own right. We all saw how she had changed during the battle. She has not been found."

Fearful murmurs crept through the crowd.

"I won't be satisfied until we find her," Wade said, gripping my hand tightly. "And brought to justice. Only then can we continue to live in peace. We do not know her whereabouts, but the Atlantean Royal Guard are keeping watch. They are stationed along the perimeter of the island. Stephanie Bowers will not step foot on this island without us knowing. And then she will be dealt with."

"Burn her!" someone yelled. "Like they used to do."

Wade raised a palm. "I understand your anger, but it is not the Atlantean way to inflict torture on our enemies. There will be a trial. And she will be sentenced accordingly."

Jordan, standing where the courtyard met the steps, scowled at Wade. "There isn't a soul on Atlantis who doesn't want to see her dead."

"That may be true," Wade replied. "But I will not lead our people into the barbarous methods of the old ways. Sadly, the High Council is gone, but with their end we have the opportunity to begin a new way of ruling. To take our island into the modern world, to show our people there is justice and fairness for all."

The crowd went wild, punching fists into the air, surging up the steps. Only Jordan remained silent. It was a good thing he wasn't a member of the Royal Guard. I didn't trust what he might do.

"Please remain vigilant, and report any suspicious activity," Wade said. "But I also want you to return to your lives and trust the army to keep you safe."

Questions barreled at us, but Wade refused to answer any and led me into the palace where we gathered in the great hall. Maya and Trent sat by the fireplace. My mother was curled into an armchair opposite them. She touched me as I walked by. Wade and I stood by a window, watching our people cast nervous glances at the ocean. Dylan and Babette sat together. Blaze, his wings now folded into his back, paced restlessly around the room. Ford was the last to enter, and he closed the heavy door softly behind him.

"We have a few things to discuss," Wade began, taking a moment to rest his eyes on every person in the room. "The first point on the agenda is the appointment of a new High Council. But I'll let Cordelia take this one."

"We need to show those who may be watching that Atlantis is strong once again, and we need a new High Council to do that." I looked at Maya, hoping she could read the inference in my face.

She took a step back. "I don't want to live in a blue bubble far away from everyone."

"I was thinking we could have a new type of High Council, one where you could live here on Atlantis," I said. "Babette is the protector of the Power of the Sea. Maya, you're our resident oracle and representative of the merfolk. Blaze, if you agree, is our last remaining dragon king, and I thought Ford could be the selachii member."

"There are no eelusionists," Dylan said.

"Edward was the last," I replied.

"I need to be with my father," Babette said, pushing her back into her chair. "I can't be here without my father. He's the only family I have left. And all those people in the tents. They need my help."

"Humans can't come here," I reminded her.

"*I* came here," she said.

I splayed a hand. "An anomaly. You're one of the united three."

"Then I'll need to leave." She leveled a challenging stare at me.

"Everyone chill," Maya said. "There may be a way."

"We can't bring people here when Stephanie is still a threat," I said. "Whether there's a way or not."

"I'm not going to let this go," Babette said.

"I didn't ask you to," I replied. "And if you don't want to wait until things are settled with Stephanie, fine, but we still need to move forward."

Babette squared her shoulders, but didn't reply. She looked at Dylan and a softness broke over her features.

"In the meantime," I said to Maya. "You're the perfect

representative for the merfolk because you can read *The Mermaid Chronicles*. So I think you would be ideal for the council."

"I accept," she said immediately. Color bloomed in her cheeks and her eyes glowed with importance.

"You can take some time to think about it," Wade said.

"I don't need to. Sign me up."

"Ford," I said to the head of our Royal Guard. He had been with us every day over the last year, never intruding, but always making sure we were safe. "I would like you to consider being the selachii representative."

"Or course," he said with a small bow.

"Thank you," Wade replied, a hand over his heart.

"Blaze." I turned my eyes on my dragon king friend. "You are the last remaining dragon king. You are the son of a dear friend. I now consider you the same. Will you do me the honor of serving on the High Council?"

"Hang on a minute, you're inviting a dragon king onto the High Council?" Babette rose to her feet. "I've got nothing against you personally, Blaze, hell I think you're a nice guy, but the dragon kings stole Atlantis. So you're happy to have him here in one of the most esteemed positions, but not the humans?"

Dylan nudged her arm. "Bette, go easy..."

She turned on her heel, her gaze cutting across us all. "I'll think how I want to think."

Dylan raised his hands. "Wouldn't want it any other way."

"We want you here too, Babette," I said through clenched teeth.

Babette swiveled to face me. "No, you don't, not really."

Maya clapped to get everyone's attention. "Please stop fighting. *United*, remember?"

"I'm sorry," I said to my friend, but couldn't bring myself to look at Babette.

"What she said," Babette said.

Turning my back on her, I turned back to Blaze. "So?"

Blaze had been wandering around the room. He stopped when I addressed him. He laughed. Everyone waited him out.

"You're serious?" he asked, his features a puzzled question mark. "I thought Babette made some good points."

"I'm serious," I said. "What else are you going to do?"

"Thought I might hunt down Stephanie and burn her out of existence."

Wade's lips set in a grim line.

"That's exactly the kind of vengeful behavior we're trying to avoid," I said, even though I wanted the same.

Blaze's lips softened, but his eyes remained as hard as steel. "Maybe I'm not the best candidate. I'm not a big believer in second chances. Look at my mother."

He'd killed his own mother. No matter their relationship, or how evil Aquaria had become, that was no easy task. Although Blaze's attitude may be a little more fire and brimstone than the others, his perspective would help balance the council. Sometimes action was better than debate.

"On second thought," Babette said. "I think you'd be perfect. It's time to shake up the archaic Atlantean viewpoint. I like me a little revenge myself."

I refused to react to her comments.

Blaze sighed.

I drew closer to him. "If not for us, for Atlantis, maybe for your father."

He dropped his chin. "Maybe."

"Babette." I steeled myself, had a strong talking to my hands, and faced her. The reluctant invitation dangled from my lips. "I think we need you. We couldn't have defeated the hound without you. And you helped rescue our people from Sean Wilson's camp. I couldn't be more grateful."

She crossed her arms. "I'm not making any decisions until I see my dad and we figure out a way for humans to live here."

I met the challenge in her eyes. "Shane gave you the Power of the Sea to protect. It is your destiny."

"We'll see about that."

"I'll help you find your father," Dylan said to her.

"We'll have to lift the veil," Maya said, walking a slow circle around the Power of the Sea.

"I understand the importance of being united, that it isn't solely for one day," I said, curling my fingers into my dress, seeking something solid and reassuring. "But Stephanie lifted the veil and there was a war."

"When she comes back, she'll only lift it again," Maya said. "We may as well stay ahead of her. With all three species here and united, we'll be better prepared for her next move."

"But it's always been a sanctuary for the water species," Wade said, his eyes catching mine. "A place for us to retreat to when persecuted. And we *have* been persecuted."

"Not by me," Babette said, with a scowl to match her mood.

"You said it yourself," Maya said. "You wanted a new High Council. We need a new Atlantis too."

"Yeah, you did say that, didn't you, Cordelia?" Babette said, authority shooting through her voice. She looked at Maya. "How do we do it?"

Maya avoided my withering gaze. "Instructions are in *The Mermaid Chronicles*."

"Of course they are," I muttered. The logs in the fireplace caught fire, the result of my misguided flames. My emotions were all over the place and the nausea slithered back into my stomach. This felt wrong. We were opening ourselves up to another attack.

"What was it you had in mind?" Babette asked. "When we fought your war for you and became united...you were going to kick us back to the mainland and go on your merry way?"

I flinched under the accusation in her tone. "No, I—"

"We all want peace." Babette glared at me. "We all want to survive. And if we can catch a bit of happiness here or there and feel a bit of laughter in our souls, then all the better. We need to heal, we need to have hope. There's nothing left on the mainland. If Atlantis can offer us hope, a place to be with possibility, I think we deserve it. Secondly," she narrowed her already narrowed eyes, "half of my father's camp is sick and dying. I think they deserve better than a stale, fetid tent for their death bed. They could be here, looking upon the ocean, trying to take in a measure of beauty before their final moments."

I stared her down. Wade hovered at my side. My fingers sparked. "I don't begrudge anyone the right to die peacefully. But what if it's not peaceful? What if Stephanie conjures another terrible beast and they attack? I don't want that for any of us."

"Maybe we can help," Babette snapped. "United, remember?"

The fire roared.

"I don't want to be blamed for more human deaths," I said through clenched teeth.

"I can't be here if my father is over there trying to make sense of life in a nuclear wasteland...after he helped you!"

"Easy, Bette." Dylan laid a hand on her arm. She shrugged him off. Ford threw a bucket of water over the fire. It was hot enough in here already. It sizzled and hissed and sent a cloud of dark smoke into the room.

Wade approached the feisty human. "Babette, you've got to understand what we've been through. I'm not against the idea of allowing the humans here, your father, *you*. But we are rather gun shy. Twice burned and all that..."

Babette jabbed a finger into his muscled chest. "I believed in you. All of you. I didn't realize there was an expiration date on our alliance."

"Fighting united against the Hound of the Ocean is one thing," I shot through my clenched teeth. "None of us would have survived if we hadn't helped each other. But bringing the humans here, the very people who hunted us and imprisoned us—you remember Nerida," I said to my brother. "She was your friend, she saved you from Zale, she looked after you in the ocean—"

"I know," Dylan said quietly.

"—and all that we went through to rescue her?"

"I know," Dylan repeated, louder this time.

"She was captured by people like the ones living over there." I pointed toward the mainland.

"That's not fair," Babette said. "You can't paint us all with the same brush."

"Your father's camp doesn't have the only human survivors. People from Sean's camp survived the battle too. I can't bring them here."

"They wouldn't come," Babette said.

"They'd be the first ones ramming down the door!" I said. "I can't allow any more of my people to die at the hands of humans. I can't drop the veil on them when they think they are safe. They deserve more."

"So do we!" Babette shouted. "And I think you'll find Sean's people have changed. Or did it escape your notice that they fought on the beach against the hound right alongside us?"

Dylan stepped between us, ready to intervene. Babette dodged him and faced me.

I had to concede her point. But I'd never say it. And it changed nothing.

"The nuclear war only happened because of all of you," she said. "I stood up and tried to fight back. I stood up in support of you. And so did my father. We didn't have to do that. I lost my mother, my sister, friends. The nuclear war only happened because of Atlantis."

"It's not our fault." I threw my hands in the air. "And you stood up in support of yourself, not us. Because you didn't like what Sean Wilson stood for and you wanted to take him down. You weren't interested in Atlantis because you were afraid of the water. But now you're here..."

Wade laid a hand on my shoulder, but I didn't want to calm down. I wanted control of this situation, of Atlantis and its future.

"That's not fair," she snapped at me. "I helped rescue your people. I was there with you at the beach, wearing your god-damn magical ring."

"Yes, you were," I said. "But we all have our own personal, selfish motivations." I looked meaningfully at Dylan. She snorted at the implied suggestion, but she didn't deny it. "I've lost people too, Babette. And I had nothing to do with the nuclear war. It was the act of a deranged tyrant. You can't blame us for that."

We glared at each other.

"Cordelia, don't forget the humans aren't just my people, they're yours too," Babette said, her tone softer. "You might be a mermaid, a very powerful fire mermaid, but you're also human."

"And you're something other than human," I reminded her. "Something more."

Our gazes were locked, but the fight left both of us.

My mother, who had remained quiet until now, rose to her feet. "Babette is important to the island. Shane saw that and entrusted her with The Power of the Sea. We need to consider her request, and not because she is requesting it, but because it is the right thing to do. It wasn't so long ago that merfolk and selachii were at war, all over an overgrown white pearl. And now look at you, united. Then the battle with the dragon kings. We had one on our side during that war and we have one now too." Mom gestured to Blaze. "I don't see why we can't be united with the humans too. The prophecies said you needed to be united with a third in battle. But it wasn't only for the battle against Aquaria and the hound, Cordelia, you need to be united for all time."

I slipped into a chair as the truth of my mother's words washed over me. Of course she was right, but there was another reason I was fiercely protective over our island. A reason I hadn't mentioned to anyone, not even Wade. I cradled my stomach, wondering how long the nausea would last.

"Okay," I said. "Okay. I get your point, Mom, but how do we protect our people?"

"Don't you see?" Babette asked. "They won't need protecting. No one will. We'll be united. The mentality that existed in Sean's camp is gone. People want to stop fighting."

I threw another flame at the logs and fueled the fire once more.

Wade frowned at me. "Cordelia...?"

"It's not how I thought it would be."

"Me neither," Babette said.

"Are you all sure?" I asked, studying my friends' expressions.

Everyone agreed.

Smiling, Maya flicked through the pages of *The Mermaid Chronicles*, at ease with the new world we were creating. I looked over her shoulder to see blank pages filling in.

CHAPTER TWENTY-TWO

Babette marched up to the Power of the Sea. "We're doing this now."

She poked a finger into the middle of the swirling orb, staring at it when it came away blue. A thin thread of glistening blueness connected her finger to the sphere. She shook her hand. The thread retreated like it had been recalled on a spool until it was swallowed by the orb.

"It's beautiful," she whispered.

"It is," Wade said.

"I can't stop staring at it." Babette gave the orb one final look before she faced me. "Are you ready, Cordelia?"

"Yes," I said. "If you're sure."

I glanced at the Power of the Sea. Thin threads unraveled from the orb like undulating seaweed, reaching for Babette. A faint blue light surrounded her. I didn't understand why she, a human, had been chosen to protect the orb. But I was learning not to question the will of Atlantis. No matter how much it irked me.

"I will accept the position on the High Council," Babette said. "When the veil is lifted."

I looked at Maya. "What do we need to do?"

"It's right here." She held *The Mermaid Chronicles* open. "A spell must be spoken aloud by the united three. I guess as you can't read it, you can repeat after me."

"Can't read what?" Babette asked, hovering over Maya's shoulder, looking at the book. "It's in English. Why couldn't we read it?"

"You can read the book?" Wade gaped at her. "Did you study languages in high school?"

"No." Babette smirked. "Geek subjects." Maya frowned at her. "Oh, sorry. No, languages weren't my thing."

"I don't know what language the book is written in, but it looks English to me," Maya said, a protective arm concealing the page.

"And me," Babette said.

"It's ancient Atlantean," Mom said. "There isn't another language like it. But for those who are granted the blessing of understanding, it will appear in their native language."

I smothered a sigh. I was the fire mermaid. I had broken a centuries long curse. I had discovered Atlantis. Re-discovered. I was the fucking *queen*. Shouldn't I be allowed to read the goddamn book?

Babette shoved Maya's arm away, looked at the open page and recited the words. "The united three must speak the following in the presence of the Power of the Sea to drop the veil to Atlantis...shall I go on?" She looked up expectantly.

Maya slammed the book shut and shot to her feet. "It's

not possible." She frowned down her nose at Babette. "How did you do that?"

"Uh...I'm not sure," Babette replied, her eyes flitting between us. "Shall I take another look?"

Maya cradled the book. "No, thank you."

"Maya," Trent said. "I thought you were all for this united three business and dropping the veil."

She tapped a foot on the floor. "I am."

"Then let Babette look at the book."

Maya reluctantly handed it over.

Babette sat in the chair Maya had recently vacated and flicked through the pages. "Fascinating!" she said. "Oh, so that explains..." and on her comments went as she gently fanned her way through the pages.

"Blaze, Ford," I called to my friends. A thought had occurred to me. "Can you read the book too?"

Blaze and Ford approached Babette and stood behind her. It was quickly confirmed they too could read every word within *The Mermaid Chronicles*.

"It's not possible," Maya said again. "It's just not possible."

"Actually, it's entirely possible," I said. "During the last year I've spent a fair bit of time in the blue chamber with Esmerelda. We came to know one another." I paused to allow the sadness of her death to drift through me. "She explained a few things to me."

"Such as?" Wade asked.

"You remember those strange blue screens which revealed every moment of our lives?" Wade nodded. "That's the way they received the prophecies too. The prophecies came from the Power of the Sea and the magic of Atlantis would unfold on those screens like a movie. As such, all four members of the High Council were privy to the information. But they didn't know how to warn us. You all heard Esmerelda when she was here and spoke of the hound and Aquaria. She was afraid to say too much, for in doing so would change our fate. The High Council created *The Mermaid Chronicles* as a way to pass information to us without altering our future. Using the Power of the Sea to reach the book wherever it may be, they entered their cryptic messages in enchanted Atlantean. They had to make the prophecies ambiguous so as not to alter our fates, but that also meant they needed a special interpreter. You, Maya." I took my friend's hand. "And your parents before you. You are our oracle. While the High Council remained in the blue chamber and didn't interfere in our lives until recently, it was especially important you understood the meaning of the prophecies."

"But the blue chamber doesn't exist anymore," Babette said. "So how are we supposed to see the prophecies?"

"By reading the book," I replied. "With the dissolution of the chamber and its portentous blue screens, I suspect the prophecies are entered directly into the book by the Power of the Sea."

Maya nodded. "Yes, that's been my understanding too. The blue chamber is gone, but the book continues to grow."

"Esmerelda, Shane, Edward, and Gal were able to understand the prophecies when they came to them on the blue screens. So it seems only natural that now Babette, Blaze, and Ford can also read the book."

"But I am still its protector," Maya said, her eyes shifting warily to Babette in the chair.

"Always. And its interpreter. You have a special intuition when it comes to the prophecies," I replied. "Here to warn us when bad shit is on the horizon."

"It's not all bad," she said, her eyes focusing on my stomach. I cocked an eyebrow at her.

"It's almost like we were chosen ahead of time," Ford said.

"I don't think you four could have refused the position even if you'd wanted to," I said.

"It *is* written—" Maya cut herself off with a laugh.

"Okay, enough about the High Council," Babette said. "When do we get to lifting this veil?"

"Now," Maya said, retrieving the book from Babette's hands. "You three," she pointed to Babette, Wade, and me, "hold hands."

Wade and I already were. I took Babette's. She held mine with a meaningful grip.

"Don't fuck this up, Cordy," she said.

"Now, repeat after me," Maya said. "I, of the united three." The Power of the Sea pulsed with vibrant color, its swirling hues of blue, from the palest of cornflowers to the darkest of midnights, overlapping each other, dissolving into each other to create blues I'd never seen before. "Do solemnly swear to uphold the unification of our three species and all other creatures who seek sanctuary upon Atlantis."

The three of us repeated her words. The Power of the Sea throbbed. It settled on one hue of blue, neither light nor dark, but somewhere in the middle. A blue that evoked feelings of serenity and hope. It pulsed through the air and wound around us all.

"In doing so, I put Atlantis and its inhabitants before myself and my own needs and promise to spend my days keeping this unification peaceful and total."

The three of us finished the last words and Maya snapped the book shut.

"That's it?" Wade asked.

"That's all the words," Maya replied. "Now all three of you need to touch the Power of the Sea."

The three of us turned to the pulsing, magical orb. We all stuck a finger into the swirling blue mass and smiled at each other nervously. It radiated a magnificent blue, the magical blue of the ocean, of the sky, of glacial lakes and all the blues in between. It pulsed and it emitted a soft, melodious tune that felt like Atlantis' anthem.

"It's done." Maya clapped her approval.

"I can go get my father?" Babette asked.

"You can," Maya replied.

Babette looked at Dylan. "Come with me, please."

"Of course," he replied. The two of them left the room.

"Now what?" I asked the others.

"Now we wait for the humans to arrive," Mom replied. "And Atlantis' new chapter to begin."

CHAPTER TWENTY-THREE

Boats filled the horizon. Wade and I stood on our balcony watching the humans approach.

"I wish they could have given us a few days," I said. "We need time. You need time. To mourn."

Wade shook his head. "I'm not going to mourn my mother. I spent three years in a heightened state of anxiety trying to save her from Zale and Caol and the ashrays. Every day I expected her to die. And when she came back, it was wonderful, at least until she started interfering in our relationship. But she eventually understood how much I love you. Her death has been avenged and I'm satisfied with that. Now, there's nothing more to do but celebrate her life. I'm going to think of the good times and try to live around the pain in my heart."

"Oh, Wade." I cupped his cheek and stroked his stubbled skin. "I love you so much."

"And I love you, Cordelia Waters."

"Finally," I smiled. "You call me by my proper name."

Wade gestured to the boats on the ocean. "It's time we went to greet the newcomers."

I slipped on a turquoise blue sarong dress and combed my fingers through my hair, trying to tame the wildness from it. I gave up as it curled around my face, and let it trail naturally down my back. Wade and I walked to the beach. The closest boat reminded me a little of my family's old boat, *The Big Blue.* As we wound through the cobbled paths, we held hands and waited, and were joined by Maya, Trent, Blaze, and Ford.

"We are the new High Council," Maya said. "We should be there to greet them."

"Ford," I said, craning my neck to look at him. "Can you call the Royal Guard together?"

"Is that necessary?" Trent asked. "I thought this was a peaceful union of all our species."

"On the surface," I replied. "But I think it might be prudent to be prepared, just in case."

"Cordy, if you have the entire Royal Guard down there to greet them, what kind of message is that going to send?" Maya frowned at me.

"One that we're not to be messed with," I replied. "Ford?"

"I knew you would be concerned," Ford said. "They're already on standby."

"Hold on," Maya said, her arms spread wide. "We can't have them out there in plain sight. The humans will think they're not welcome, and if I were one of them, I would wonder what kind of land I had come to if I were greeted by a couple hundred Atlantean guards. If you insist on having them present, keep them out of sight, *please.*"

I considered her words, battled against my instincts. "Okay. Ford, instruct them to stay out of sight until you give them a signal."

"*If* you give them a signal," Maya sighed. "You shouldn't have to."

"No, we shouldn't," I said.

As we walked by the Fountain of Youth, Maya removed a cup from the makeshift shelf. She filled the cup full.

"What's that for?" I narrowed my eyes at her. "An ocean shifter only needs one sip to heal them completely. Why do you need so much?"

"That all depends on you," she replied.

"On me?"

"Yes, on you and how you react."

"How I react to what?"

"There's going to be a small skirmish caused by one lone individual. His actions are not supported by the masses. You will need to let it go."

I looked from my friend to the clear liquid in the cup.

"We may only need one sip," she said.

"For an Atlantean. An Atlantean is going to be injured," I realized aloud.

"It all depends on you, Cordy," Maya said.

"Why?" I asked.

"I know this wasn't what you wanted, and right now you're an emotional muppet—I mean that in the nicest way possible—but still, an emotional muppet because your emotions are all over the place. I get it. Mine are too. But you have more reasons than most—"

"I really am," I said. "An emotional muppet."

"Don't worry, it will pass. As soon as our old enemies die hard."

"What does that mean?"

"It refers to a shifting prophecy."

"Shifting?"

Maya pointed to the cup in her hand. "Yes, shifting. Not everything is decided yet."

"Old enemies die hard? So Stephanie is coming back?"

"Not yet."

"And she's going to die? So much for a trial." Although I had wanted to kill her before, the thought of her in shackles was more appealing.

I shifted my weight from one foot to the other. The Royal Guard descended the palace steps and concealed themselves along the pathway leading to the beach. Their presence was essential. Not only to protect ourselves from any funny ideas the humans might have, but if Stephanie decided this was her opportune time to show up, we would be ready.

"It's up to you, Cordy," Maya said. "If you want to avoid another war, you need to keep your cool."

"I can do that. Now that I know."

Maya continued along the beach path, but she didn't throw out the water from the Fountain of Youth.

We followed her to the beach. A few minutes later, we arrived at the docks as the first boats entered the marina.

"Here they come." Wade reached for my hand, tugged me against his chest and wrapped an arm around my waist. I leaned back against the solid reassurance of him.

We stood on the dock, united, waiting for the one person who made us the united three. Babette stood at the bow of the leading boat, her face a neutral mask, her blonde hair whipping in the wind.

The boat arrived. My stomach knotted. I squeezed Wade's hand. Flames darted over my fingers, which I had to consciously will away.

The boat moored into a slip. Babette jumped onto the jetty. Her father came behind her. They walked the length of the floating platform and turned toward us and the beach. Dylan emerged from the water with a squeaking Flipper. The dolphin splashed us all with water and then leaped high into the air. Babette giggled. After rubbing its snout, Dylan waded out of the water to meet us and slung a dripping wet arm around Babette's shoulders. She didn't seem to mind.

When they drew close, Babette threw an object at me. "Catch, Cordy." I caught the object. It was my old Navy cap.

"Where did you find this?" I asked.

"Dylan did," she replied.

"I made a detour," Dylan said.

"Thank you," I said, placing the cap on my head and giving my brother a hug. "Eww, you're still wet."

"I think he's managed to dry most of himself off on me," Babette said, gesturing to her soaking wet clothes. Dylan pulled her into our hug. My skin prickled. I never thought Babette and I would share a hug.

"Welcome." Wade offered a hand to Rob.

Rob shook Wade's hand as his gaze drifted to the palace towering behind us and the city beyond. "This certainly is some island."

I remembered my first glimpse of Atlantis, when everything

had fallen to ruin, and the columns were broken and the plant life was dying and the whole thing was drowned under three feet of water. And then the transformation. It was breathtaking; the purity, the perfection of it all. It was indescribable. And the feeling had ballooned in my chest until I thought I might faint or explode or implode or something with the incredulity of it all.

Rob dropped to his knees. "Thank you."

Wade chuckled. "There's no need for all that. I haven't even got my crown on today."

Rob remained on his knees.

"I can go grab the red carpet if it will make you feel more comfortable?" Trent chuckled.

Babette laughed. "Get up, Dad. Your daughter is on the High Council, remember?"

Wade socked Trent's shoulder, then turned to Rob. "We're very casual here on the island. Please do get up."

Rob rose to his feet and struck his fist against his chest. "I may have helped you in the past, but we couldn't have fought against the hound without each other, and I wouldn't have a second chance at life, with my daughter, without all of this. I'm eternally grateful and indebted to you. I will serve you in any capacity you wish."

Wade put a hand on each of Rob's shoulders. "Rob, this is your land now too. That's what being united means."

Rob nodded. "Still, it's all so much."

"I know," Wade agreed. "And if you want to help, I can't think of anything better for you than building the Atlantean army. Ford is joining the ranks of the High Council and we need a leader for our united army. If you could train *our* people together, from the bottom up, I would be indebted to you."

"There is only Stephanie left to deal with," Babette said, a hand on her hip. "She is one person. No more war, right?"

I thought of the Royal Guard hidden in bushes and behind the vine-covered columns that lined the path to the beach. I glanced at the cup of healing water in Maya's hands. It was all going so well. But she had spoken of a skirmish.

"For now," Maya said.

Babette frowned. "For now?"

"You've seen *The Mermaid Chronicles*," Maya said. "You know how it works."

"It changes," Babette said. "Every decision of every being on this island affects the future of Atlantis and the people in it."

"Exactly," Maya said. "The prophecies are the collective output of our inhabitants' decisions. Some predictions the book is very sure of, others need further clarification from future decisions to become more obvious or to be fully understood." She looked from the cup in her hand to me and flashed me a tentative smile. "Some prophecies are so out of scope that the book doesn't even bother informing us of it, or if it does, very loosely. For now, there is nothing written in the pages of *The Mermaid Chronicles* that affects our immediate future, but we should always be watchful."

Old enemies die hard.

Rob looked her up and down for a few seconds. Finally, he turned to Wade. "I'd be honored to build and train an army. With a weapon like this book of yours, we'd be undefeatable."

"It's not a weapon," Maya whispered.

"Thank you." Wade stuck his hand out again. "Now, let's get the rest of your people ashore."

Rob waved to the boat. Other vessels docked in the marina. People disembarked from Rob's boat and walked along the dock. Most shook hands with us and thanked us before they approached the beach.

"How are they all going to fit?" I asked Wade as the last boat docked. I turned to look at the palace. Not only were the rounded roofs stretching higher into the sky, but the entire island was growing. The city expanded, and the mountains and hills beyond that. It grew and enlarged until our island was big enough to accommodate us all. That was the magic of Atlantis.

When the last stragglers left the final boat and began the walk along the jetty, I glanced at the cup in Maya's hand. I cut my gaze to the last clump of approaching people. A man hovered at the back. He was trying to dodge around those in front. His right arm swung wildly while he kept his left glued to his side.

The metal of a gun winked under the strong sun. Before I could raise an alarm or evoke my flames, he fired six rapid-fire shots at us, at Wade.

The bullets sped by my cheek, singed my hair, drew blood along the top of my shoulder. Wade ducked as bullets whizzed over his head. Close. Too close.

A member of the Royal Guard leaped from the bushes, clutching his arm. Maya rushed to his side and made him sip from the cup. He was instantly healed.

Maya rose and drew close to me. Flames twitched at my fingertips.

"You don't need those," she said.

But I could only focus on the man. Gun abandoned, he stood in the middle of the dock.

Fear swarmed over my skin. Anger heated my eyes. How could I have been so stupid as to let the one species who had persecuted us onto our island? Why had I ever thought it was a good idea?

I stared at the would-be assassin. Ford grabbed the gun from the ground and wrestled the man's arm behind his back. The rest of the Royal Guard emerged from their hiding places and marched to the beach.

Babette crossed her arms, an angry line forming across her forehead. "What the hell is this?"

"A response to that." I pointed at the now handcuffed man.

"And then what? Are you going to kill him right here on the beach?"

"He tried to kill Wade!"

"I'm okay, Cordelia, there's been no harm done," Wade said. He caught one of my hands and recoiled. I had burned him with my flames. But I was too angry to apologize, too angry to see if he was okay.

"No harm done? He could have killed you!" I pushed my hands behind my back and glared at my husband, at the High Council, and at Babette. "This is exactly what I was afraid of. This is what I told you would happen."

"I'm so sorry," Rob said. "We vetted everyone before they boarded, but well, with the lack of resources, maybe it wasn't thorough enough. I'm sorry. This should never have happened. Rest assured; he will be dealt with."

"I'm okay," Wade said, sucking on the burn on his hand. "A little shaken, but okay." He pushed the cup in Maya's hand toward me, made me sip until the line of blood on my shoulder was healed.

"That was too close," I said to him.

"What were you going to do with the Royal Guard, Cordelia?" Babette asked.

"They were here for Stephanie," I half lied.

Babette clicked her tongue in her cheek. "So why were they hiding?"

The man resisted Ford's hold as our guard pushed him toward us.

"Just a precaution," I said. "A precaution I hoped wouldn't be needed. I'm not happy I was right."

"It's one person," Maya said.

"Stephanie is one person," I said.

"Look, Cordelia." Maya gestured to the beach where the humans had gathered, watching us, watching the man in Ford's captivity. Fearful whispers hurried from mouth to mouth. They were scared. Because of me.

I glanced at Blaze. There was no sign of his fire, but he stood tall, his wings outstretched, signaling his differences and his strength.

The Royal Guard stood in a line, weapons at their sides, ready for my order.

"Are you sure there won't be any more protestors?" I asked Rob. But I was looking at Maya. The weight of her stare caught my attention. Flames remained on my fingers.

She shook her head. She hadn't collected the Fountain of Youth until I'd decided to bring the Royal Guard to the beach. An Atlantean was hurt. It could have been Wade. And then my fury would have known no bounds.

"I'm sorry I burned you," I said to Wade.

"S'okay," he replied. "I'm okay."

I made him drink until he was healed. "It's not okay. I'm sorry."

Ford arrived with the accused man.

"We don't have a jail here on Atlantis," Wade said to him. "And we can't exactly allow you to roam the streets freely now, considering your actions."

"You killed my friend." The man spat at Wade's feet. "At the camp."

"What friend?" Wade asked.

The man's eyes turned stormier than the ocean. "My best friend."

Wade laid a hand on his shoulder. "I'm truly sorry. I was protecting my family and my island."

The man said nothing. He glared at Wade, then spat in his face.

With exaggerated slowness, Wade wiped the spittle from his cheek.

"If you don't mind," Rob said, snapping his heels together. "I have a suggestion."

"I'm all ears," Wade replied.

"Let's send him back to the mainland. I'll take him back myself."

Wade considered, his head tilted thoughtfully.

"No," I said. "He could sail back here and try again."

"I think we should consider it," Maya said.

"I've already got one threat hanging over my head. I don't need another," I said.

Babette faced me. "Have you got another suggestion?"

I chewed on my lip as my flames danced on my fingers. "No."

"Trust me, Cordelia," Rob said. "Let me take care of this."

I stared at the ocean, the beach, the gathered humans. "On your head be it."

Rob took the man from Ford's hold and marched him back to a boat. The two of them boarded. I could see Rob shouting at the man and clipping him around the head. The man, with a steely look in his eyes, remained quiet.

"That was close," Trent said, once the boat had pulled away. He nudged me. "For a minute there, I thought you were going to go all flame-on."

I blew on my fingers and the flames winked out.

"I'll say," Babette said. "I thought I was going to have to relinquish my position on the High Council. And I've so been looking forward to it."

"Not on account of me." I smiled pleasantly, ignoring the challenge in her tone.

Babette marched away, calling to her people, leading them up the beach and toward the palace. The rest of us followed.

Wade drew close. "You okay?"

"I'm uneasy."

"We've been through this."

"I can't help the way I feel."

"Maya would tell us if there was a problem. You know she would."

"I know," I whispered. "But Maya doesn't know everything. And some things are too far in the future to predict with accuracy, but I can still feel it coming in my gut."

"You're going to drive yourself crazy if you keep waiting for the next disaster."

I stopped in the sand, took my husband's hand. "There will always be a next disaster, so I might as well prepare for it."

Wade's selachii eyes flashed. "Cordy, you can't live like that."

"You lost your mother, Trent his parents, Maya her foster family...so many people have lost so much. I won't allow any more loss. Not if I can help it."

CHAPTER TWENTY-FOUR

I prowled the beach every morning looking for signs of Stephanie. I couldn't imagine life returning to normal until she had been dealt with. She was patient, clever, and knew how to bide her time. But I would be waiting.

The sand whirled around me in a sudden gust and Blaze landed next to me where the water met the beach.

"You wanted to talk to me?"

"I did," I said. "Are you settling in okay?"

Blazed pulled his wings close and sat in the sand, burying his feet. "I am. I've never lived anywhere so beautiful."

"I'm glad you like it."

Blaze poured sand over his feet. "Does everyone get the personal touch from the royal couple?"

I smiled. "Not everyone."

"But I'm special."

"You know you are." I sat next to him and drew circles in the sand. "I loved your father. I still do."

"I know," Blaze replied, his gaze locked on the horizon.

We sat shoulder to shoulder, our arms brushing, content in the comfortable silence between us, listening to the sound of breaking waves.

"And I can't help but have strong feelings for you too."

"And I you," he said, nudging me gently with his elbow.

"But I know so little about you."

"And I so much about you." He smiled. His lips were lopsided, lending him a mischievousness that warmed my insides. "The one time I saw my father in the last twenty years, he couldn't talk of anything but you. It was before you two had officially met. But he had been watching you from the High Council's chambers. He knew you would be the one to break the curse."

"I did."

"I know."

"Why did you only see him the once?"

"Because he was a member of the High Council. He couldn't come out often."

"Didn't that bother you? That he chose the council over you?" I cringed at the bluntness of my words, but then Blaze was a man who appreciated the hard truth.

Blaze rubbed a hand over his broad chest. "I don't see it that way. He would have died quickly if he'd chosen to live with me outside the protective blue chamber. I understood that."

"But he did come outside. He came out to help me."

"You needed help. He saved your life."

"He did."

"And I'm glad." Blaze looked at me, his eyes full of fire. "Because in you, I have a little of him."

"And in you, I have a little of him too."

Blaze blew a small flame from his mouth. It skipped across the water like a stone, finally sinking several yards out. "The better part of my parentage."

"Was Aquaria always a sea witch?"

Blaze shook his head. "She was once a mermaid. A mermaid who fell in love with a dragon king and got pregnant."

"And then what?"

"Although my father spent brief visits in the human world, he wouldn't relinquish his duties to the High Council. My mother was...upset. Furious. She cursed them all. Her anger was her strength; her curses always came true. She cursed them to their blue chamber, unable to leave without aging rapidly in the outside world. That action secured my mother's path in becoming a sea witch."

"But Gal left when he needed to. To see you."

"And to help you," Blaze said.

"So you were left with your mother."

Blaze snorted and a lick of flame sparked out of his nostrils. "I left my mother's den as soon as I could. I think I was about seven, in human terms."

"How did you escape?"

"It took a few attempts." Blaze wrapped his arms around his knees. "I didn't notice the evilness in her at first. The changes had been so gradual; the hair darkening and then wriggling with snakes. It was only one snake to start with, then more and more, until I thought they might have always been there. But finally, I took one long look at her and realized she wasn't the same. Her anger had consumed her."

"I'm sorry, Blaze."

"Each time I ran away, she brought me back." He scooped a handful of sand and poured it over one knee. "I still wanted a mother."

"Everyone needs their mother," I said, thinking of when Zale had ripped mine from me so violently. I often pictured Zale's jaws wrapped around her ankles, tugging her mercilessly into the ocean. It still filled my dreams.

"I left for good several years ago, when her sister attacked the merfolk in Australia. My mother helped her. I'd had enough of her malicious ways, and I told her so. After that, I caught the occasional glimpse of her. Sometimes we'd talk. But she knew to leave me alone."

"All because Gal wouldn't stay with her?"

Blaze shook his head. "She would tell you that. My father would tell you that, such was his guilt. But it was all her. They were her evil decisions to make and only hers."

"Like Stephanie," I said.

"We'll find her."

"I'm scouting the island every day."

"And me."

"Maybe if I'd treated her differently..." I recalled the day she and Jordan left to climb the mountain, before the storm had tried to obliterate our island and everyone had feared her dead. I had noticed the darkening of her hair and dismissed it as a stylistic venture. If I'd looked a little closer or paid a little more attention, maybe I would have seen she was beginning to transition into a sea witch. But I was glad Stephanie hadn't been in my life during the past year. I was relieved she had finally decided to let Wade and me be. I hadn't sought her out, I hadn't checked to see if she was okay. She had her own friends to lean on. How woefully ignorant I had been of the growing grudge she carried with her every day, plotting our demise.

"It's not your fault," Blaze said. "It wasn't my dad's fault with my mother, and what Stephanie has become isn't your fault either."

I tilted my face to the sun and let the warmth ease the tension from my cheeks. "There's something I want to ask you."

"I had a feeling you didn't call me here just to hear my life story," Blaze said, now pouring sand over my feet.

"It's of a delicate nature." I wrapped my arms around my stomach. "No one else knows yet. You must keep it a secret."

"I'm intrigued." Blaze shifted his weight to face me. His wings hovered above our heads and seemed to hide us from the surrounding world. "I think we're safe under here."

I laughed and placed a hand on his arm. "If it's okay with you, I'd like to use Gal's name. I'd like to call my son Gal."

Blaze's eyes widened. "You're pregnant?"

"I think so," I said, cradling my stomach. "I can feel him." I pressed the palm of my hand against my stomach. There wasn't a bulge yet. But it wouldn't be long.

"And you know it's a boy?"

"I do," I replied, raising my eyes to his face once again.

"I'd be honored for him to have my father's name." There were tears in his eyes, and he did something surprising then, something I'd expect only Wade to do. He placed a hand on my stomach and followed it with a gentle kiss. But it felt right. He was Gal's son. He was family.

"I haven't even told Wade yet," I said.

"I understand. I'll keep your secret."

"I haven't found the right time. I tried once, back on the mainland, right after we met you. But I was so tired, and he told me to go to sleep, and for once I did what he told me."

"You will." Blaze patted my hand. "And this little guy will make himself known soon enough."

During the following week, our new inhabitants settled into the island. The healthy among them were assigned new residences and found jobs to occupy themselves, as well as to keep our island functioning. Those sick with radiation poisoning were nursed in a large wing of the palace until a hospital could be built. With the existence of the Fountain of Youth, no Atlantean had needed a hospital before.

After my daily walks searching for signs of Stephanie's reappearance, often in the company of Blaze, I spent the afternoons in the hospital tending to the sick. Raina and I spent several of those afternoons together, making up for lost time.

Many died the first night, perhaps having only waited to reach Atlantis so they could die in a place with dignity. There were more deaths on the second and third nights. After that, the mortality rate slowed as the remaining patients adapted to their new surroundings.

Statues of the old High Council were erected along the main path to the beach. Esmeralda wore the mermaid brooch at her neck, Shane held the Power of the Sea in his hands, Edward stood with a smaller version of the Power of the Sea ready to hurl at the unrepresented hound, and then there was Gal. He stood taller than the rest, his stone wings unfurled, giving the impression he could fly, when in reality he couldn't. I spent time with them every day.

"Life is returning to normal," Maya said during a meeting of the High Council.

Babette poked her finger into the swirling mass of the Power of the Sea. "Perhaps we should host a celebration. To honor those we lost and welcome those we gained."

Ford frowned.

"Stephanie is still out there," I said. "And if we start relaxing and partying, I can guarantee you, she will find a way to ruin it."

"Unless she's finally learned her lesson." Wade hovered by my side. Ever since we'd returned, whenever we occupied the same room, he was rarely beyond touching distance. The war had shaken both of us, and we needed the physical reassurance of each other's presence. "Maybe she'll stay away."

"You know her better than that." I squeezed his hand.

"Hell, maybe she's already dead," Babette said.

"I'm not concluding that until I see a body," I said.

Babette's penciled eyebrows rose high. "We can't sit around twiddling our thumbs."

"Maya, what does the book say?" I asked.

All eyes swiveled in her direction.

Maya sighed. "That as long as Stephanie is free, she is a threat."

"Let me see that." Babette wrestled the book out of Maya's arms and flipped to the relevant page. "For fuck's sake."

"The problem is, it doesn't give us a timeline," Maya said. "So I say we get on with life. Rob is training the army. They can keep an eye out for anything during the party."

"It's too dangerous," I said.

"Cordy." Wade touched my arm. "Our people need some light relief."

"And how am I supposed to keep them safe when there's a murderous sea witch planning an ambush?"

"You don't know that," Babette said.

"Yes, I do."

"It's not only your responsibility." Wade's hand rested on my hips. "You have me, the High Council, the army. Ford."

"We need this," Maya said. "I need this. Trent needs it. Your sister needs it, and your parents. Come on, Cordy, it will be okay."

"Maya is right." Babette got up in my face. "I lost my mother and sister. Most of the people in my camp lost their entire families. We need closure. We need something to give us hope." She threw a hand at me. "You, you get your whole family. And you *gained* a sister."

Tension ran through my jaw. "Make no mistake. I am well versed in grief. I spent five years mourning the loss of my mother and twin brother. I know about grief, Babette."

"Yeah, but the rest of us didn't get our families back."

"Having them back doesn't make the trauma go away."

"Cordy, Babette, please," Wade said, a hand tugging at my curls—his way of telling me to shut up. "We're united, remember?"

"Uh-huh," I muttered.

"I'm not likely to forget," Babette said.

There was a party. My anxiety didn't leave during the preparations. If anything, it worsened. Was this what life held for me now? Always looking over my shoulder? Or was it the pregnancy hormones running rife in my body? Either way, I was a nervous wreck. I didn't sleep for the entire week the party was prepared. I spent the mornings stalking the beach, the afternoons in the hospital, the evenings in the great hall trying to understand *The Mermaid Chronicles* for myself, and most of the nights staring out of my window at the ocean. Waiting. Waiting for Stephanie.

During the celebration, Wade put food on my plate, which I didn't eat. Dylan put champagne in my glass, which I didn't drink. I sat with my family and stared at the flame of the single candle on our table. Blaze flew overhead, lighting new torches Trent had built to line the pathways and water channels. The lanterns hung from cables crisscrossing the roofs of Atlantis, and the total effect showed a city in competition with the stars.

My mother, father, and sister managed an easy conversation, perhaps to make up for my quietness. Dylan and Babette whispered to each other across the table. It didn't escape my notice that his glass held only sparkling water.

"It's beautiful," Raina remarked as she watched Blaze soar through the sky.

"The lights, or Blaze?" I asked.

She grinned. "Both."

We commemorated the High Council, both old and new. The toasts carried on until we ran out of things to toast for. I knew of one more, but I needed Wade alone. Our champagne glasses were empty. Dylan fetched another bottle. He filled Babette's, but didn't touch his own. He lit a cigarette and muttered something about the Fountain of Youth not being able to cure addiction. But it was enough for now. One step at a time.

Babette was responsible for pulling my brother out of his deep, dark hole of misery. She was responsible for tempering his drinking. I didn't think Babette and I would ever see eye-to-eye, but I would always hold her in the highest esteem for saving my brother.

The celebrations continued as the band struck up. I couldn't focus on the conversation, but kept my eyes trained on the shadows.

Wade put a hand on my thigh. "Relax, Cordy, the Guard is on watch."

"Hmmm," I muttered.

"There's new changes in the book," Maya announced across the table.

I stared at her. "Stephanie."

"Nothing new about her," Maya replied. "This is good stuff."

"Good?" Raina asked, giving me an encouraging smile.

"I can't believe you haven't told me yet." Maya winked at me. "I'm putting in my request for godmother now."

I lurched upright. It took Wade a few seconds, then his mouth fell open.

"Huh?" he stuttered, then stared at me, his gaze falling to my stomach. "You're *pregnant*?"

"You didn't know?" Maya asked Wade. "Shit, I'm sorry, Cordy. I thought he knew."

Shaking his head, Wade clutched the table.

"It's okay, Maya. I've only recently realized myself," I said. "How did you know?"

Maya rolled her eyes. "It's written in the book."

"Naturally," I said.

"You're pregnant?" Wade asked again, his hand reaching for my stomach. It was still flat, no outward sign I carried a child within me.

Mom pressed tears out of the corners of her eyes with a fingertip. "Oh, Cordelia. That's wonderful. Chris, isn't that wonderful?"

Dad beamed at me. Wade's eyes filled with tears, and he swept me onto his lap and wrapped his arms tightly around me.

"You're happy?" I asked.

"Of course, Cordelia Blue. I couldn't be happier."

"It's a boy," I said to my husband. My index finger suddenly sprouted one weak flame. Wade smiled and blew it out.

"It is," Maya said. "And you being pregnant also explains why your fire power has been a little wonky."

"A *little* wonky? It won't appear when I want it and it explodes across the room when I don't, or I'm mad or scared or emotional." I looked at my fingers, expecting them all to have flickered into life, but they remained oddly normal. "You see? Nothing!"

"Exactly," Maya agreed. "Your emotions and hormones are going to be in turmoil for the next few months."

I sighed. "Maybe I need to wear gloves."

"There's no need for that," Wade said, and kissed the finger that had recently exhibited a flame. "You'll get the hang of it again."

"And his name?" Maya asked. "I'm assuming Wade doesn't know that either."

"He has a name already?" Wade's eyes flashed selachii black. "Was I around when that decision was made?"

"Wade, if it's okay with you, I'd like to call our son Gal."

He smiled. "That's perfect."

"It is," Maya said. "It's written."

"I think it's time for *our* news now," Trent said.

I leaned across the table. "News?"

Maya thrust her left hand in our faces. A brilliant diamond ring sparkled on her ring finger.

"Congratulations." Wade slapped Trent on the back. "You kept that quiet, buddy."

"I'm happy for you," I said. "For both of you."

As I leaned around the table to hug Maya, something dropped from the sky and landed in the middle of the table. A snake. A long, black, evil, venomous snake.

"Stephanie," I said.

CHAPTER TWENTY-FIVE

"Stephanie!" someone screamed.

Another snake zoomed through the sky, taking a chunk out of Raina's cheek. Blaze flew in circles overhead, but couldn't risk his flames hurting the Atlanteans.

Jordan appeared at our table, a scowl severe enough to cut glass. "Where is she?"

The air became alive with the sound of violent hissing as snakes flew through the darkness and targeted their victims. But I couldn't locate Stephanie. Jordan and I stood back-to-back, studying the screaming crowd as they toppled tables and hopped over fallen chairs. Plates and glasses smashed to the floor as people dove and ducked for cover.

Jordan removed a large hunting knife from an inner pocket.

"Where did you get that?" I asked, as I attempted to will my flames into existence, but my firepower wasn't listening.

"I have my ways," he replied.

Wade stood by my side, his hand resting on my stomach. "We need to get you inside."

"Not until Stephanie is dealt with," I replied.

Wade yanked my arm, tugging me against his chest. "I can't lose you. I can't lose our child."

A snake flew past his hair, snapping at his cheek, and lodged onto Trent's hand. Screaming, his eyes bulged, and his veins turned black.

"Get to the fountain!" someone yelled.

"Go, Jordan." Maya pointed him toward the beach. "Go now. I need to get Trent to the fountain."

Jordan took off, both arms pumping, the knife glinting in the moonlight. I ran after him, and Wade ran after me, calling for me to stop.

I needed to see Stephanie for myself. I needed to see her arrested, thrown in a dungeon with nothing to keep her company but diseased rats.

We found her on one of the cobbled paths, the main one that wound from the beach to the courtyard.

She stood her ground, her black eyes focused, her snake hair seething with rage.

"Stephanie," Wade called to her.

Her snakes hissed, dozens taking flight from her scalp and streaming toward the party. "Wade."

"We need to talk," Wade said.

Stephanie took a couple of steps in our direction, but remained at a safe distance. She was well acquainted with Wade's strength and my flames. She wasn't stupid. And Jordan stood in front of her with the large, gleaming hunting knife.

"I don't think so," she replied. "We've said all we're ever going to say to each other."

I slipped my hand into Wade's and gave it a gentle squeeze.

Jordan jabbed at the space between him and the sea witch. "There were so many things I wanted to say to you, so many things I wanted you to understand, but now that you're here...what does it matter anymore?"

Stephanie laughed.

"This is about me," Wade said.

"Don't flatter yourself, Wade-y," Stephanie snapped.

"Have you ever loved anyone, or is what you see in the mirror enough for you?" Jordan asked. "It's not pretty."

Her eyes cut to Wade.

"You told me you loved me," Wade said, a hand on his chest. "But this isn't love, Stephanie."

Her black eyes filled with midnight. "Not anymore. Now it's about revenge."

"Just because I didn't love you back?" Wade asked. "Come on, Steph."

"Don't call me that," she snarled.

"Look at you. You're disgusting." Jordan raised the knife.

"Jordan," Wade said. "No one has to die here tonight."

He looked at us over his shoulder. "I never promised that."

Stephanie settled her bug black eyes on me. "You won't take me willingly."

"Fine with me," Jordan growled.

"What are you doing here?" I asked, finally producing a flame on my hands. "What do you want?"

Her smile widened. "You can hurt me, but it won't be over. Yours is coming."

"What have you done, Stephanie?" Wade asked, daring a few steps closer.

She coiled a hissing snake around her finger like it was no more than a strand of hair. "Wouldn't you like to know?"

Her snakes hissed. Atlanteans screamed. Chaos ruled behind our backs. How many humans had been hurt? How many had poison streaming through their veins that the fountain could not help?

"I didn't bother calling on Scylla and Charybdis, seeing how easily you dispatched my hound," Stephanie said. "But I have other friends, other beasts to do my bidding. Let's see... have I called on the great kraken, the most formidable creature of the sea? Or perhaps where Aquaria failed, Calypso will succeed. The Irish selkies, or the blue men of Minch may come to my aid. And there's always the Lady of the Lake." She tapped a finger against her jaw and her snakes hissed with approval. "If I'm feeling particularly vengeful, there are always the ghost pirates." She leveled a look at my stomach. Did she know? How could she? "So many choices. Or perhaps I just wanted to come home." She stopped pacing and faced us.

"There's no place for you here," Wade said, shaking his head sadly. "I thought perhaps there was...at one time...that you would see the error of your ways and could be forgiven. But I see that's not possible anymore."

"You deserve to die," Jordan yelled as a gust of wind plucked at his clothing.

Sand stung my eyes, bit at my bare legs. Tore at the flames on my fingers.

"What? Does Atlantis have the death penalty now?" Stephanie sneered.

Before anyone could answer her, Jordan lunged with the knife. My flames burned on my hands, but there was little I could do to stop Jordan without hurting him. I was about to shout a warning when Maya appeared and grabbed my wrist, earning a scorch mark along her arm.

"Shit," she squealed.

I turned to my friend, one eye on Jordan. "I'm so sorry, but why did you—"

"Jordan!" Wade called, leaping after his cousin.

Jordan lunged and stabbed the knife into the center of Stephanie's chest. Her snakes hissed, biting his arm as he buried the blade between her ribs.

"Jordan, *please,*" Stephanie begged as black blood dripped from her mouth. Her hands covered his around the hilt of the knife.

The snakes bit him. Again and again. Finally, he let go of the knife and dropped to his knees. Someone went for the Fountain of Youth.

Stephanie stared at us. "I didn't think..." her words came out in a gurgle. The snakes remained on her head, wriggling with a new intensity, inspecting the blood pouring from her mouth and chest. She yanked on the hilt of the knife and removed the blade, dropped it in the sand, then fell to her knees. Clutching her hands against her chest, she attempted to stem the blood from the fatal wound.

Color leached from her face. Black snakes wriggled free

from her hair, fell to the ground, and buried themselves in the sand. Her hair returned to blonde. She lifted one bloodied finger and pointed at Jordan. Silent words spilled from her lips that had no impact. She fell, face first, into the sand. By the time Wade and I reached her she was dead.

Jordan sat in the sand only a few feet from her body. His eyes registered shock.

"I killed her," Jordan said. "And I'd do it again." He dropped sideways and his body convulsed under the effects of the poison.

Stephanie's blood puddled in the sand, turning it black and releasing a reeking odor. Her blank black eyes remained fixed on the ocean.

Maya poured water from the fountain into Jordan's mouth, ceasing his convulsions and eradicating the poison from his body.

"Is Trent okay?" I asked Maya.

She nodded and took her own sip of magic water, her arm healing instantly.

"Is that the end of it?" I asked, staring at Stephanie's body. "All those creatures she mentioned..."

"There's a page on each and every one of them in *The Mermaid Chronicles*," Maya said. "I can show you if you like. Every single ocean creature, but that doesn't mean they're coming after us."

"It doesn't mean they're not."

STRANGELY, Stephanie's death did little to ease my anxiety. It built daily until I had frequent panic attacks. Maybe it was trauma, everything I had been through, the uncertainty that still hovered over me, the child in my womb. I refused to let any harm come to him. I needed to prepare.

"Everything is okay," Wade said to me one night as we readied ourselves for bed. "With Stephanie's death, closure and peace have been brought to our island."

I sat next to him on the bed. "I know her death was hard for you."

He rubbed his hand across his thigh. "I accepted a long time ago that she had changed. That I could no longer trust her." He shook his head. "But I never expected her to go this far. I never thought she would..."

"You think the best of people." I held his hand. "It's one of the things I love about you."

He ran a hand through his hair, fiddled with his wedding ring. "It's what's got us into trouble before. I won't let that happen again."

"We're in it together."

"We are," he said, facing me. "So please tell me what's on your mind. In sickness and in health, the good times and the bad, remember?"

I mustered a smile. "I know."

"Cordelia? I wasn't kidding when I took my vows. I love you. I love you inside and out, to the moon and back. I'm not doing this without you, so spill. Now."

My Wade. We had been through so much. Overcome so many obstacles just to be together. Nothing could tear us apart. He was my life.

"I can't explain it. But I have a bad feeling," I said. "We lost five humans during Stephanie's attack."

"The fountain can't protect them."

"There are grumblings," I said. "They don't think it's fair."

"It's not."

"But there's nothing we can do about it. There's nothing in the book to suggest the fountain can be altered to work for humans too."

"Maybe there will be in the future."

"Maybe," I said. "But I think we need to watch our backs."

He pulled away to look at me. "You're still worried about the humans being here?"

"Not so much." I stroked the small swelling in my stomach. "I don't know what I'm worried about. I have a bad feeling I can't put my finger on."

"Do you think it's something to do with our son?" Wade asked, his hands folded in his lap, his eyes on my minute bump.

"Yes, I'm sure of it." I frowned. "How could it not be?"

Wade stood, all pretense at placating me gone. "We've started training the new army. I'm impressed with the recruits, and I'm impressed with Rob. You know he's a martial arts expert too?"

I nodded. "You and I and Blaze are more powerful than any Atlantean army."

"Well then," he said. "That should give you comfort. We can protect our son."

"It should," I said. "But it doesn't." I tried to imagine what could defeat me. What would I be so afraid of that I would be unable to use my powers, unable through fear or because I was incapacitated? Did it make a difference which?

"Talk to Maya," Wade said. "Let's talk to her in the morning and see what she says. But Cordy, if she says there's nothing in the book, you've got to let this go, okay? You need rest during this pregnancy. Not stress."

"Yeah, sure," I said absently as I crawled into bed.

Neither of us slept. Wade shuffled around, his breathing erratic and irregular. My words, my concerns, had frightened him.

The next morning, Wade and I were due for a meeting with the High Council and the new senate. Babette, Maya, Blaze, and Ford all sat at a table flanking the side of the marble fireplace. My mother was the head of the senate, and she assembled her new recruits. Trent, Marina, and surprisingly Jordan, sat at another table together with my mother. Wade had suggested Jordan's appointment to my mother. She had liked the idea immediately and thought it would be a good distraction for him. The senate were tasked with the policy and government of the island, the High Council everything else.

Apart from Wade, Maya, my mother, and I, no one knew Jordan was responsible for Stephanie's death. We thought it better that way.

Wade and I sat in two chairs in the middle of the two tables. We were the King and Queen of Atlantis and would preside over all matters of the senate, the High Council and thus, Atlantis. The Power of the Sea swirled atop its marble pillar in the center of the room. I couldn't concentrate on any of the matters discussed; the dungeons that had been discovered off one of the underground tunnels, the new police force that would work in conjunction with the new army, the hospital that had sprung up and how humans were bringing in medical supplies from the mainland, and as much as I loved the idea of a yearly celebration which we would call the Day of Unification, my mind was elsewhere. Wade's father had returned to the water and promised to report of any news from the seas.

When the meeting was over, the senate and the High Council filed out of the room. Wade took my hand. "Let's talk to her now."

Tension wound through my muscles. "Maya, can you stay?"

She looked at us, then retraced her steps. She sat on a chair in front of us. "What's up?"

"We have a few questions for you," Wade said. He glanced at the door to check it was closed. "Just for you. This conversation doesn't leave this room, understood?"

"Of course," Maya said.

"Cordy's worried about our son."

Maya half rose. "Has something happened?"

"I'm fine," I said. "The baby is fine. For now. I'd like him to remain that way."

"What can I do?" Maya asked.

"Have you read anything in the book?" Wade looked directly into her eyes. "Anything at all that shows he might be in danger sometime in the future?"

Maya shook her head. "No, nothing."

I leaned closer to my friend. "I was there on the beach

when you explained to Rob and Babette about the book, about its scaled probabilities. That it can hint at future events."

"That's true." She fidgeted in the chair.

"I need to know. Everything." My thumbs chased each other in my lap, tiny sparks shooting from my fingertips. "If there's anything at all, I need to know. I couldn't bear it if anything happened to him." Anxiety swarmed up my throat, causing a painful lump. "I need to know."

Maya edged closer. "I would never keep anything from you. You know that."

"I know." Tears pricked. "My emotions are all over the place right now."

"It's not only your responsibility to keep him safe." Maya moved to the edge of my chair. "You've chosen me and Trent and Blaze to be his godparents. It's our job, as well as yours, to guide him and keep him safe. Plus, he has loving grandparents and two extremely tough aunts and a don't-mess-with-me uncle. With all of that..." she trailed off and averted her gaze.

"With all what?" Wade asked, his arm tightening around me. "What is it, Maya?"

"It's too soon," she said. "There are things in the book, but it's too early. We could prepare for one eventuality ten years in the future. But the likelihood is it will change another ten times along the way. We'd exhaust ourselves trying to prepare. You need to trust me. I will guide you when I know it's the right time."

"But there is *something*," I said. Fear sapped the air from my lungs.

"There is going to be several years of peace," Maya replied, holding both my hands. "That I can guarantee you without a doubt. Your marriage may have been linked to Stephanie's attack and the Hound of the Ocean, but as a result of that battle, we are rewarded with peace." She met my eyes. Hers were fierce and determined. She was telling the truth.

"Can't you give me a clue?"

"Not yet." Maya frowned. "I'm worried if I say too much, it will change things for the worse. Give it time. Give *me* time."

"I don't know how to do that," I said.

"We don't have a choice," she replied.

"Cordy," Wade said gently. "I think we can let this go for now. Our son will be safe. We'll make sure of it. He has so much love and protection around him, how could he not be safe?"

"Wade's right, Cordy," Maya said. "We have years of peace to enjoy. Please stop worrying."

There was nothing more she could tell us. I had to put my faith in her. Her and the High Council.

"Thank you, Maya." I hugged her. "I'm okay now."

She kissed my cheek before she left the room.

"Are you *really* okay?" Wade asked.

"Of course not," I replied. I threw small flames from my fingers at the logs in the fireplace and watched them come to life. The morning was cool, the sun refusing to penetrate the palace windows to chase away the shadows or my fears. But the fire did nothing to warm my soul. I stared at the flames for a long time.

"Do you feel any better at all?"

"No." I leaned back in the large wing chair.

"Neither do I," he said.

I blanched. "You're worried?"

"Yeah." He prodded the armrests, making a jerky rhythm with his fingers. "I believe everything Maya had to say."

"So do I. I don't doubt her for a moment."

"But I also trust your instincts, Cordelia. You've always been special to the merfolk, and the Atlanteans. Esmerelda told you as much. And you may be unable to see the prophecies like the High Council can, but I trust your instincts."

"I wish I had something more concrete than a gut feeling to go on."

"You'll get there." He kissed the back of my hand. "You've always had a knack for our world and how it works."

"You think so? One day, I just found myself in the middle of it. Since then, I've always felt like I'm the one trying to catch up."

"No. The rest of us have been playing catch up to you. You have a certain intuition which I've come to respect and rely on."

"Even when they told me you'd stolen the pearl?" I mustered a smile.

"That might be your one exception," he laughed. "But these instincts of yours, I can only think they're heightened in pregnancy. You are going to be a wonderful mother, Cordelia, I've no doubt, and that fact will only be made more so by your feelings and instincts. If you're feeling something now, I think we need to listen to it."

Wade took my hand and laced his fingers through mine.

"What do we do?" I whispered as a chill traced the length of my spine.

Wade didn't say anything. His eyes flashed black to blue. I watched the reflection of the flames flicker in his pupils. His fingers twitched in mine.

"There's nothing we can do," he said. "We can't prepare for every eventuality without exhausting ourselves to the point that we won't be ready for the actual moment when it arrives. Rob is training the army. And as you said, you and I and Blaze have powers. We need to surround our son with love and protection. That is all we can do."

"And we wait."

"We wait," Wade agreed.

"What do you think it will be?" I asked. The question hung between us. We listened to the flames crack and spit. The silence stretched on until I thought perhaps Wade hadn't heard me.

"No, Cordelia. I'm not going to do that. I need to be able to sleep at night. And so do you. We must try to enjoy life. Otherwise, what will have been the point of any of this?" He swept his hand around the room to encompass the Power of the Sea, the palace and everything that existed on Atlantis.

In all the time since I had discovered I was a mermaid, I hadn't once wished it away or prayed I could be someone other than I was. But in that moment, I longed to be Maya. Or to have her ability, so I might see the future as it came and prepare myself for whatever lay ahead. The agony of not knowing layered me with a fresh coat of anxiety every day.

I had never bitten my nails or worried over a necklace or twisted my hair into knots or any of those little nervous habits which people used to quell their anxiety. But I could feel something building inside me, a powerful feeling that needed an outlet. I didn't know how to let it out, but I couldn't contain it either.

"We go to Maya and Trent's wedding." I tried on a smile. "I will be her matron of honor."

"Yes." Wade squeezed my hand again.

"And we wait for Maya to tell us what comes next."

"Yes, we wait for Maya to tell us what comes next," Wade echoed. "And maybe we can finally take a honeymoon."

I swept a hand over my stomach and smiled at the life within. While he was still inside me, he was safe. I could take comfort from that.

The End

Read on for a sneak peek of *Ghost Pirates*, book 4 of *The Mermaid Chronicles*...

THANK YOU!

Thank you so much for making it all the way to the end. I hope you have enjoyed Cordelia's third adventure and are excited to discover the rest of her journey (2 more books to come). If you did, leaving a review is the best possible present for an author! You can do it here:

https://geni.us/FightforFreedom

Cordelia and her friends have been living in my head for years now and I'm so thankful to be able to share them all with you. Without you, my dream of being a novelist would never have happened, so from the bottom of my heart: Thank You!

Maybe the next time you're at the beach, you'll cast your eyes at the ocean and wonder where Cordelia is in that moment, or if you can spot Atlantis.

If you're interested in my other books, you can read the first chapter of all of them on my website at **www.marisa-noelle.com**, or buy from any bookshop. Please sign up to my mailing list to get the latest news, free stories, novellas, and chapters from all my other books. Every month I hold a competition and three lucky readers get an **e-book completely free**!

You will receive the first three chapters of The Shadow Keepers FREE!!!

Read on for a sneak peek of *Ghost Pirates*, book 4 of *The Mermaid Chronicles*...

ACKNOWLEDGMENTS

Well, folks, they say it takes a village to raise a child, but I'm here to tell you, it takes a whole circus to birth a book! So, grab your popcorn, because I've got some shout-outs and thank-yous that are more entertaining than a juggling act on a unicycle!

First up, my writing group, The Rebel Alliance. You guys are like the Jedi Masters of encouragement, and I couldn't have done this without you. You've had my back for so long that I'm pretty sure you have a permanent imprint of my book cover on it!

And speaking of covers, Fay, you're the Picasso of book design. Seriously, the cover is so gorgeous it's practically doing the cha-cha on its own. Bravo!

Now, let's talk about Team Swag. We navigate the treacherous waters of publishing together, and boy, do we make a splash! When it comes to sharing knowledge, we're like the Avengers of advice-giving. What a fantastic bunch of writers and friends!

Neil, my rock, my Steady Eddie. You stole my heart in a single night and have been guarding it like a precious gem ever since. I love you more than a mermaid loves the ocean (and that's saying something).

To my kids, Riley, Lucas, and Quinn, thanks for being the

wind beneath my writerly wings. You're my plot problem-solving superheroes, and you always rescue me! Just promise me you won't be embarrassed if I show up at your school fairs with a stack of books.

Mom, you're the eagle-eyed proofreader of my dreams, even if we occasionally find a typo or two. Let's just blame it on Dad when that happens, shall we?

To my early supporters, you're the MVPs of my writing journey. Sasha, Michelle, Nikki, Adrian, Darcy, Hetty, Louise, you've given me advice and feedback that's worth its weight in gold doubloons!

Twitter, oh Twitter, (and you will always be Twitter) you've been my trusty sidekick in this adventure. The writing community there has made rejections feel like mosquito bites at a barbecue—annoying but manageable. You all know who you are, and I couldn't have asked for better virtual friends. Thank you!

And then there's Booktok! What a wild and wonderful place I've stumbled into. You've made me buy so many crowns I'm starting to feel like royalty. Thanks for supporting my journey, engaging with me, and even buying my books. You're the crown jewels of my author life!

A big shout-out to my A-level English teacher, Michael Fox, who taught me to first think for myself and second defend my ideas. You're the reason I can write more than a grocery list!

Last but not least, a standing ovation for my readers. You are the true stars of this show, and I wouldn't be here without you. Stick around, because there are more books in my circus tent, and I promise they'll be worth the price of admission.

Oh, and if you fancy learning more about my books and want to be in with the chance to win exclusive giveaways, sign up to my website below!

(www.marisanoelle.com)

Read on for a sneak peek of *Ghost Pirates*, book 4 of *The Mermaid Chronicles*…

ABOUT THE AUTHOR

Marisa Noelle is the author behind a treasure trove of middle-grade, young adult, and adult novels that dance through the realms of science-fiction, fantasy, horror, dystopian, and mental health. From unraveling mysteries to diving deep into the human psyche, she's your go-to wordsmith for adventures that'll tickle your imagination.

Marisa's literary exploits include "The Shadow Keepers," a spine-tingling tale to keep you up all night, and "The Unraveling of Luna Forester," a masterpiece that snagged the prestigious First Place Incipere Award, rocked the WriteBlend Finalist stage, waltzed as a BBYNA Semi-Finalist, and took its place on the Bookshelf Finalist shelf. With dystopian being one of her favorite genres, you can expect fast-paced thrills from the world of "The Unadjusteds Trilogy," a rollercoaster ride featuring "The Unadjusteds," "The Rise of the Altereds," and "The Reckoning," perfect for fans of Divergent, Maze Runner & The Hunger Games. And don't forget to dive into "The Mermaid Chronicles," a series that will plunge you into the depths of "Secrets of the Deep," lead you on a wild "Quest for Atlantis," challenge you to "Fight for Freedom," send shivers down your spine with "Ghost Pirates," and leave you craving "Vendetta." She also writes steamy romance under the pen name Savannah Warner.

When Marisa's not weaving literary spells, she's helping mold the future of MG and YA authors as a mentor for the Write Mentor program.

When not writing, Marisa likes to imagine herself as a mermaid, and can often be found in the local pool...or lake... or ocean. Despite her undeniable bookworm credentials since she was knee-high to a grasshopper, the author gig took Marisa by surprise. You see, she had a secret past as a bit of a science geek during her school days. But hey, science and storytelling make a surprisingly magical concoction! Currently, Marisa calls Woking, UK, her home sweet home, where she resides with her trusty squad, including her husband, three amazing kids, and a furry four-legged friend named Copper.

Marisa loves to hear from her readers. You can find and connect with her at the links below.

Twitter & Instagram: **@MarisaNoelle77**
Tiktok: **@MarisaNoelle12**
Website: **www.MarisaNoelle.com**

Read on for a sneak peek of *Ghost Pirates*, book 4 of *The Mermaid Chronicles*...

THE MERMAID
CHRONICLES
BOOK FOUR

GHOST
PIRATES

MARISA NOELLE

Angelica cradled her nephew close, shushing him with meaningless platitudes as if he were conscious and could hear her soothing words. His ashray wounds were extensive. They covered such a vast span of his mottled skin that she couldn't say for sure if he would survive. Unlikely. She knew that deep down. But she refused to let the truth surface. Better to stuff it down deep with all the other pain. But pain had a limit. Loss could break a person. Grief was a physical thing. Guilt was another entity altogether. A nasty, dark, hard, growing *thing* made of nothing but meanness.

She squeezed her eyes shut against her morbid thoughts and sang to him, even though her voice trembled and didn't carry its usual timbre. What else could she do? An ashray wound was incurable. The ghostly rays attacked during the hours of darkness, burning human or orca flesh—it didn't make a difference to them—and left angry wounds that lasted for at least a year. For those who avoided infection, the pain alone was often unbearable, leading many to contemplate jumping off towering icebergs or drowning themselves in the sea. Her own sister...driven insane by the pain. But she wouldn't let that happen to her nephew, Frost. Not if it was the last thing she did.

The small ice shelf they rested on rocked with an unseen force. Angelica braced herself and held onto Frost, careful not to touch his wounds. As the ice shook beneath them, she cast a quick glance at the remainder of her resting clan. They were dotted among the icebergs, most of them with their orca tails still visible, but a few had transformed into their human forms. Not long ago, there were over fifty of them. Now their numbers were a mere twenty-five. The war. The ashrays. The dark mutterings of the deep.

A few acknowledged her panicked look, noted her trembling iceberg, and jumped into the frigid Antarctic water to come to her aid. Who knew what new monstrosity might arise? But before her clan reached her, a familiar head breached the surface of the water. Zale.

"You scared the shit out of me," Angelica said.

Treading water, Zale raised both palms. "I apologize."

Angelica relaxed back onto the ice but didn't lessen her hold on Frost.

"What do you want, Zale?" Angelica eyed the enormous selachii. His size was a new thing. All the time he'd spent with the Denizens of the Deep had finally paid off. According to him. Granting him not just their trust, but an extraordinary size. Megalodon size. No wonder the ice rattled when he swam. "I'm not in the mood."

"Is it not enough for me to enjoy your scintillating conversation?" He smirked.

"I've got other things on my mind."

His gaze fell to Frost, still unconscious on her lap. Zale shuddered. "Ashray, huh? Nasty fuckers."

"More than one." A wall of tears built behind her eyes, but it would do no good to shed them. "I don't know what to do. His wounds are so extensive. After my sister...I can't lose him, Zale."

Zale leaped out of the water and landed on the ice beside Angelica, rocking it again. His great white shark tail dangled in the water. He lifted both Angelica and Frost into his arms. "It's going to be okay."

She rested her head against his chest. "No, it's not, and it's all my fault."

His hand brushed the back of her head, a rare tender gesture, nothing he'd ever done during the nights they'd been intimate. "It's not your fault. You're only doing what you need to do to survive."

"Diving into uncharted territories? Taking him to dangerous or forbidden zones? Hunting the ashrays because all our food sources died after the war?"

"You're the clan leader. You must make difficult decisions."

"We've lost over twenty in five years," Angelica said, pulling back from him to look at his dark eyes.

His expression hardened. "You can blame the humans for that. And the merfolk. And the selachii."

"*You* are a selachii."

He shook his head. "Not anymore. I'm something else. Something bigger. Something better. Something far more powerful."

"What difference does that make?" Angelica glanced at Frost. His lips were blue. His skin was ice-white, even the mottled bits that made them so unique. The vitiligo that marked their human flesh when they weren't in their orca form. Distinct, beautiful, elegant. Yet on Frost, the markings were fading. A sign he was near death.

"I'm sorry." Zale lifted her chin with his finger so her eyes met his. "I know a way to help him."

"You do?" Angelica curled her fingers around his wrist, squeezed, trying to wring the answer out of him. "What is it?"

"Atlantis."

Angelica's heart sank. "Atlantis is a myth."

"I assure you, it is anything but a myth. It is entirely real."

"Then why aren't you there?"

"I have no interest in being there. Not yet."

"How can an island help Frost?" Angelica asked.

"Because the Fountain of Youth resides on Atlantis," Zale replied.

Hope pricked a thorn in Angelica's heart. "It's real?"

"It's real. And it can cure ashray wounds."

Angelica looked at Frost, at his frigid appearance, at the life leaching rapidly from him. "Tell me how to get there."

Zale grabbed the back of her neck, a gesture meant to intimidate, one she was more familiar with. "You must do something for me first."

Angelica raised her gaze from her dying nephew to meet the ice in Zale's eyes. "If it will save Frost."

Zale placed an object in her palm. A small hard thing with rough edges and glints of obsidian. A rock of some kind. "When you get to Atlantis, put it in the fountain."

"What is it?"

"Nothing you need to concern yourself with," Zale said. "All that's important is healing Frost. The rest will take care of itself." He slipped off the ice into the water, rocking the iceberg once more. "That is what you want, isn't it? To heal your nephew?"

Angelica nodded. Zale gave her directions to the hidden island, then slipped away beneath the frigid waves.

The rest of her clan surrounded her small ice shelf, casting her worried looks. Angelica kissed her nephew's forehead, then held the rock high in a tight fist. There wasn't a single member of the orcana who hadn't been wounded by an ashray. "To Atlantis. To heal all our wounds."

"To Atlantis!" They cheered back at her, smiles brimming with hope.

I blocked the punch, evaded the low sweep, and ducked under a threatening kick to my face. Each move was calculated, each strike met with precision. The shadows of my opponent danced around me, mirroring the intensity of the fight. No time to draw breath. Only time to react. The next kick connected with my stomach. Air left my lungs in a violent gust as darkness ebbed at the corner of my vision. I didn't feel pain, just a white-hot anger. But my fire would be no use here.

"Come on, Mom!" Gal called. "You can do it!"

Spinning, I caught myself on the stone balcony which overlooked the courtyard and ocean. The stone felt cold to my heated skin. I gripped the ledge as I struggled to breathe. Sweat poured down my face, ribboned down my spine, coated every inch of skin. Small sparks flickered on my fingers and streaked out the window. As I struggled to inflate my lungs, I watched the tiny flames head to the ocean and disappear under the water.

"Are you okay?" Ford put a hand on my back.

I faced my loyal and skilled bodyguard, the man who had saved my life multiple times. Not just mine, But Wade and Gal's too.

"I need a minute."

"Enemies don't give you a minute." He turned back to the practice mats.

A truth I knew all too well.

His words stirred anger in me. Before he could reach the middle of the room, I sprang, sweeping out both his legs. He landed flat on his back.

"Go, Mom!" Gal called.

I stood over Ford. "Never underestimate your opponent."

Ford's tough instructions were not only about physical prowess; they were about cultivating the mental strength needed to face any challenge life threw at us. The opportunity to learn from him was worth enduring the bruises and exhaustion. And I was glad to finally get one over on him.

He yanked my leg, and then I was beside him on the floor. "Never lose your concentration."

"Dammit," I muttered.

Ford launched to his feet; a neat little acrobatic maneuver that made him seem more elegant than a mermaid. He turned to Gal. "Your turn, buddy."

"I'll get him for you, Mom," he said.

Getting to my feet, I gave my son a high-five and made my way to the bench on the side of the room. Thirst crawled up my throat as sweat pooled at the small of my back. My entire body ached. But I wouldn't visit the fountain. If Gal had to endure the training sessions without being cured by the Fountain of Youth, then I would bear that with him.

Every morning, five days a week, before the sun crested the horizon, Gal and I wound our way through the palace to the turret and spent an hour battling it out with my personal bodyguard. Ford had been with Wade and me ever since we'd discovered Atlantis, and he'd never let us down.

I didn't need the training, not with my ability to conjure fire to my hands in less than a second, but Gal had no such powers to defend himself. He had insisted if we forced him to train for an hour before school every day, then I had to join him.

It became the one part of the day where I could momentarily free myself from overthinking. Sometimes. A time when I could concentrate on the rhythm of hits, the ducking, the blocking, the kicking. Breathe in the ocean's scent, the sweat in the room, the damp in the stone walls. Forget the book, the island, the unrest, the prophecies, and concentrate on defending myself, on teaching Gal how to defend himself.

I watched Gal as he warmed up. He jumped on the spot, swung his arms in both directions, performed a few deep lunges. Ford took out his leg, and he tumbled to the floor.

"Hey!" Gal protested. "I wasn't ready!"

Ford ruffled his auburn hair. "Do you think your opponent is going to play fair?"

Gal's shoulders slumped. "I guess not."

"Not so hard," I said to Ford.

Ford faced me. "I can't teach him to fight with feathers."

It was a comment I'd heard before. Several times. Almost daily.

"I know, I'm sorry. Carry on," I said, and braced myself as Gal readied himself to fight.

A mix of pride and concern surged through me as I watched my son. Each hit, thwack, punch, and kick reverberated off the stone walls and burrowed into my heart. I memorized each one, calculating how many new bruises Gal would incur. He'd been learning for more than two years. And even though he was getting better at blocking, bruises still littered his tanned skin on a permanent basis. But it was a small price to pay for his safety.

"We're going to start a martial arts competition, right?" Gal said, as he jabbed at Ford's chest. "And you can be the judge, and I'll win all the medals. Although it would be nice to have a worthy opponent. Maybe I can talk Ember into coming too—"

Ford swept out his legs, and Gal landed on his ass. Again. "Hey!"

"Less talking, more concentrating," Ford said. "Unless you plan to bore your opponent to death."

"Hey!" Gal said again, launching to his feet and running at Ford. Effortlessly, Ford held out a hand and caught Gal's fist in his palm. Gal swung, but he couldn't reach the wall of Ford's burly chest.

"No fair," Gal said.

"Think outside the box," Ford said.

I watched my son, urging him to think things through. Not that you had much time to think during a fight for your life, but these scenarios must become second nature to him. He was the Prince of Atlantis. There would always be challenges. Enemies. Prophecies.

Glugging on my water bottle, I attempted to push the anxious thoughts away, but with the brightening day, they stuck to me faster and harder. It wouldn't be long until Gal was at school for the day. Gone for seven hours. Out of my sight. Out of my protection. Anything could happen.

Gal stopped swinging at Ford. He looked up at the muscled man with an inquisitive expression, took a deep breath and, ran up his legs. With his hand still caught in Ford's palm, he flipped over the bigger man's arm, twisting out of his grasp. He landed with a triumphant smile, and thank God, wasn't foolish enough to gloat. He threw himself back into the fight, both arms jabbing.

"Good boy," Ford said.

"See, Mom?" Gal turned to me. "No one is going to sneak up on me! Whatever that book dishes out, I got it covered."

I wanted to smile at my son's enthusiasm. He was such a typical boy; all restless energy and endless stamina, an innate instinct to wrestle and fight. The smile that formed on my lips took effort, made my cheeks ache with practiced agony. I prayed he couldn't tell the difference between my real smiles and my forced ones, but deep down, I knew he was smarter than that.

"You've definitely got it covered," Ford said. "Hell, you should be *my* bodyguard."

"Yes!" Gal punched an arm in the air. "Best job ever!"

"No!" I launched to my feet.

They both stared at me.

My fears swelled, and I struggled to find the right words to convey my concerns without appearing overbearing. I swallowed my fear and gathered my thoughts. "The Prince of Atlantis must rule the island."

Gal rolled his eyes. I didn't blame him. Truthfully, I didn't care what he wanted to do. I wanted him to pursue his dreams, do what made him happy, and if he didn't want to be Prince, then I would find a way to make that possible. But at that moment, I couldn't think of another reason to explain why the idea of him fighting for his career wasn't an option I could get on board with.

"It's because of the fountain, isn't it?" Gal muttered. "I never get to do anything fun."

I winced. "You're here, aren't you? Having fun?"

"You know what I mean," Gal said, and slumped onto the bench. "What's the point of training if I'm not allowed to fight for real?"

So many thoughts tumbled through my brain, I didn't know which one to focus on first.

Ford raised an eyebrow at me, then lowered his voice. "How much have you told him about the book? Does he really need to know the details?"

"He is the *prince*," I said, my tone sharper than I intended. "There will always be threats. And I may not always be there to protect him."

"That's not your job."

"Of course it is," I said. "That's my *only* job."

"Cordelia—"

I raised a palm. "I don't want to hear it, Ford. Train my son. Make him indestructible. That's all I want from you."

"Cordelia—"

I glared at him. "Ford."

"Okay, okay." He raised both hands and took a step back. "I'm only asking because I care."

"I know." I went to my son and kneeled by him. "Why would you want to fight for your job?"

He looked at me with his big blue eyes. Wade's eyes. As mesmerizing as the ocean. "Because I want to help people. Protect people. Like Ford does for you and Dad. Or Rob leading the army. Protecting people is good."

I took both of his hands in mine. "It is. It's very good. I love that you see that. But we also must protect ourselves."

A little frown appeared above the bridge of his nose. I had the urge to kiss it away, but he was at the age where my kisses weren't so welcome anymore.

"But why am I the only one who has to train?"

"Because you are the prince."

"But I'm no different to Ember or Una or any other person here."

I sighed. "You know that's not true. You are being forced to grow up quicker than I would have liked. But some realities we must face, no matter how old or young you are. Your life will always be in danger—"

"I know. You don't need to remind me."

"I'm sorry. I am. I want you to be happy." I rested my forehead against his and squeezed his hands. "I love you, Gal."

"I love you too, Mom."

"Let's go get ready for school."

He stood, grabbed his water bottle, and headed out the door, calling a 'thank you' to Ford on his way. I looked over my shoulder, held Ford's eyes. He nodded. I couldn't bring myself to smile. But I knew he understood my fears. That I didn't have to voice them aloud. He knew me almost as well as Wade. And that if anything happened to either my son or my husband, I wouldn't survive it.

To carry on reading, click here:
https://geni.us/GhostPirates